"Frasier's w̶... —Jayn...

"Anne Frasier delivers thoroughly engrossing, completely riveting suspense."—Lisa Gardner

Praise for *Pale Immortal*

"Frasier delivers twist upon twist. . . . This is the kind of book that builds to a slow boil, and then bubbles incessantly and will keep you turning pages to the end, desperate to find out what happens. . . . Frasier is an expert at haunting the reader. . . . *Pale Immortal* is the kind that lingers. The characters are rich, complex. The story is masterfully spun."
—Spinetingler Magazine

"Easily the best work I've read in 2006. This is just simply a masterpiece. I can't wait for the sequel so I can walk Tuonela's streets again."
—Maximum Horrors

"[An] exciting and thrilling tale. . . . Ms. Frasier proves why she is one of today's bestselling authors, in a book that will have you jumping at every noise but unable to put it down. Magnificently written story and characters."
—MyShelf.com

"One of those nifty page-turning thrillers that keep you reading nonstop till you turn the last page. And Anne Frasier is a writer talented at creating vividly fractured characters and a dark, disturbing atmosphere and theme. . . . If you want to taste something a little different, then *Pale Immortal* is a heady and sinister brew."
—BookLoons

"Anne Frasier has written a very scary novel with gothic and supernatural overtones. . . . This is a stupendous work, worthy of an award nomination."
—The Best Reviews

"Few books keep me turning pages from dark till dawn, but this one did. Be prepared, for it could happen to you too."
—Armchair Interviews

"Frasier's latest rivets with suspense and paranormal elements as vampires—both real and imagined—become a force to be reckoned with. She masterfully creates the perfect atmosphere for suspicious death and compelling mystery in this nail-biting thrill ride."
—*Romantic Times*

continued . . .

Other Books by Anne Frasier

GARDEN OF DARKNESS

Anne Frasier

ONYX
Published by New American Library, a division of
Penguin Group (USA) Inc., 375 Hudson Street,
New York, New York 10014, USA
Penguin Group (Canada), 90 Eglinton Avenue East, Suite 700, Toronto,
Ontario M4P 2Y3, Canada (a division of Pearson Penguin Canada Inc.)
Penguin Books Ltd., 80 Strand, London WC2R 0RL, England
Penguin Ireland, 25 St. Stephen's Green, Dublin 2,
Ireland (a division of Penguin Books Ltd.)
Penguin Group (Australia), 250 Camberwell Road, Camberwell, Victoria 3124,
Australia (a division of Pearson Australia Group Pty. Ltd.)
Penguin Books India Pvt. Ltd., 11 Community Centre, Panchsheel Park,
New Delhi - 110 017, India
Penguin Group (NZ), 67 Apollo Drive, Rosedale, North Shore 0632,
New Zealand (a division of Pearson New Zealand Ltd.)
Penguin Books (South Africa) (Pty.) Ltd., 24 Sturdee Avenue,
Rosebank, Johannesburg 2196, South Africa

Penguin Books Ltd., Registered Offices:
80 Strand, London WC2R 0RL, England

First published by Onyx, an imprint of New American Library,
a division of Penguin Group (USA) Inc.

First Printing, December 2007
10 9 8 7 6 5 4 3 2 1

Copyright © Anne Frasier, 2007
All rights reserved

For the Pimp Squad

Prologue

Where does the wind begin?

A dank breeze rose from the ground like one long exhaled breath. It lifted fallen leaves and swirled them up into the night sky. The leaves moved as if they knew where they were going, as if they had a destination. They flew past open windows where children were tucked into bed, hushed words snatched from sweet mouths and replaced with new ones.

"Where does the wind begin?" one child asked another.

"The Tuonela River," the other child replied.

"What's going on up there?" a mother called from below.

The children looked at one another in fear. "Nothing." But they felt strange. Had a soft hand caressed them? Just a brush down the cheek, leaving a trail of goose bumps behind?

Sweet, sweet babies.

He drew nearer and inhaled their soap scent, and his breath stirred the fine hair on their heads.

Time was different here.

He could smell the river: wet driftwood, shells and bones gleaming on the shore. In the black mud of the river bottom, giant catfish slept the deep sleep in filtered light that was bent and reshaped. Never surfacing, the catfish waited patiently for prey to come close enough to catch and swallow whole.

Sweet, sweet life.

The damp night wind was tinged with sorrow and loss and longing.

Oh, to be complete, to be whole.

Some people said he was bad. But that was like saying a bear was bad when it caught a fish. It was like saying a cat was bad when it ate a bird. The bear wasn't bad. The cat wasn't bad.

He wasn't bad.

Two places called to him, the old and the new.

For a moment he was confused. In his mind the two places meshed and he couldn't separate them. Time moved forward and backward, and the passage of a hundred years seemed like hours. Time unfolded and turned in on itself and his loss became something that hadn't yet happened, and the strength and power he'd once known could possibly be found again.

He left the children and soared from the house, up through the roof but not as far as the stars. He joined a flock of night birds as they moved out of town, shifting and changing, blocking the moonlight.

On the ground far below, a man walking his dog

felt the curious movement of air. He looked up, his face a white oval. He seemed to shrug and dismiss the sudden heaviness. But when the dog whimpered, he turned and hurried home.

Something was coming. Something had been coming for a long time. Something big. Powerful. Something that would shake the residents of Tuonela.

He soared.

To the old place.

His home.

Over the house built from native stone. Over the bare, rolling hillside that met dark woodland. Through the trees, silent and secret.

A light in the night.

A lantern and the sound of a shovel striking rocky ground.

This must be what it was like to astral project. To find yourself watching yourself. Because the man below was him, but not him.

The dead—they were everywhere. He could see their faces in the bark of the trees and the patterns made by the twisting leaves. Like him, they were looking for bodies to inhabit. Unlike him, they would take any vessel. He wanted one and only one.

The man on the ground seemed unaware of the dead surrounding him. He remained focused on his digging, never looking up. His heart pounded from exertion; steam rose from his shoulders.

Go inside.

The coaxing command seemed to come from the faces in the bark and the faces in the leaves. Who were they?

Don't you remember us?

Don't you remember your followers?

One face in particular became more distinct, the voice seeming to separate from the singsong chant of the others.

The scent of sage and lavender invaded his head. And somehow he could feel the softness of her skin under his fingertips.

Come inside, Richard.

Richard. That's who he was. Richard Manchester, the Pale Immortal. And this was his land—the land of the dead.

Come inside.

The man below stabbed the shovel into the ground, then released it and straightened, wiping his forehead with the back of his hand.

The night birds were gone. They had done their duty by bringing him here, and now they were asleep in the trees, heads tucked beneath black wings.

Richard hovered above the man with the shovel. *Foolish person. Digging for secrets on the ground when the secret is above you. When the secret is in you.*

Chapter One

"We should have stopped at the gas station," Brenda said.

With both hands on the wheel, Joe peered through the windshield. "I thought this was the road, okay? And all roads lead somewhere. We're going in the right direction."

She'd known it would be like this. She wanted to be home in her own bed. Joe kept forcing her to do things she didn't want to do. Everybody kept forcing her to do things she didn't want to do. And now they were lost. It was the middle of the night, and they were driving down a narrow two-lane, going who knew where.

A movement. On the road in front of them.

"Did you see that?" Unconsciously she put a hand to Joe's shoulder.

He leaned forward in his seat. "The sign?" He pointed. "You talking about that sign?"

She sighed, removed her hand from his arm, and settled back. "I thought I saw a—" She stopped herself. She'd almost said *little girl.* ". . . Person. Thought I saw a person."

She was always seeing kids. Little girls. Ever since her miscarriage. That's what this trip was about. To get her out of the house. To get her out of bed. A change of scenery. But the two of them? Alone together? Well, it wasn't working out. They hadn't been married all that long. Three years. But it was plenty of time for regret. Sometimes she hated him, and she didn't even know why.

The miscarriage certainly hadn't been his fault.

A girl.

Why'd she ask? Why'd she want to know?

Joe didn't abuse her. He'd never cheated on her, as far as she knew. He was boring. Did you leave somebody for being boring? For being too nice? All the time?

He slowed for the sign. "Tuonela. Sounds familiar."

"Isn't that the town where all that weird stuff happened?"

"Didn't they move the town?"

"One is Old Tuonela, and one is just Tuonela, or something like that."

There it was again.

A flash of white.

"Look out!"

Joe slammed on the brakes and the car screeched to a halt, skidding sideways on loose gravel, throwing them both forward, seat belts locking.

"I saw something!" Brenda cried. "I saw a little girl! Back up. Back up!"

"There's no little girl," Joe told her sadly. "What would a kid be doing out here in the middle of nowhere?"

"She must be lost. Like us." Maybe they were supposed to come this way. So that they could find this child. Save this child.

She unbuckled her seat belt and twisted to look over her shoulder. "Back up!" She motioned frantically with one hand. "Back up!"

He sighed and reversed. The front tires spun and they shot backward.

Something thudded against the trunk.

Brenda screamed.

Joe slammed on the brakes, the car rocking.

"You hit her! Oh, my God! You hit her!" Brenda threw open the door and jumped out. She ran to the rear of the car.

The only light sources were the interior dome and the brake lights. What if the child was caught under the car? "I can't see!" Brenda shouted. "It's too dark! Get a flashlight! Bring a flashlight!"

She saw Joe reach across the front seat for the glove box.

Brenda leaned toward the darkness under the car. She strained her eyes.

Was that a shape? A darker shape? "Don't worry, sweetheart," she crooned, her voice cracking. "You'll be okay. You're going to be okay. We're going to help you. We're going to take care of you."

She felt a blast of frigid air against her face. Her hair blew back. That was followed by scraping, mixed with frightened, heavy breathing.

The shape moved.

It brushed past her, footsteps sounding soft and flat and bare against the blacktop. The car's headlights fanned into the heavy woodland, glancing off the child's white gown and long blond hair.

"Stop!" Brenda called.

In a blur of white, the child reached the edge of the headlights' range and plunged into the blackness beyond.

Brenda ran after her.

Across the road, legs flying, heart hammering.

Past the headlights and into the thick grove of trees that moved into an infinity of straight rows.

Back at the car, Joe stood with a dead flashlight in his hand, trying to comprehend what was happening. He wasn't good at making decisions without Brenda's help.

Should he move the car? Someone might come around the corner and hit it. Should he forget the car and go after his wife?

He stepped to the side of the road. He paused and listened.

Nothing.

He walked across the shoulder, down the ditch, and back up, stopping where the thick trees began. They were all the same. Some kind of aspen, their trunks as big around as a person.

"Brenda!"

His voice bounced back as if hitting a solid wall.

His heart was beating hard now. Cold sweat crept down his spine. "Brenda! Don't go in there! We'll get somebody to help. We'll call the cops!"

He reached into his pocket and pulled out his cell phone. No signal.

"Brenda!"

He moved forward, forcing one foot in front of the other. He stopped at the trees; he wasn't sure why. "Brenda!"

Then he heard a scream. From deep within the trees. A bloodcurdling cry of terror followed by silence.

Chapter Two

In Tuonela, night came early and dawn came late. While the rest of the county was awash in morning sunlight, the steep valleys and ravines of Tuonela remained cloaked in thirty more minutes of darkness.

Under the glow of a street lamp, Rachel Burton carried a cardboard box containing her African violet and Christmas cactus to the U-Haul, and slid it across the front seat. Her body hummed with sudden urgency, telling her to jump in the truck and get the hell on the road even though she wanted to give her apartment one final perusal.

Should have left earlier.

She'd planned to leave last night, but she'd told herself that was foolish.

Wait until morning. Wait until light.

The sense of urgency increased.

Rather than going back inside, she hurried up the steep steps that led to the three-story Victorian and what was now the city morgue. She locked the wooden door and slipped the key through the mail slot. Without giving the building and her upstairs apartment another glance, she turned and walked away.

Free.

Almost.

She pulled herself into the cab of the short truck. Her belongings didn't fill it, but a van hadn't been big enough. She let the engine idle a minute, then put it in gear and turned up the hill to climb from the deep valley that stopped at the Wisconsin River.

Heading west. To California.

The vehicle groaned and creaked, laboring its way out of the dark hole, finally reaching level ground, sunlight glinting off the rearview mirror. Her heart began to hammer more seriously now.

She was leaving. For good. She was going to make it this time.

Evan didn't even call to tell you good-bye.

To hell with him. To hell with Tuonela.

Very soon she would be a thousand miles from this place. Very soon it would no longer seem quite real, no longer seem so important. It didn't deserve to take up so much space in her head. Soon she would remember it for what it was: a dying town. A bleak, sad, dying town where bad things had happened.

The vehicle took her through the slumbering flatlands, where houses had been built on a grid and streets didn't turn in on themselves. Out past the Quik Stop and Burger King, Applebee's and Perkins.

The flatlands looked like a million other Midwestern towns, built overnight strictly for convenience.

This part of Tuonela hurt your eyes and pained your heart in a way only a true lack of beauty and individuality could. But it was better than the other part. The part that mesmerized you and tricked you and lulled you into thinking it was normal and okay.

She passed an invisible line that marked the edge of town.

She adjusted herself, settling in for the long drive. She let out a deep breath. She reached for the radio.

And heard a siren.

She checked the side mirror.

A patrol car was coming up fast behind her, lights flashing. She glanced down at the speedometer. Fifty. The road was a two-lane with no shoulder. She slowed her pace, expecting the officer to drive around. He didn't. She slowed even more, finally reaching an intersection with room to pull aside. The car screeched to a halt behind her. Someone got out and approached her truck.

Alastair Stroud. He'd recently returned from early retirement in Florida to take the job of interim chief of police.

Rachel rolled down her window. "Come to see me off?" Her heart slammed in her chest again.

He had that look on his face. A look she'd seen on her father's face too many times. A look that said bad shit was afoot.

"I was hoping to catch you before you left Tuonela."

I was hoping to get out of here before you caught me. I should have left last night.

"There's been a murder," Alastair said. "I need your help."

"Get somebody else."

"There isn't anybody else."

Not true. The medical examiner from the adjoining county was filling in until they found a new ME and coroner. Everything was temporary. People filling in until the real person came along. That wasn't going to happen. There were no real people here.

"Becker Thomas."

Alastair shook his head. "Becker's busy. A nasty accident on Highway Ten. Besides, I'm afraid Becker might not be able to handle this. I'm afraid it might be too much for him. He's used to more normal deaths."

Normal deaths.

"I'm sorry," he said. "I know you want to get out of here. I understand that. Especially after your father's murder and everything that happened in Old Tuonela, but—"

The word *but* hung in the air between them.

But we could really use your help. One more time. One more for the road.

All roads led back to Tuonela. That's what Rachel was discovering. Like a board game with paths that kept returning you to Start.

Alligator swamp, go back ten squares. Quicksand, go back to Start. Sucking chest wound, go back to Start. Nutcases who think they're vampires, go back to Start.

It was crazy to think a place could control you. That the ground was somehow more than just soil and plants. More than just a place for vegetation and burying the dead.

She could see that Alastair could see the resignation in her eyes. He took advantage of it. "There's an abandoned farmhouse up the road about a half mile. Pull in there and I'll pick you up. I'll take you to the crime scene."

Rachel put the truck in gear and moved forward.

She should just keep driving, but that wasn't who she was. Instead, she spotted the narrow gravel drive, overgrown with weeds, and pulled in. She locked the truck, hoping her plants wouldn't get too hot, then walked to where Alastair was waiting.

Aspen Grove.

Rachel recognized the place. Part of the state forest bordered by the highway and Evan Stroud's land, which included Old Tuonela. Several acres of aspen trees planted in carefully checked rows. It was relatively easy to plant straight rows of anything, but checking them meant they lined up perfectly no matter where you stood. It was an old technique, done with string. One that had been abandoned once people started planting by machine.

Unlike the heart of Tuonela, the ground here had been worn flat. The soil was black and as fine as sand, and if you looked down the rows of trees from any angle you would swear they went into infinity.

"Are those quaking aspens?" Rachel asked.

The sun had risen completely, and the leaves against the white trunks were almost blinding in their brilliance and contrast to the gray sky.

"Big tooth," Alastair said.

Side by side they waded through dry, knee-deep weeds at the edge of the road. Alastair bent and picked up a soft yellow leaf and handed it to her. "Like the quaking aspen, except for the teeth."

The leaf was heart-shaped, edged with scalloped points. It didn't seem right, like suddenly finding out butterflies had fangs.

Stepping into the grove was like diving underwater. The temperature plunged, and Rachel's ears felt plugged. Sounds she'd been unaware of until that moment were cut off.

"A guy shows up in town just before dawn," Alastair told her. "Hysterical. Said his wife had vanished."

Rachel was aware of the strength and life and vitality of the trees. They absorbed sound, sucking the resonance from Alastair's voice, making it fall flat.

The husband may have killed the wife and dumped her. Trees that bordered old highways were popular spots for the uninitiated. A first kill. Panic. Dump it the first place you find just to get rid of it. It was common. But if this was so common, why hadn't Alastair waited for Becker?

"So he brought me out here." Alastair was a little breathless, walking and talking, plus carrying the additional weight of his belt and gun. Her dad used to complain about the equipment adding forty pounds, giving cops bad backs and bad knees.

They walked for so long that Rachel began to think they should have reached the other side. Her head began to feel funny, and she had the strange notion that they were caught in some kind of loop. Things got weird when she hadn't had her morning coffee, she tried to tell herself. But she knew better.

This wasn't Peoria.

Rachel was about to ask the age-old question, "Are we there yet?" when the visual repetition of trees changed.

As they moved closer, she made out a patch of solid beige that ended up being a police uniform worn by a young officer who looked familiar but whose name she couldn't place. He was jittery. Some of the tension drained from his body, and his shoulders visibly relaxed when Rachel and Alastair got close enough to be recognized as the good guys.

The grove would have been disquieting under normal circumstances, but to be left there alone to guard a dead body . . . Well, no wonder he was anxious.

She spotted something on the ground, near the base of a tree. At first glance it looked like a hundred-pound skinned squirrel, but then she realized it was human.

She had to turn away, a hand to her mouth.

"We came out here and searched the entire area," Alastair said. "This is all we found. No skin." When she didn't reply, he continued: "I've never seen anything like it, but I thought maybe you had. Since you used to live in L.A."

L.A. got a bad rap. L.A. had nothing on Tuonela and Old Tuonela. But Tuonelians had to always think there were worse places out there. It gave the residents something to feel good about.

You think it's bad here? Pshaw. You should live in California. Crazy shit happens there. Crazy shit, lemme tell ya.

The young cop shifted in his beige uniform, hands resting on his belt, elbows out. "This is some crazy shit."

Rachel frowned. Had she spoken her thoughts out loud? Was he just agreeing? She looked at Alastair. He was staring down at the remains.

Rachel had been a coroner a long time. She'd seen a lot of awful things; she'd seen a lot of weird, crazy shit. "I've never seen anything like this."

Selfishly, she thought about the U-Haul truck with the African violet and Christmas cactus waiting to resume their journey to California. And she knew that wasn't going to be happening anytime soon.

Chapter Three

We were a few miles from Tuonela when we spotted the flashing emergency lights just as our rented minivan crested the hill. I leaned forward from the backseat to get a better view and saw a cluster of vehicles and dark dots of people against a rural backdrop of dead grass, yellow leaves, and blue sky. Cop cars and an ambulance were parked in the ditch alongside the road.

"Slow down," I said.

"It's almost noon." Stewart didn't let up on the gas. "We're gonna be late for the museum opening."

"Really late if you get us killed or run over somebody." Did I need to point out the obvious?

From the passenger seat, Claire glared to remind me that she was in charge.

I've always had a problem with authority, especially if that authority comes from somebody close to my own age. I'm also paranoid about dying. None of the other three in the van knew I'd already died twice, once from electrocution, and once when

I fell through the ice and was underwater for almost an hour.

Sometimes it felt like death was chasing me, and now I was going to be spending two weeks in a town that meant "land of the dead." So wrong. But they were paying me a hundred bucks a day. An unemployed, starving artist couldn't turn her back on that kind of money. Not to mention that this could be a chance to unfuck my life.

Stewart slowed the minivan.

Ian and I had been in the backseat for several hours, and even though we were all close to the same age, it was a flashback to childhood. It felt like he and I were the kids, Claire and Stewart the parents. Too weird. Especially strange since I'd met Ian and Stewart only that morning.

I was surprised when they'd accepted my application to be part of the documentary crew, but I'm cheap. Cheaper than anybody else in Minneapolis. And I have most of my own equipment, plus I can shoot both video and film. Some people can't. But it's still pretty funny that a group of journalism majors would hire a college dropout to shoot their documentary.

Now that we were closer I saw a white van with the words COUNTY CORONER painted on the side in black lettering. A somber group of people emerged from a stand of trees. They were carrying a gurney. On top of the gurney was a black body bag.

Welcome to Tuonela.

Never one to miss a photo op, I dug out my camera. "Pull over."

Stewart shot Claire a question. *Should I?* Claire shrugged. "Might be something for the documentary. I'll wait here."

Stewart stopped the minivan and I jumped out.

The camera was a small handheld. I kept it down, hoping nobody would notice. It's my job to be invisible. Most of the time people don't even acknowledge my existence.

Watching the viewfinder, I made the shot long and low, capturing the foreground and keeping the lens wide open for maximum depth of field.

Stewart came up behind me. "I don't see any wreck."

I zoomed in on a policeman. His face registered shock and horror. Other faces held the same emotion.

"I don't think it's a wreck."

I panned, then paused on a woman who seemed to be in charge. She stood off by herself, legs braced, arms crossed, watching the body being loaded into the van. The wind blew, and dry prairie grass rustled. Distantly I knew the capture would be nice in review.

The breeze lifted the woman's short, dark hair and created waves in her navy blue jacket, molding the fabric across an obviously pregnant belly. She didn't look shocked like the others. Instead she appeared worried and maybe even resigned.

"Kristin." Stewart tapped my arm and pointed to a guy who was doubled over, hands on his knees. "That cop is puking. Wouldn't you like to know what he just saw?"

"Not really."

"Hey!"

We'd been spotted.

A policeman strode toward us, arms pumping. "What are you doing? You can't film here." He waved his hands, shooing us away.

I lowered the camera but didn't shut it off. "Sorry." I expected him to demand the videotape, but he didn't.

Stewart was already scrambling for the vehicle. Before the cop realized he might want to confiscate the footage, I turned and ran. The minivan wheels rolled as I slammed the door.

"What the hell do you think that was all about?" Stewart's voice trembled.

On the seat beside me, Ian stirred and came awake, looking about groggily. "What?"

"Must have found a nasty dead body, that's for sure," I said. "We haven't even reached Tuonela, and weird things are already happening."

"What's so weird about a dead body and people getting sick?" Claire looked over the seat. "I mean, it's unusual, but not weird."

This was going to be a tough gig. Claire was already bugging the hell out of me. And it wasn't just her attitude. I don't like to judge people on outward appearances, but it was almost impossible for me to ignore her expensive blond hairdo and upscale business clothes. Right now she was wearing a cashmere sweater, black skirt, and black knee boots that were probably equivalent to two months' rent.

"I always miss everything," Ian muttered.

"We should ask about it when we get to town," Stewart said. "See if anybody knows what was going on."

A few more miles and we hit the outskirts of Tuonela.

I was disappointed to find that it looked as nondescript as any other Midwestern town, with a bunch of flat, boring buildings. But that ended up being the new area. The same street finally narrowed to a two-lane that dipped toward the river. We hit steep hills that pitched us forward and dropped us into Tuonela, the *real* Tuonela.

The road was suddenly lined with Victorian houses perched precariously as they struggled to cling to their foundations. Buildings were stone or dark brick, several stories tall, some with jagged peaks, some flat. At the bottom of the valley, a decay enveloped us. The sky darkened, and I found myself looking up to make sure the sun was still there.

A dying town.

There were thousands of them scattered throughout the United States, where you could feel the hope and vibrancy of the past, and the desolation of the future.

"Hey—karaoke." Claire pointed to a two-story bar with gray clapboard siding and a neon OPEN sign.

"Tomorrow night," Ian added. He laughed in delight. "I'm definitely going to check that out."

They were here to make fun of people. To expose ignorance and put it on the big screen. *Let's go to this*

*little town in the Midwest. People say a vampire used to
live there.*

That was what they'd really come for. To make a
documentary on a man called Richard Manchester,
a man who'd died a hundred years ago.

Our plan was to focus on Manchester, the town,
and the culture of fear and superstition that went
along with small-town ignorance. We would interview people. We hoped to interview one guy in particular: a man named Evan Stroud some people
claimed was a living vampire.

It would be a hoot.

That was the one part of accepting the job that
made me uncomfortable. I sure as hell don't believe
in vampires, but I have a documentary ethic. I don't
make fun of people unless they ask for it. If vampires were a part of someone's culture, so what?
Document it. That was fine. But don't ridicule.

"Look!" Claire pointed to another building.
"Vampire Candy Shoppe." She laughed. "We have
to get that on video. And we have to get some
candy. Hopefully an interview."

We followed the directions Claire had gotten off
the Internet. It was easy to find the museum.

"Oh, my God." Claire stared out the window at a
line of people that went around the block.

"This must be the place," Stewart said. "What a
goddamn circus. Looks like we're not the only ones
here to immortalize the event. I told you we should
have done our project on something more obscure."

The WXOW news team had set up with a van,
live-feed dish, and black cables snaking across the

parking lot. People were selling hot dogs and cotton candy. It was like some huge street fair.

Not everybody was happy with the opening of the new exhibit. A man with a ragged gray beard paced with a sign that read, REPENT SINNERS, on one side, BURN THE VAMPIRE on the other.

I taped it.

"They burn vampires?" Ian asked. "I thought they burned witches and staked vampires."

Claire laughed. "Guess they can't keep their folklore straight."

The museum ramp was full. We ended up parking blocks away.

"Save me a place in line." I rewound the videotape. "I want to see what I got back there."

The others went on without me.

What I love about film and video is how it captures action and small scenes the human brain can't process at the actual time of the event. I'm always surprised when I play back footage. It's new and different—almost as if I'd never been there at all. Sure, there was the stuff in the foreground, the main action that I always remember, but it's the small dramas that often tell bigger stories.

I viewed the footage of the two men sliding the body bag into the white van. The faces of the cops, raw and stark. I reversed and watched the section again.

How could the recorded emotion seem so much more intense than the live scene? It amazed me.

Recording an event changed it. I'm not sure how, but it allowed a person to see things they'd missed before. Almost as if the real event wasn't the real event, and the video was reality.

Some people might argue that the viewing allowed you to sort things out, that it gave you time to focus. I'm not so sure about that. I often find myself toying with the idea that the recording actually brings about a change.

I let it play all the way out.

This time I reached the sad woman with the short black hair. She had a beautiful, angular face and large, soulful eyes. As I watched, she put an unconscious hand to her stomach, and something flitted across her face as her thoughts seemed to turn inward.

Maternal fear.

The grass blew—but not exactly the way it had blown when I was filming. The timing was slightly off; the shadows were deeper. Bits of conversation I hadn't been aware of at the time could be heard.

"Never seen anything like it."

"Didn't look human."

"What could possibly do that?"

"A wild animal."

I caught a glimpse of something in the shadows of the yellow woods behind the pregnant woman.

A small figure with long hair.

I blinked and it was gone. I rewound and replayed, but didn't see anything the second time through.

I tried again.

There.

Stop.

Rewind.

Pause.

A shadowy figure in the woods, appearing in only a few frames. Too vague to make out.

Artifacts often showed up in strange places, especially if tape had been used before. Even new tape wasn't foolproof when it came to picking up odd shapes that weren't really there. Freaky, but it happens.

Strange how it looked so much like a person.

Like a little girl . . .

Chapter Four

It was weird how the presence of people created energy. They didn't even have to be moving around. Most were just standing in line waiting for the museum doors to open, but Graham Stroud could feel them out there, creating a tingle in his brain.

Collective unconscious? Was that it?

"One minute until doors open!"

That cry was carried from the front of the museum and passed from person to person until it reached Graham in the dark depths of the lower level, where he and the others stood guard at the as-yet-to-be unveiled exhibit.

"Last chance," Amy said. "We could peek. See it before everybody else does."

The guards were dressed alike, in black slacks and blue polo shirts with the museum logo printed discreetly above the left breast. The room had been given a fresh coat of paint, but it hadn't been enough to cover up the damp smell of basement. A kind of wet rock combined with mildew. And the lighting didn't help. Round, recessed ceiling lights brushed a faint orange glow across surfaces and failed to illuminate corners and indentations.

"Are you afraid?" Amy shot him an I-dare-you smile.

He knew her from school. The class clown. Smart, but always stirring up trouble. He was surprised they'd hired her. The other guard—a kid named Bradley—shifted nervously, but didn't say anything.

Lighting for the room had been a big issue. It was finally decided that low light would keep the exhibit from rotting and disintegrating, and also add to the atmosphere.

Are you afraid?

His dad and grandfather had asked him how he could take this job with all that had happened.

He was drawn to fear. Wasn't everybody? Was that attraction something left over from the time humans didn't live in houses or towns? If something scared you, you had to examine it, make sure it was worthy of the fear so it could then be labeled as either harmless or a threat.

Beyond the psychological, Graham just felt a need to get out of the house and make some money. Typical teenager. And maybe that's all it was. Maybe he was blowing things at home out of proportion. He basically had two choices: museum guard or fast food guy. Wasn't too hard to figure out why he'd chosen museum guard.

He thought too much. Sometimes he wished his brain would just shut off.

Amy bent down and fingered a velvet corner of

the fabric covering a case that stood seven feet high. In the poor light, parts of her face seemed to be missing, and Graham had to try to fill in the blank spots with memory of the way she'd looked moments ago.

He couldn't do it.

An air horn honked. Amy let out a shriek, dropped the corner of the cloth she'd been clutching, and straightened as if on springs. Bradley giggled. Then the building exploded as the ground-level doors opened.

They looked above their heads—hundreds of footfalls thundered over them, creating one continuous roar as people rushed forward in hopes of getting a good spot.

The room filled.

The mayor and his bunch broke a path through the crowd. A TV station crew followed with a camera. After a short but boring speech about the museum and tourism and the revitalization of Tuonela, along with something about embracing history, Mayor McBride stepped forward and with a flourish whipped the velvet fabric away to reveal a glass box containing an upright mummy dressed in an antique black suit.

The Pale Immortal.

That brought about a gasp, followed by a long silence.

Someone finally let out a murmur that broke the spell. Conversation gradually increased until the room hummed.

Graham thought he'd been prepared. How bad could it be? He'd seen mummies before. On TV, and at other museums. Hell, he'd even sat beside this guy. But it had been dark, and at the time he'd thought he was *alive*.

Just a piece of leather in a suit.

But as he looked at the corpse, he wondered if people like his dad and Rachel Burton had been right: The Pale Immortal was nothing to take lightly or put on display.

Patrons filed through.

Some were nervous. Some giggled. A couple of little kids cried, and their mothers whisked them away. Who would bring a little kid to see a shriveled-up dead guy? That was evil.

People kept coming.

So far so good. Nobody was breaking any rules. Nobody was trying to step over the rope or sneak in food. Then he spotted a girl with bright red hair dressed in thrift shop clothes, pulling a camera from an army green messenger bag.

"Miss?" *Miss*?

Should he call her *miss*? She wasn't old enough for *ma'am*. "You can't take pictures in here." They'd allowed one news crew inside. That was it.

She removed the lens cap. "I don't have a flash."

"That's not the point."

She was holding a small video camera. The green light was on. *Damn*. Now what was he supposed to do? "No videotaping."

"Oh? I thought we just weren't supposed to use a flash."

She was playing dumb while she let the camera

run, cradling it unobtrusively at her side, the lens pointed in the direction of the display case.

He stepped between the camera and the mummy. "No cameras."

He was only a few feet from her. He'd guess she was twenty-one or twenty-two. Not from Tuonela. Definitely not from Tuonela. She even smelled different. Sweet, like a mandarin orange.

Her gaze shifted from his face to his name tag, back to his face. "Stroud?"

He could see her connecting the dots, figuring out who he was.

Times like these he thought maybe he shouldn't have changed his name to Stroud. Maybe he should have kept his mother's name. Or maybe something completely new. He'd be going off to college in the fall, and it would be nice to ditch the freak label. Leave it in Tuonela, where it belonged.

Yep, he was bitter. Young and bitter. His girlfriend couldn't hang out with him because of his history. He didn't really blame her parents. If he had kids, he wouldn't let them hang out with him either. But without Isobel's stable influence, and with his dad doing the stuff he was doing, Graham was pissed off most of the time.

"I know the camera's running," he said.

Her cheeks turned bright red and she laughed.

Maybe now that she knew who he was, she'd pay attention to him.

Now *that* was funny.

She shut it off. "Sorry." Her smile was lopsided

and sheepish. She replaced the lens cap and stuck the camera in her bag.

"We're making a documentary," she told him. "Part of a senior project at the University of Minnesota."

Looking for a freak show. They weren't the first or the last.

"Are you related to Evan Stroud?"

"He's my dad." No sense in lying. She'd find out anyway.

"We'd love to interview him for the project." She pulled out a business card. "We'd love to interview both of you."

Interview his dad? "That won't happen." He tried to hand the card back, but she wouldn't take it.

He'd expected things to get better once he found his dad, but in a lot of ways they were worse.

"We'll be in town for two weeks and are staying at the Tuonela Inn. My cell phone number is on the card."

When he saw she wasn't going to take the card back, he pocketed it. It would have been rude to throw it away in front of her. "You're a senior at the U of M?"

"Not me."

She twisted around and looked over her shoulder for someone, then back. "I'm not a student. Well, I was, but I dropped out." She shrugged as if to say, *You know how it is with college.* "I'm working for some students. They're back there somewhere in that mob. They're going to be really pissed that I didn't get any footage of this. It's the main reason we came. They'll probably fire me and dump me without a dime."

She was playing him. He wasn't an idiot.

"It's not like we're selling it to *Geraldo*. Nobody will see it other than the professors. It's for school."

The room was packed; people were growing impatient. Someone bumped the girl from behind.

"You'd better get moving," he told her.

"Kristin!"

Near the entry to the mummy room a girl waved both arms in the air. "Did you get it?" she shouted over the crowd.

Kristin turned back to Graham and rolled her eyes. "An interview with your dad would really save my ass." She adjusted the strap on her messenger bag. "Call me." She moved past him and the mob surged forward.

Graham didn't want her to get in trouble and lose her job. Maybe he'd let her interview him, but he wasn't letting anybody near his dad.

Chapter Five

Rachel covered the skinned body with a sheet. Without removing her blood-splattered disposable gown, she left the basement autopsy suite and stepped into the hallway, where Mayor McBride and Alastair Stroud waited.

She'd invited them inside for the exam. The mayor had passed. The police chief had given up after two minutes. Her assistant had lasted ten before dashing from the room.

The carcass hadn't bothered her. Not even the smell, which was strange given her condition and the way her stomach heaved when she caught a whiff of strong perfumes.

Both men glanced at her belly, then back up, discomfort on their faces.

Except for a couple of friends, nobody in town had questioned her about the pregnancy. And nobody—*nobody*—knew the identity of the father.

The mayor pocketed his cell phone. "Well?"

He was an outsider and a relative newcomer, if

you used the Tuonela time line. He'd lived there about ten years. A young businessman with a lot of plans for change, and he didn't want those plans screwed up.

"I've never seen anything like it." Rachel thought about her moving truck parked outside. How far would she be by now? Halfway across Minnesota? Selfish of her, maybe. But she wasn't thinking of just herself anymore.

Alastair Stroud patted his shirt pocket and produced a small notebook and pen. "Was it a wild animal?"

"It was, wasn't it?" the mayor asked.

"I don't know."

"But it could have been, right?"

"The skin was removed quickly and efficiently, with what looked like great precision. I don't know how something like that could have been achieved. I'm not sure the most skilled surgeon in the world could have done something like that. And if it could be done, it would take hours. It would be tedious and sloppy. Skin will sometimes slip off after a body has been dead for a few days. I often remove the entire skin glove in order to get good prints, but this . . ." She shook her head.

"The husband said she was gone for only a short time before he found her." Alastair clicked his pen. "What could do that?"

"Coyotes," McBride said from the comfort of a stylish suit. "Had to be coyotes. I grew up on a farm. I know what a pack of them can do in just a matter of minutes."

"I couldn't find any evidence of bite marks. Coyotes would have eaten at least part of the body."

"Maybe the husband scared them off," Stroud suggested. "Maybe it wasn't coyotes, but wild dogs. Or even tame dogs. Tame dogs don't kill for food, they kill for fun."

True.

"Chief Stroud and I have been talking, and we're hoping you'll stick around until we can find a replacement," the mayor said.

Finding a replacement wouldn't be easy, since she played the unusual dual role of both coroner and medical examiner.

"It would bring some reassurance to residents and visitors," the mayor continued. "We don't want to alarm people, not when we're just getting the whole tourist thing off the ground. Your departure, on the heels of this ghastly death, will look odd."

"But I was leaving before it ever occurred."

"Most people won't know that. Most people will look at it and think you ran. That maybe you were scared. And we know there's nothing to be scared of. I'm going to put together a team. We'll scour the area and find the coyotes or dogs and round them up."

That didn't sound like a good idea. She was already imagining a mass slaughter of innocent animals.

"You feeling okay?" Alastair asked. "You look a little pale."

It was all too much. *I thought I was getting the hell out of here*, she wanted to shout.

She had to get away before the baby was born.

She'd hoped to be settled in California, find a good obstetrician and pediatrician. She couldn't have the baby here. Not in Tuonela.

She tugged off the disposable gown and wadded it up. "I'll be fine."

"So you'll stay?" the mayor asked.

"I'll think about it."

The mayor's cell phone rang. He excused himself and stepped outside for a better signal, leaving Rachel alone with Alastair Stroud.

He'd aged since she'd last seen him. He was still a nice-looking man, now with a thick head of snow white hair that seemed to have turned overnight.

"How's Graham?" she asked.

Alastair closed and pocketed the notebook. "I'm trying to talk him and Evan into moving back to town. There's plenty of room for all of us in that big house. It's not really my house anyway; it's Evan's. I don't know what he moved out there for. I guess he thinks he's saving an important part of history."

"It shouldn't be saved." It was no secret that she and Evan had disagreed about Old Tuonela.

Alastair looked uncomfortable. "He and I don't talk about it."

The mayor poked his head back inside. "I gotta go. Gotta write a press release. Please put together a quick report, something I can include in my announcement. Thanks, Rachel. I hope you'll stay. Please think about it. We'll make it worth your while."

He left.

"I hope you'll stay too," Alastair said. "Not just

because of this new development, but because of Graham." His cell phone rang. He told her good-bye and hurried out the door, phone to his ear.

Once he and the mayor were gone, Rachel walked out to the moving truck.

Her African violet and Christmas cactus were still on the front seat where she'd left them, only now they were dead.

Damn.

Don't think.

She hated her weakness. She'd just autopsied the skinned body of a woman without shedding a tear. Now, as she looked at the poor plants, a sob escaped her.

Chapter Six

In Old Tuonela, one never knew how the day would end. Sometimes it was quick, sunlight vanishing like an extinguished candle flame. Other times the light became hazy and clung to the day, unwilling to let go.

Evan Stroud hated the evenings that lingered. They taunted him with a promise of darkness. When the night finally came, he was like a released animal.

Now that the sun was gone, Evan strode angrily from the crumbling mansion, shovel and lantern in hand, heading for the stand of trees that marked the actual boundary of Old Tuonela.

The anger helped in so many ways.

He unlocked the gate, slipped through the opening, and relocked it.

He didn't want any surprise visitors.

A dirt path with cupped edges cut through grass and weeds. It was late fall, and a few hard freezes had killed back vegetation.

He was running out of time.

Old Tuonela was a ghost town originally settled by Richard Manchester, the Pale Immortal. Once Manchester was killed the town packed up and moved five miles away and started over, abandoning history and the past, leaving dark secrets buried in the ground and walls of the decaying buildings.

Evan was after those secrets.

Frustration and anger made the digging go quickly.

He couldn't explain why he dug where he dug. It was kind of a Zen thing; one spot was probably as good as any other.

He'd started the project in a structure that had once been someone's home. From there, he'd moved to the mill and now the churchyard.

This felt right.

But he'd thought that before.

He dug.

Tuonela and Old Tuonela lay in a section of a vast zone known as the Driftless Area—ground that had somehow eluded the touch of glaciers. Streams still twisted, and cliffs were craggy. Strange, unnamed plants and rare species of animals inhabited untouched deep, dark ravines. Cold pockets of air left over from the Ice Age sometimes escaped and wrapped around an ankle.

Using the shovel as a lever, Evan loosened a large stone. With both hands he removed the stone and carried it to a growing pile. He tugged the shovel free and continued the pattern.

He dug until the sky began to grow light in the

east. He turned off the lantern. Curls of steam rose from his sweat-soaked body.

Evan Stroud had two obsessions: Old Tuonela and Rachel Burton.

On more lucid nights, he could admit to himself that his obsession with Old Tuonela was used to drown out his obsession with Rachel Burton. On less lucid nights, when exhaustion numbed his mind, he could almost forget she existed. And he liked forgetting she existed. He needed to forget she existed.

The night's dig uncovered nothing.

Maybe tomorrow.

His bones ached and his hands were raw and bloody. But at least he'd be able to sleep. And when he woke up, he would dig again.

He headed home.

He slipped through the gate, locked it behind him, and began the ascent up the hill. A darker shadow stepped away from a boulder. Evan lifted the shovel, poised to strike, when the shadow spoke.

"I knew you were staying out there more than just a couple of hours," came Graham's voice out of the darkness. "I knew you were staying out there till dawn."

Evan swayed in exhaustion. "How long have you been waiting here?"

"All night. Freezing my ass off."

In the increasing light, Evan saw a blanket wrapped around Graham's shoulders. Graham relieved him of the lantern. Side by side, they walked up the treeless knoll toward the house.

"What are you looking for?" Graham asked. It was a question he'd asked before.

"The past." That was all Evan knew.

Graham shook his head. "What difference does it make? The past is over. It no longer exists. What about your book? Aren't you supposed to be writing a book? Isn't it due . . . like, in a month?"

Evan brushed a hand across his brow. Book? Yes. He had a vague recollection of a book. An editor. A publisher. A contract. That was his old life. How foolish of him to have toiled so many years on books while this project had been lying dormant.

"I could help you with it," Graham said. "Not the writing, but organizing your notes. Stuff like that."

"Maybe when winter comes."

Hopefully Graham would forget about it by then.

The day lasted forever, and it was so hard waiting for darkness. Evan had just left Old Tuonela, yet he already felt the urgent need to return to the dig site. He'd work around the clock if it were possible.

Graham looked up. "You stayed out too long."

The light was coming.

Graham removed the blanket and tossed it over Evan's head. He grabbed his father's arm and led him back into the house, where Evan collapsed in a chair at the kitchen table.

"I'll make some breakfast." Graham glanced down. "You need to wash your hands."

Evan looked at his dirt-caked, bloody palms. Yes, he needed to do that.

He continued to stare at them.

"Here." Graham helped him to the kitchen sink.

He stuck Evan's hands under the faucet and shot green dish soap on them. "I talked to Alastair today."

Evan watched Graham wash his hands. Interesting. "He's your grandfather. You should call him Grandpa, or Grandfather."

"I can't get used to that. Think I'll stick with Alastair for now. Anyway, he thinks you and I should move back to Tuonela. He thinks we could all live together in your old house." Graham shut off the water, grabbed a towel, and dried Evan's hands.

"I can't leave here. You know that."

Graham flipped the towel over his shoulder. "You need to quit going out there."

"I can't."

"You have to."

"You could come with me." Evan sat back down at the table. "Help me."

"You know I won't do that. Why even mention it?"

Graham cooked some scrambled eggs, then transferred them to the plate in front of Evan.

"Bad stuff has happened in Old Tuonela," Graham said. "Not just to me, but to other people."

"I know." Evan had no interest in food, but he picked up a fork and took a bite for Graham's sake. "That's why I'm doing what I'm doing. Those other people have a story to tell. Those people need to be heard."

Graham stood with arms and ankles crossed as he leaned against the sink. He swallowed. "Aren't you afraid?"

"Of what?"

"Of letting them loose?"

Evan thought a moment. "I think that's what they might want."

Graham blinked back tears of fear. "Did you ever think they might be bad? Because I happen to know there's bad shit out there."

"Don't cuss."

"I'll fucking cuss if I want to."

He was shouting now.

Something crashed inside Evan's brain. Blood roared through his veins. He unfolded himself and shot to his feet. With a single motion he swept his arm across the table and knocked the plate of food to the floor. In the next movement, his hand lashed out. He grabbed Graham by the throat and shoved him up against the wall.

"What did you just say to me?" He asked the question even though Graham couldn't physically reply. "I don't want to ever hear you talk that way to me again, understand?"

Graham's face was bright red. He nodded.

"Understand?"

Graham nodded again.

Evan wanted to keep squeezing. To hold Graham until he went limp, but he forced himself to let go. Graham dropped to the floor, sucked in a few deep breaths, then jumped to his feet and ran.

Chapter Seven

Police Chief Alastair Stroud headed out of town. Old Tuonela was located five miles away, in a rugged, unfarmable area of Wisconsin where deep ravines cut the earth and ancient tree trunks were cloaked in moss and shadows. There had been much speculation as to why anyone would have settled in such a remote, hard-to-reach region when the river valley was just five miles away.

Seclusion. Isolation.

Alastair suspected Richard Manchester had wanted to create an actual physical barrier for his little town. The Tuonela and Wisconsin rivers were close, but not close enough to be a doorway to the rest of the world. A man couldn't step from his home, hop on a boat, and get away.

Or go for help.

A place of madness.

Nobody knew exactly what had gone on there, and nobody needed to know. Close the door and lock it. The residents had been right.

He turned off the highway onto a narrow lane that wound through towering cottonwoods and aspens. A frost had dipped in from Canada, the chill bringing a change. A hushed layer of leaves covered the path. The golden yellow of the leaves on the trees and ground combined to create light that seemed to radiate from the earth. Poison sumac and Virginia creeper had turned deep shades of purple and red. Closer to the ground were goldenrod and love lies bleeding.

Beautiful.

A place of death shouldn't hold such beauty.

Fall had once been Alastair's favorite time of the year, but he hadn't really noticed the seasons in a long time. Now he looked around and realized with shock that fall was nearly over and winter was almost here.

He pulled up to the sprawling mansion that rumor said had once belonged to the Pale Immortal. Some even called it the Manchester house. Much of the building was in disrepair and uninhabitable, with broken windows, crumbling masonry, and weed-infested grounds.

Alastair cut the engine and sat there a moment.

Evan's car was nowhere in sight, but that didn't mean Evan wasn't home. Graham had recently gotten his driver's license and was using the vehicle for school.

No one answered the front door.

Alastair left the porch and walked around back. He knocked on the kitchen door.

No answer.

With his hands on his leather belt, he looked off into the distance, trying to gauge how far it was from Evan's house to the place they'd found the skinned body. Probably two or three miles as the crow flew.

He tested the kitchen door. Unlocked; he opened it and stepped inside.

A shattered plate lay broken on the floor, along with what looked like scrambled eggs. Black ants were busy grabbing what they could carry back to their home. There must have been thousands of them, moving in one crooked line.

"Evan!" Alastair stepped around the shattered plate. He walked down the hallway, then up the stairs. "Evan!"

They say you never quit worrying about your kids no matter how old they got. It was true. And you would do whatever it took to keep them safe.

Alastair's heart beat fast with an old dread, an old fear.

He hurried up the stairs, hit the landing, and turned. More stairs, then another hallway. He quickly located Graham's room.

A computer. Band posters. Clothes on the floor. Books and notebooks. On a desk was a framed photo of Graham's girlfriend.

Poor kids. Isobel's parents had taken her out of the country to get her away from Graham and Tuonela.

A third room was Evan's. The windows had been painted black; not a sliver of light penetrated the glass.

Alastair could barely make out a bump under the

covers. He flipped on the dim ceiling light, strode to the bed, and put out his hand to touch the shape. "Evan?"

The covers exploded and Evan shot straight up. Alastair recoiled.

Evan recognized him and relaxed. "What the hell are you doing here?"

"The door was unlocked. Not a good idea."

Evan laughed. "Nobody's coming in this house."

"Are you okay? I saw the plate on the floor—"

"A little accident, that's all." Evan swung his bare feet to the floor.

How long had it been since Alastair had last seen him? Two weeks? Three? It looked like he'd lost twenty pounds. His cheeks were sunken; he had dark shadows under his eyes.

Evan reached to push tangled chunks of black hair away from his forehead, and Alastair noticed that his fingernails were packed with dirt. Ribs showed under white skin. Raised red scars on his chest and forearm told of more recent tales.

"Did you hear about the woman who was killed?" Alastair asked.

"What woman?"

"A woman. Dead in the woods. She was skinned."

Evan looked up sharply. "Murder?"

"We don't know yet. Could be wild animals. Have you seen any packs of coyotes or dogs running around?"

Evan frowned and shook his head. "Where was this body?"

"A few miles from here." Alastair watched Evan closely.

There had been a time when he could read his son, easily read him, but since he'd come back from Florida he sometimes felt Evan was somebody he no longer knew, and trying to read him was like trying to read a stranger.

"Did you see anything?" Alastair asked. "Hear anything the night before last?"

"No." Evan frowned with suspicion. "Why are you asking me these things?"

"I'm a cop. It's what I do."

Evan grabbed a pair of jeans from the floor, stepped into them, got to his feet buttoning and zipping. "This is more than that."

"I'm concerned about you and Graham living out here. I don't think it's a good idea. Especially with winter coming on. You'll get snowed in. And now with this . . ."

Evan gave his words some thought. "I'm not moving back, but you might be right about Graham. Maybe he should live in Tuonela for the winter."

"You should come too." Alastair glanced at the plaster walls. "I'll bet this place isn't insulated."

"Graham would be better off with you."

"Not just Graham. You too."

"Somebody has to stay here."

"Why?"

"To guard Old Tuonela."

"Nobody needs to guard it."

Evan considered him for a long moment. "Why did you come back from Florida?"

"To help out."

"I think it was more than that. I think it had to do with something that happened a long time ago. When I first got sick."

Alastair's heart pounded and his mouth went dry. "What are you talking about?"

"The Pale Immortal."

He couldn't know. How could he know?

Alastair's mind raced, justifying the past. A father did what he could to save his son.

Evan picked up a glass of water from the bedside table, took a long swallow, then looked at his dad. "The heart. I'm talking about the heart. I'm talking about the broth you made from the heart of the Pale Immortal and fed to me."

Oh, Jesus. Jesus, no.

Alastair swallowed. He could feel the sweat rolling down his spine. "I don't know what you're talking about. If you heard some crazy rumor, then that's all it is. The Pale Immortal is all myth and rumors. That's just another one."

"I found it. I found the remaining heart, because you didn't feed it all to me. My bet is you got scared and stopped." Evan came and stood directly in front of him.

His eyes. Evan's eyes were different. They were darker, the pupils large and druggy. There was somebody else in there.

"I found it," Evan said. "I found it, and I drank it. Oh, I didn't know what it was at the time. I just thought it was tea." He laughed harshly. "You know how I like tea. I thought it was just some exotic brew with mushrooms and herbs. But it didn't take long for me to put it together."

"Did you drink it all? The entire container?"

"What do you think? Look at me. Do you think I consumed it all? Then you might want to ask yourself if you really want me to come to town and live with you. You might want to think really hard about that."

Alastair reached behind him. He took several steps back until he hit the door.

"What am I?" Evan asked. "That's what I'd like to know. What did you do to me?"

Alastair turned and walked blindly down the steps. Out the front door.

To the car. Get in. Turn the key.

Drive.

Away, away, away.

Before he left the last stretch of lane, before he got to the hard road that led back to Tuonela, he stopped and put the car in park.

He closed his eyes and leaned his forehead against the steering wheel. A sob tore from him and his shoulders shook.

Chapter Eight

Graham stepped from the school building, flipped open his cell phone, and called the camera girl from the museum.

He sure as hell didn't want to go home, and since he was pissed at Evan he wasn't feeling all that uncomfortable about spilling his guts in an interview.

Her name was Kristin Blackmoore.

He did feel a little weird about calling a girl, but this wasn't anything like that. Not like he was asking her out or anything, or even attracted to her. But when she answered, his heart beat in double time, then settled down.

"Can we meet at your house?" Kristin asked. "We like to capture people in their own environment."

Wouldn't that be wild if he just showed up in Old Tuonela with a camera crew? Evan would be on one of his rants, tossing plates. Or maybe he'd be muttering about what he'd dug up that night. Graham laughed just thinking about it. "No, we can't go to my place. How about upstairs at Peaches? It's a coffee shop on Main Street three blocks from the inn where you're staying. You can pretend it's in my house. Oh, and I don't want a bunch of people there, okay? Just you."

"I don't pretend. This isn't a fictional piece."

"Okay. Whatever."

He was doing her a favor, for chrissake. "Do you want to do it or not?"

He'd been so pissy lately. He knew he should be ashamed of himself, and probably would be tomorrow. But not now. Now he was pissy and he liked it.

He disconnected, hopped in his dad's black car, and drove to Peaches.

Peaches was an old two-story house that had been turned into a café. The floor was worn down to unstained wood, the couches were threadbare, and the chairs were wobbly.

Nobody was upstairs.

He settled at a small table in front of a window that overlooked Main Street. If anybody else showed up he and Kristin could step out on the balcony.

He thought he caught a glimpse of red hair.

Two minutes later Kristin appeared upstairs, a can of diet cola in one hand, a green canvas bag over her shoulder. She spotted Graham right away. Crouching, she slid her can of pop across the table, then sat down and began to unpack her bag.

Her hair was the fakest red he'd ever seen in his life. He liked it.

Was she a crust punk? Crust punks were dirty. She didn't look dirty. Her jeans were full of holes and patches, and her green tennis shoes were faded and frayed, but she looked clean.

"That was fast," he said. "You must have been close."

"I was at the inn. I had a headache this morning, so the others left to scout locations without me." She pulled out her camera and began fiddling with it. "Headache's gone now, but it will probably come back. They usually do."

"You live in Minneapolis? I'm thinking of going to the University of Minnesota."

"Saint Paul. In a neighborhood called Frogtown." She laughed. "Known for ethnic diversity, poor people, and hookers. You should come and check it out." She pulled out a small telescoping tripod, opened it, tightened the locking rings, and positioned the legs on the floor. "What are you thinking of majoring in?"

"I don't know." He shrugged. "I just need to get away from here."

"Tuonela is beautiful." She screwed the camera to the tripod. "I could stay here a while, I think. But it probably gets boring."

Sweet hell. He wished.

"This will be heavily edited—or maybe not even used," she warned.

She turned on the camera and began by asking some pretty boring things. After a while he relaxed and forgot the camera was rolling. That's when the questions got more personal. By that time he'd let down his guard and was beginning to enjoy himself.

It was like being with his therapist, only a lot more interesting.

He was pretty much a newcomer to Tuonela, so he talked about the town and the people as seen through the eyes of a newcomer. But when it came to talking about his dead, abusive mother and Evan, he stopped. While Kristin waited for him to continue, Graham thought about how strange it was that he'd traded one crazy parent for another.

He hadn't seen that coming.

"I was looking for a fairy tale," he finally said. "Because if anyplace could handle a fairy tale, you'd think it would be this place, wouldn't you? With all the crazy shit that happens here, you almost expect it. I said *shit*. Can you edit that out? Want me to do it again? No? Anyway, this is really just like any other place. It is. Swear to God. I mean, things are weird, like all the Pale Immortal stuff, but people are people. They play softball. They have picnics. They go fishing. They love and hate. Just like any other place."

"But other places don't have vampires."

"Do you believe that? Do you believe in vampires?"

She smiled. "Do you?"

"Come on."

"What about your dad?"

"Are you asking me if he's a vampire?" Graham shook his head. "I thought you said you were after something real. You're putting your own slant on this. You're going to make us look like a bunch of idiots." He watched her closely, and could tell he'd hit a nerve. "You *are*. That's what this is about. Just another freak show."

"I'm after the truth," Kristin said. "I want proof that none of this vampire stuff is real."

"You do know my dad has a skin disease, don't you? He's allergic to sunlight. It has a medical name, but most people just call it vampire disease. Look it up." He crossed his arms over his chest and leaned back in his chair. "I'm done. Shut off the camera."

She could see he was serious.

She shut off the camera, removed it from the tripod, popped out a tape the size of a small container of stick matches, and inserted another. "I want to show you something." She watched the viewscreen, then turned the camera around.

Graham leaned forward and craned his neck to see. It took him a moment to realize he was watching footage of the museum opening. Low angles, low light, and a bobbing camera made it tough to put together the exact location. But there he was, telling Kristin she couldn't use a camera in the museum. There she was, ignoring him. The camera kept running, and somehow she was able to focus on the case containing the mummified corpse. A reflection on the glass created confusion and distortion, but suddenly the face of the Pale Immortal seemed to take on a human quality.

"Isn't that freaky?" Kristin asked.

"It's a reflection," Graham said. "Somebody in the crowd."

"Is it?"

She rewound and replayed the footage. She froze the video on the face.

He stared at it for a long time. For some reason,

the reflection reminded him of his dad. He didn't mention that.

"It's just a reflection," he repeated as he watched her pack up the camera and telescope the tripod legs.

"I think we're going to a karaoke bar tonight." She zipped up her case. "Want to come?"

"I'm seventeen."

"I have a computer program that I use to make fake IDs. If you want one, just let me know."

"You're just trying to get that interview with my dad. It's not going to work."

She laughed. Threw back her head and laughed.

Maybe it *was* working.

"You're funny."

"Yeah, people tell me that. I don't really get it."

"And you're older than seventeen. Inside."

She was right.

He'd done something most adults had never done. Something that was going to haunt him for the rest of his life.

She hadn't asked him about that. Maybe she didn't know. That was nice. To be around somebody who didn't know.

"I have to work at the museum. After that I have to go home."

"Okay." She got to her feet. "I'm not trying to corrupt you or anything. Thanks for the interview. If you change your mind about karaoke, let me know."

After she left, Graham headed to the museum, where he put in a four-hour shift. He didn't want to go into the mummy room, but that was his station.

The numbers weren't as bad as they'd been on opening day, but the building was still uncomfortably crowded. After Graham got over his initial nervousness, he tested his reflection theory, standing in different locations and watching as people entered the museum, but he couldn't re-create the effect from the video.

When his shift was over, he drove to his grandfather's house and parked in front of the sidewalk.

He used speed dial to call Evan. No answer. Graham left a voice mail. "I'm probably going to stay in Tuonela tonight with Alastair. If that's not okay, let me know and I'll come home." He disconnected, grabbed his backpack, and got out of the car.

The house was located on Benefit Street in the very spot where a sharp valley gave way to flatland. Just months ago Graham's mother had dropped him off there.

Months . . . It seemed like years. Now she was dead. How many people were gone? Four?

The house was old—dark beams and stucco, with a huge front porch and woodland on three sides.

It took a while for his grandfather to answer his knock.

Even though his hair was white, Alastair Stroud probably wasn't all that old. He was kind of wiry and still kinda tan from time spent on golf courses in Florida. He wore a lot of crisp plaid shirts and always smelled faintly of aftershave. Right now he smelled like alcohol, and it took only a few seconds for Graham to realize his grandfather was wasted.

Nice.

Did any of the adults in his family act like adults? That was what he wanted to know. And his grandfather was a cop. But he guessed cops got drunk just like anybody else when they weren't on duty. Weird to think about.

Alastair tried like hell to appear sober, but he was too far gone. He blinked and dropped awkwardly into an overstuffed chair. "Have a seat." He waved a drunken hand.

Graham hovered near the doorway. "I don't know. I think maybe I'll just go."

"No, stay! Stay!"

So much for spending the night. No way was he doing that now.

"I was just getting ready to pop a frozen pizza in the oven."

Graham dropped his backpack on the floor and walked across the living room to the adjoining kitchen. Every single cupboard door was open. The floor and counters were strewn with dishes and crap that had been pulled out. "What are you doing?"

"Looking for something." Alastair jumped to his feet. "You haven't seen a small tin tea canister, have you? About this size?" He made a shape with his hands.

"Silver?"

"Yes!"

"I think I saw it with some of my dad's stuff. At the other place."

His grandfather crossed the room and grabbed him by both shoulders. "If you see it again, stay away from it." He gave him a small shake. His eyes were bloodshot and glassy. "Understand? Stay away from it."

"Okay, you know what?" Graham bent his knees and slipped from his grasp. "I can't do this." He walked to the door and picked up his backpack. "Go to bed. Go to bed and sleep it off."

"If you see it, call me. If you see the tin."

"I'll do that."

He left.

Out the door and back in the car.

He made a three-point turn and headed down the hill that took him past the morgue, where Rachel Burton had lived. Parked outside the Victorian mansion was what looked like the same moving truck he'd seen there before. Was Rachel still in town?

He pulled into the back driveway, then ran around the brick path that led to the massive wooden front doors. He rang Rachel's apartment. The front door buzzed to let him in.

He strode down the dark, carpeted halls, briefly thought about taking the elevator, then decided to sprint up the stairs to her place on the third floor.

She opened the door, and it was immediately obvious she'd been crying. Her eyes were red; her nose was red.

And her stomach.

What the hell?

"You're having a baby?" The words just came out.

"Didn't you know?" She turned and shuffled away to grab a box of tissues. "I figured everybody in town knew."

Holy shit.

He thought back to the last time he'd seen her. She'd been driving the coroner van. Her stomach had been hidden.

He didn't even know she had a boyfriend. Maybe she didn't. Maybe this was one of those artificial in-seminations. Oh, that was just too bizarre. He felt heat creeping up his face, and he lingered by the door.

"Come on in."

The apartment was empty except for a red retro table and chairs. In the middle of the table were two dead plants.

"You know what . . . ?" He pointed a thumb over his shoulder. "I think I should go. . . ."

"Stay a minute." She blew her nose and tossed the tissue aside. Now he caught sight of a big pile of wadded-up tissues on the floor next to a chair.

"I saw the truck outside. What happened? Aren't you moving?"

"I can't get out of here. I have to face it. It's not going to happen." She made a useless gesture with her hand. "I can't leave. Tuonela won't let me leave."

He wanted to ask her about the baby, but how did you do something like that? "I have to go." He backed up. "I'm sorry for disturbing you. I'm glad you aren't moving. Well, I'm sorry for you, but glad for me. I gotta go."

He gave a little bounce, spun around, and got the hell out of there. Back in the car he pulled out his cell phone and punched in Kristin Blackmoore's number.

They hadn't left for the bar yet.

He caught up with them at the inn, where Kristin made a fake ID for him. It took only minutes to print it out on the inn's printer and slip it into a used laminate sleeve. He was twenty-one and his name was Kevin Graham.

Pretty sneaky.

The bar was less than a mile away, so they walked. Claire—the person in charge of the shoot—didn't go. She was working on getting a psychic to come to Tuonela to do a reading on the town. So it was just the four of them—three guys and a girl.

Until that moment, until they were all walking down the sidewalk together talking about nothing, Graham hadn't realized how lonely he'd been. Especially since Isobel had left. He knew kids at school, but nobody really hung out with him. Kids his age were afraid of him. He was an outsider. One with an unpleasant past.

Maybe that was why he found the idea of spending time with the documentary crew appealing. They were outsiders too. And they didn't know about him. Not everything.

The fake ID got him inside.

"Told you there was nothing to worry about," Kristin said. "They don't care if you're old enough to drink, as long as you have something that keeps them from getting in trouble."

He got drunk. Wasted, actually.

Briefly he thought of Alastair, about how truly unattractive a drunk person could be, but he quickly brushed that memory aside. They bought something called Immortal Punch. It came in a giant bowl and knocked them all on their asses.

He couldn't sing worth shit, but he got up and sang the Pogues song "Dirty Old Town."

The night grew late, and people began to drift away and return to their homes. Ian and Stewart headed back to the inn. Graham and Kristin stayed until the karaoke machine was unplugged, the beer coolers refilled, and the OPEN light turned off.

They clung to each other.

Under the glow of a full moon, they talked and laughed as they made their way back down the steep sidewalk to Main Street.

Leaves whispered even though there was no breeze, and shadows crept out of sidewalk cracks.

They were so loud and so caught up in their drunkenness that they would never have known if anybody had followed them. They would never have known if something less than human was drawn to the noise, watching and skittering along behind them with a sound that resembled rustling leaves.

They stopped under a street lamp.

"I killed somebody," Graham announced.

Kristin stared at him. "I died." She swayed, then held up two fingers. "Twice."

They burst out laughing and continued down the hill, where the moon was obscured and the shadows were so dark they could no longer see their feet in front of them. Where their steps took them off the edge of the earth.

"Shhhh," Kristin said when they reached the inn.

She fished a key from her pocket and unlocked the door as if she lived there. Graham was impressed. With great exaggeration, they tiptoed up the stairs to Kristin's room on the third floor.

Once they were inside with the door closed, Kristin toed off her sneakers and slipped out of her jeans, leaving them in a pile on the floor next to the bed. "You should really come to school in Minneapolis." She crawled under the covers. Graham peeled off his jeans and followed.

Chapter Nine

A scraping sound pulled Evan from a comatose sleep. He lay in bed, ears alert.

There it was again. Coming from downstairs. Like a bare branch scraping against a window.

He checked the clock by the bed. Two a.m. Normally he waited and waited for darkness. How had he slept so late?

He got up and got dressed.

In Graham's room he found a neatly made bed and no sign of Graham. He would call Alastair. But at the last moment he thought to go downstairs to check his voice mail and found a message from Graham saying he was staying in Tuonela with his grandfather. Evan relaxed.

The scratching started again. Now that he was closer he could tell it was coming from outside. He followed the sound to the front door.

On his porch he found a stinking, fetid mass of boneless, formless skin with black, opaque pits where the eyes should have been. He put a hand to his nose and pulled back a few inches.

Is this a dream? Have I finally completely lost my mind?

As he watched, the skin turned and tumbled down the porch steps to collapse in a pile on the walk. A minute passed; then it began to move again. A hand reached out, nails digging into the ground. It pulled itself several feet, then repeated the movement.

Evan grabbed the shovel and lantern and followed from a safe distance.

He watched as the skin crawled under the gate, then made its way down the lane toward the heart of Old Tuonela.

Matthew Torrance had been the museum's custodian for almost twenty years. He liked the job. He liked being by himself. He liked being able to listen to music with headphones on while he cleaned. He liked being able to smoke a joint if he felt like it, or take a nap. Nobody to bug him.

He was single, never married, and was into heavy metal. He read science fiction, and had been to two *Star Trek* conventions back in the early nineties. He'd met a girl there, but after three years he'd decided *Star Trek* wasn't enough to have in common. He wasn't even sure he liked girls. Or guys. Or people in general.

He went out on the roof of the museum and lit up.

The sky was clear and the moon was full. And the pot was new and potent as hell. *Damn*. After a few hits he started feeling almost too fucked-up. If there was such a thing. He put out the joint, tucked it into a little plastic film canister, and slipped the canister into his pocket.

Whoa. Had to sit down. Had to *lie* down.

He sprawled out on his back on the tar-and-pea-gravel roof.

The stars above his head swirled.

He put on his headphones and turned on his iPod. Tunes. The tunes would stabilize him.

He lost track of time.

Maybe he'd been there three minutes or three hours.

He checked the luminescent dial on his watch, but immediately forgot what it said.

Gotta go clean the museum. Gotta go get stuff done.

He shoved himself to his feet and went back inside. Instead of using the stairs, he took the service elevator down to the basement level, where he'd left his supplies.

He dug out his insulated lunch bag and began eating everything in it.

Maybe if he ate enough he'd come down.

Pretty soon his chicken sandwich was gone. The chips were gone. His diet soda was gone, along with a giant peanut-butter cookie he'd picked up at the gas station near his house. Now he was stuffed, stoned, but still thinking about food.

Something chocolate would be nice. . . .

He pulled out his duty list.

Buff the floors.

Shit. He didn't feel like doing that. It was hard

enough when he was straight. The buffer had a mind of its own, and sometimes it got away from him. He'd do it tomorrow. Maybe he'd just drag the dry mop across the floors tonight.

That's what he did.

And became absorbed in the rhythmic pattern of the red mop sliding across the maple floor, the contrast of deep red against the pale wood, the way the handle's shadow shifted from right to left as he swept, stark and sharp.

The shadow vanished.

Had a bulb gone out? Then he realized something was blocking the light. His own body?

With mop handle in hand, he shifted slightly.

Nothing changed.

Something wrong.

Something very wrong.

And yet he didn't want to turn and look behind him. If somebody was back there he didn't want him to know he was onto him.

He casually shut off his iPod. Then *sweep, sweep, sweep.*

Turn and look.

Nothing.

Nobody.

He swung back around. Something still blocked the light.

He wanted to run. He wanted to get the hell out of there. Instead, he forced himself to walk around.

He checked the restrooms. He checked the storage closet. The last place he looked was the new room.

He let out a gasp and dropped the mop. He took two steps back, his mouth hanging open.

Son of a bitch.

Gloria Raymond woke up, tossed back the covers, and got out of bed. Without putting on shoes or a coat, without pulling up her hair or even covering it with a hat, she walked out the front door, then down the sidewalk to the center of the street.

A mile took her through the park and through vacant lots and woodland, across railroads tracks and broken glass. Feeling no pain, her feet cut and bleeding enough to leave footprints, she walked to the levee and climbed the chain-link fence that had been put up last year when a three-year-old had drowned. Her pink cotton nightgown snagged and ripped as she dropped to the other side.

Even though she would be seventy-five next month, she jumped nimbly to the bobbing dock and walked to the end that jutted out into the Wisconsin River.

The moon reflected off the surface.

A full moon, round like a face. The water rippled, creating a pretty, repeating design that was mesmerizing.

Under the surface of the water Gloria saw her husband smiling up at her, his eyes wide open. He reached for her hand, and she reached back. . . .

Evan followed the skin to Old Tuonela, where crumbling buildings had been reclaimed by nature. The skin collapsed in a dark corner near a stone wall.

Evan finally understood.

He jabbed the shovel in the ground and began digging.

Rachel couldn't sleep.

She kept dreaming that someone was in her apartment. She would awaken with a jolt, lie there and listen to the ticking clock, then go back to sleep, only to have it happen again. The dream itself was so real that even after waking up she felt a presence and imagined the sound of breathing coming from nearby.

Earlier in the day the mayor had sent a crew over to unload the moving truck. Within an hour of their arrival her apartment was almost back to the way it had been before she'd tried to get the hell out of Dodge. They'd even put the dishes in the cupboard and returned books to the bookshelves. Boxes that had taken her weeks to pack were unpacked, broken down, and waiting to be picked up by Recycling.

Erase and rewind.

Part of her was shocked that she'd given in so easily. That same part wanted to call a cab and head for the nearest airport, get on a plane, and that would be that. Job done. Because once she had some physical distance between herself and Tuonela, the pull wouldn't be as strong. She knew that from experience. Close proximity brought about confusion and mental chaos.

But there was another part of her that was almost smug about the way things had turned out. Maybe she could have a better life somewhere else, but this was where she belonged. All roads led back.

She drifted off to sleep again.

Tossing and turning, she began to dream of food. That dream mingled with the dream about the man in the house, and then it shifted to the skinned body in the basement morgue, then back to food.

There was nothing to eat in her apartment.

She got up, slipped on a pair of jeans and a jacket, and drove to a twenty-four-hour grocery store in a strip mall on the edge of town.

The streets were deserted, and the moon created deep shadows that moved and lingered in her peripheral vision. She heard faint voices and checked to see if the radio was on.

No.

She listened intently.

The van's engine, along with the tires singing over pavement, sounded like voices. Or maybe it was the wind, which let out a whistle whenever it hit the driver's window just right. Or maybe it was the whisper of leaves as they marched through intersections. . . .

The parking lot was empty; she pulled into a spot near the entrance.

Automatic doors and metal railings.

Inside, fluorescent lights were a blinding assault.

"Looking for something in particular?"

She was startled to find herself staring at the meat cooler.

Somehow she'd traversed the length of the store.

With no memory of the brief journey, she looked up at the stock boy. "Just browsing."

Anything that happened in the middle of the night took on a strange quality. Had she been asleep? Had she driven here in some dreamlike state? Humans weren't nocturnal. Humans weren't supposed to be awake after the sun went down.

She caught a distorted glimpse of herself in the chrome trim of the meat case. Ashen skin and dark-circled eyes.

The stock boy left and she glanced back down at the meat—and began to salivate. She grabbed both pint containers and flat trays, and carried them to the checkout counter.

Why couldn't she crave pickles and ice cream, like most pregnant women?

The clerk commented on her purchases as she scanned. "You must be doing the raw diet. I started my dogs on that three months ago, and you should see them now. They have the shiniest coats and brightest eyes. Course, I'm going broke feeding them." She rattled off the amount due. "What kind of dog do you have?"

Rachel looked up from staring at a pool of blood that had leaked onto the conveyor belt. "What?"

"Dog. What kind of dog?"

"Oh." She fished out her credit card and handed it to the woman. "A mutt." She couldn't believe she was lying about having a dog. "He has some shepherd in him. Maybe some collie." She didn't want to tell the woman the meat was all for her.

The woman slid the card through the reader and

passed it back. "Mutts are good. When you get special breeds you can run into all sorts of trouble. Blindness, hip problems. And you're supposed to kill them if they have a defect. I can't imagine doing that."

"That would be awful," Rachel agreed, unable to fully concentrate on the conversation.

The woman double-bagged the dripping meat and handed the plastic bags to Rachel. "Wait." She ducked and produced a dog biscuit from under the cash register. "I keep them there for working dogs, but give your guy a treat from me when you get home." The automatic door banged. Both women turned, but no one was there.

"The wind is crazy tonight," the clerk said. "And every time I turn on the vacuum, I think I hear a buncha people talking."

Rachel remembered the radio—or what she'd thought had been the radio.

On the way back to the morgue, she could smell the rich scent of blood. She drove too fast, but the streets were deserted.

Lights continued to control intersections, even though there was no traffic. Impatient, she gunned the van and ran a red light. She listened for a siren, and watched the rearview mirror for police.

Nothing.

At home she got out a frying pan and put it over a flame on the gas stove. Then she pulled the lid from one of the plastic containers. With a fork, she lifted out a piece of liver that unfolded until it was twelve inches long and six inches wide.

It sizzled when it hit the pan.

She picked up the container and carried it to the sink. She started to dump the contents, paused, then lifted the plastic tub to her mouth—and drank the blood.

She used to get out-of-control chocolate cravings before her period. One candy bar or brownie was never enough. This was like that, multiplied by a thousand. Once she tasted the salty richness of the blood, she had to have more.

She shut off the flame under the pan and slipped the still-raw liver onto a plate. She cut a piece and took a bite. It was rubbery, but the chill of refrigeration had been seared away. She chewed and swallowed. Unsated, she picked up the liver with her bare hands.

Evan's shovel hit something hard. Probably a rock. He brought the lantern closer and scraped loose dirt away.

A skull, crushed by the impact of the shovel blade. He continued more carefully, uncovering the rest of the body. That was followed by another skeleton, this one smaller.

He'd found a mass grave.

Rachel slept, her mind full of strange dreams that were mixed with combined images of the Pale Immortal. She awoke confused, her body humming from a touch that seemed as real as the room and the bed.

It had to be the pregnancy.

Her nightgown was soaked with sweat. Tendrils of damp hair clung to her neck. The bedsheets were twisted and soaked.

She turned on a night-light and removed the damp gown, dropping it to the floor near her bare feet. From a drawer she grabbed a large T-shirt and tugged it over her head, then reached under her arms for the hem, looked down, and let out a gasp.

On her stomach were two red areas of discoloration that looked like handprints. As she watched, the imprints faded until they were gone.

Chapter Ten

Alastair was drunk.

Not proud of himself for that. He'd had a drinking problem that had started shortly after Evan's illness had manifested itself, but he'd finally pulled himself together and gotten the problem under control. Now he was afraid he'd opened the floodgate. But his drinking was the least of his worries. There was something going on, something that seemed to have started about the time the body of the Pale Immortal had been moved from a secret location to the museum. It could be argued that it had really started months ago, with a gang of kids and one crazy guy who thought he was the reincarnation of the Pale Immortal. Or some might even argue that it had started a hundred years ago.

Alastair's phone rang.

Let it go.

He wasn't going to answer it, but then he remembered he was chief of police, and if he didn't answer it somebody would probably start pounding on his door. He sure as hell didn't want that to happen.

Reports coming in of sightings, he was told. Not UFO sightings, but people claiming to have seen the Pale Immortal, or someone who looked like the Pale Immortal, roaming through town. There were other reports, even more disturbing, of someone wandering around dressed in what looked like a human skin.

That sobered him up.

He disconnected and immediately got another call from his deputy and assistant, Brian Finn. "Got a report from the museum. The Pale Immortal moved." There was laughter in the man's voice, but also a hint of doubt.

This *was* Tuonela.

"Moved? What does that mean?"

"I'm not sure."

Alastair got out of bed, drank some strong coffee that had been sitting in the pot for who knew how long, gargled with Listerine, slapped on some after-shave, popped gum in his mouth, and headed downtown.

His attempts at covering up the stink had probably helped, but he could still smell alcohol on himself, seeping out of his pores.

When he arrived at the museum, the sun wasn't up yet. Two cop cars were parked near the door, and a smiling young officer let him inside, looking sheepish and saying something about a wild-goose chase.

The Pale Immortal was in the Plexiglas case,

where it was supposed to be, looking like it was supposed to look.

"Sorry to get you down here for nothing," the custodian said.

Matthew Torrance was a good guy, but he had a drug habit everybody in town knew about and pretended didn't exist, since he kept it to himself and wasn't dealing. You did what you had to do to get by. To get through life. But in this case, drugs made Matthew an unreliable witness.

"I could have sworn . . . " Matthew's words trailed off, and he hung his head in embarrassment.

"Lot of weirdness going on tonight," Alastair said in an attempt to make light of the situation. "Something in the air." He was just talking, making noise to reassure the guy, but he also knew there was some truth to what he said.

Matthew nodded. "It's a hum. A buzz. Like a buncha people talking. Ever go to sleep at night, and just as you're drifting off you hear them? Like a huge auditorium full of people? I used to think I was hearing other people's thoughts, you know? Like the collective unconscious. You get to that place, that door between sleeping and waking, and you can hear them. That's when you connect. But now I'm not so sure. Now I wonder . . ." He glanced at the mummy.

They were all related. The people of Tuonela. Like some strange dynasty of horror, most of them could trace their ancestry back to Old Tuonela.

And those reports of the Pale Immortal walking through town . . .

Mass hysteria.

Occasionally Alastair thought of time as liquid, the past reaching into the future and vice versa. Were the residents of Tuonela seeing imprints of the past? Reenactments of past events? Were uneasy spirits wandering through town, searching for answers to their own unanswered questions?

Alastair looked down at the floor inside the case. Was that disturbed dust?

He didn't point it out. He didn't say anything. Instead, he left the museum and drove to Old Tuonela.

The sun was up, but it hadn't yet reached the shrouded, overhanging lane that led to Evan's house. Steam curled from the wet ground and lay heavily in dips and valleys, clinging to low vegetation.

Once again, Evan's car wasn't there. Alastair suddenly remembered Graham stopping by his place last night. A fresh wave of shame washed over him.

A lantern and a dirt-encrusted shovel had been left by the front door—signs of Evan's excavating.

Alastair walked toward the stand of timber that marked the edge of Old Tuonela. He climbed the gate and headed down the worn path that led into the woods, the heavy dew soaking into his pant legs.

Towering pines and cottonwoods that hadn't lost their leaves blocked the sunlight. The air smelled of damp earth, crushed plants, and compost.

Decay and fermentation. Life and death.

Alastair had been jerked from a drunken sleep, and he realized he hadn't been completely sober at the museum. In fact, he'd been pretty lit. Now he was crashing, his body beginning to ache. His head hurt like hell, and he felt a little queasy. The shameful thing was that he wanted another drink. Vodka with a beer chaser. He could almost taste it. . . .

He paused and braced his hands on his knees, catching his breath but also struggling with the sense of dread that had been living in his heart ever since he'd come back to Tuonela. He wanted to pack up his son and grandson and take them away from here. Take them far away to a town so different they would soon forget about this dark, rotten place.

But Evan would never leave. Alastair knew that. He could dream about a different kind of life for his son, but in his heart he knew it wasn't going to happen.

Alastair crested the final hill and stopped.

Before him was a small, timber-filled valley dotted with the crumbling carcasses of structures that had once been buildings. Buildings where people had once worked and lived. Now the homes were nothing more than misshapen objects covered with moss and tangled vines, encased, protected, yet also devoured.

Holes.

Everywhere.

Some as large as small buildings. Others smaller, more the size of a grave. How many? A hundred? More?

Jesus.

How had one man possibly moved so much earth?

And his next thought, the thought that had been lurking for a long time: His son had lost his mind.

Back at the house, Alastair entered without knocking. The eggs from yesterday had been cleaned up—a good sign.

This time he didn't call Evan's name. Instead, he moved quietly through the silent structure and up the stairs.

Graham's room was empty, his bed made.

It seemed strange that a kid would leave so early in the morning. Kids liked to sleep. But maybe he was meeting friends at Peaches before school.

A stench hit him. He pivoted. He put his hand to his face to cover his nose. Death. That's what he smelled.

And heard.

Because he knew that sound. The low buzz of flies.

With his hammering heart sick with dread, he forced himself to move forward, in the direction of Evan's room.

There was his son.

In bed.

Quiet and still.

The thing he'd spent years fearing had finally happened. Evan was dead. But just as the agonizing thought filled his head, Evan made a small sound and rolled to his side, asleep, one bare white arm above the covers.

The flies . . . Alastair could still hear the flies. . . .

The room was black, slivers of light cutting

through cracks in the walls and separations between warped boards.

Alastair stepped closer, the floor creaking beneath him. He tracked the buzzing to the opposite side of the bed. As his eyes adjusted to the darkness, he was finally able to make out bloat flies circling a pile of clothing.

Alastair stepped closer.

He pressed a fist to his mouth.

Not clothes.

On the floor in front of him was a skin. A rancid, rotten human skin.

Chapter Eleven

Dr. Ted Jacobs ran the ultrasound transducer across Rachel's stomach while they both watched the monitor.

"Looks fine," he said.

Rachel relaxed.

"There's the heart." He pointed. "See all four chambers? Here's the brain and spine. See the eye? It's open."

"Oh, my God. And there's a hand."

"Can't make out the sex. Legs are crossed." Dr. Jacobs turned off the ultrasound machine.

"I've had strange cravings and strange dreams."

"Not unusual. Maggie was the same way." He wiped the gel from her stomach, hit the foot pedal on the metal trash can, and tossed the paper towel. "I thought you were leaving town."

She pulled down her top and pushed herself higher on her elbows. "I tried. You know how it is."

"All roads lead back to Tuonela?" He laughed. "Tell me about it." He'd tried to leave too. He'd spent a couple of years at a practice in Milwaukee before coming back. "We need new blood; otherwise we'll soon have people running around with two heads and webbed feet."

"Nobody wants to move here."

"I'm hoping the increase in tourism will bring some new residents and new life into the town."

A nurse peeked into the room, handed him a sheet of paper, and left, closing the door behind her. "Looks like your iron level is way down," Ted said. "Everything else looks good. Have you been taking your supplements?"

"I may have missed one or two. I've been craving meat." She couldn't bring herself to admit that she'd been craving *raw* meat.

"That's understandable when your body is suffering from an iron depletion. Have you been tired?"

"Yes, but I've been busy. Moving—or trying to move—and then with the body that was found outside of town." She put a hand to her stomach. "I worry about the baby."

"Are you talking about your job? I wouldn't worry about it unless dealing with death is suddenly bothering you in ways it didn't bother you before. A lot of mothers work right up until delivery day."

"No, I'm fine with autopsies. It's just . . . everything. I'm stressed out. I worry about the stress."

"It's none of my business. I'm speaking as a friend rather than as your doctor, but have you told the father?"

"No." She sat up all the way.

"Are you going to? Not that I don't think you're

perfectly capable of raising a child on your own, but I just thought this secrecy might be the source of some of your stress. And I know that if a woman were pregnant with my baby, I'd want to know."

"I plan to tell him."

"You're in your third trimester." A gentle reminder.

"It's not that easy. I've made a couple of attempts, but he hasn't returned my calls." It wasn't as if she and the father had a relationship. It wasn't a love affair that had soured. It had just been Tuonela doing what it always did—screwing with people's heads. "I agree he has a right to know, but I have the feeling he won't even care."

"You know what I always remember about you from school?" He smiled. "How fearless you were." His smile changed. It became concerned. He could see she was hiding something. "But I see fear in your eyes now."

Yes, she was afraid. Of more than he could guess. "Pregnancy changes a person. I worry about everything now."

Protect the baby. She had to protect the baby. And the last thing she wanted was people saying her child was a vampire.

Chapter Twelve

Now he knew how a killer felt.

The blind panic. The need to immediately dispose of the body, get rid of the evidence. *Now.* The illogical thinking that seemed logical.

Hide it. Get rid of it. Pretend it never happened.

Alastair drove out of town and kept driving. He drove fifty miles while the stench seeped from the trunk and filled his car. It soaked into his clothes and made his throat burn.

At the fifty-mile mark, he started looking for some isolated area off a back road. His plan was to dump the skin somewhere remote. Maybe in a river or a lake. Water was a good way to get rid of evidence. But now that he'd been on the road over an hour, he started to calm down and think more clearly. Dumping the skin was too risky. He needed time.

So he turned around and headed home.

Think.

He had to think.

The criminals who'd been able to hide their crimes for the longest times were the ones who didn't panic, who didn't get in a hurry to get rid of the evidence. They were the ones who kept the body close.

He returned home and parked his car in the unattached garage. The house may have been in town, but it was surrounded by timber Evan had called his buffer zone.

Alastair went into the house and returned to the garage with several large black garbage bags. He stuffed the skin into a plastic bag, then followed up with two more layers of plastic. When he was finished, he wrapped tape around the whole package, then labeled it DEER. He took the package inside, went to the basement, and tucked it into the bottom of the chest freezer, stacking deer meat on top of it.

A father did what he had to do to protect his son.

Alastair took a shower and threw his clothes in the washing machine. But he could still smell the skin. The stench was embedded in his sinuses.

His phone rang.

A body had been found in the river.

Had Evan struck again?

Alastair's car reeked of death. He drove to the river with all of the windows down. He could have driven to the police station and picked up his patrol car, but he didn't want to leave his stinking vehicle in the parking lot.

When he reached the crime scene, he parked a block away from everybody else.

A cluster of people stood near the dock. The

coroner van was there. Two patrol cars, and way too many gawkers. He found Rachel Burton in the crowd.

"Gloria Raymond," Rachel said.

"Any obvious cause of death?"

"Looks like a straightforward drowning, but I'll be able to tell more after the autopsy."

A police officer spotted him and stepped forward. "Neighbors say she's been a little goofy since her husband died."

"Suicidal?" *Please let the woman be suicidal.*

"Not overtly, but she was suffering from depression."

Alastair rubbed his chin. "You say it happened last night? That might explain the reports we got of someone wandering through town. It was probably poor Mrs. Raymond."

A police car pulled to a stop and another officer jumped out. "We checked her house. The front door was wide open. No sign of a break-in. Nothing appeared disturbed. Looks like she just walked out the front door and headed for the river."

"Where did she live?" Alastair asked.

"Corner of Fairmont and Adams."

"That's a long way for somebody her age to walk."

"It fits," Rachel said. "Her feet are pretty badly cut up. She probably walked all the way here, poor woman."

"Sad," Alastair said. At the same time he was humming inside. It wasn't Evan. Evan didn't do it.

"I don't get it," a young officer said. "If you're

going to kill yourself, why not do it at home? Why walk so far? Why not at least drive?"

"We don't know that it was suicide," Rachel reminded him. "Maybe she was sleepwalking. Or suffering from dementia."

"Let me have a look at the body before you load her up," Alastair said.

He and Rachel walked to the gurney, where her assistant and two officers stood. Rachel unzipped the black bag. A tangled, torn, twisted nightgown was wrapped around the woman's body.

"Part of her gown was found on the fence," Rachel said. "Over there."

"She climbed a fence?" Alastair shook his head. "Amazing."

Gloria Raymond's eyes were open and covered with a white film. But her mouth was smiling sweetly. It gave Alastair the creeps. "Why does her face look like that? Rigor mortis?"

"No, she's not in rigor." Rachel stared at the woman. "I think she's just happy."

Skin in the freezer.

A human skin in the freezer.

What had he been thinking? What was he doing?

"Are you okay?"

He blinked.

Rachel was staring at him. Could she smell him? Could she smell death on him?

He was wearing his horrible crime like clothing, a flag, and anybody who glanced his way would know what he'd done. It radiated from him.

He was overwhelmed by his own shame. He was a *cop*, for chrissake. Chief of police.

Suicide didn't seem like such a bad idea. He just wanted all of this to stop. But he couldn't leave his son. He couldn't leave Graham.

"Alastair? Are you okay?"

He still hadn't answered her. "I got up early. Had a little problem at the museum. Now that I think about it, I haven't eaten today."

She was watching him with concern.

There had been a time when he was fairly certain Rachel would end up his daughter-in-law. Things changed. Disease came knocking. Among other things. Yet he thought of her as a daughter. Her father had been his close friend. His best friend. What would Seymour think about what he was doing? He wouldn't approve. Rachel wouldn't approve either.

"I haven't eaten either. How about some breakfast?" Rachel smiled at him. "My treat."

Chapter Thirteen

Things had gotten out of hand last night.

I didn't need anybody to tell me that. I drank too much. Now it was morning, I had an awful hangover, and we were getting ready to head out for the day.

You know how it is. Those first few minutes when you get up and think you might be able to make it, that maybe you don't feel so bad. But then fifteen minutes later you realize you had no business getting out of bed.

Everybody else had already left the inn and was outside waiting for me. I took it easy on the stairs. My skin felt too small for my body, and when a wave of heat rolled over me I stopped halfway down, a hand on the banister. I took a few deep breaths and continued.

Outside, the cool morning air hit my face, and for a second I thought I might live.

The van was parked and waiting at a curb.

I thought Graham had left.

No.

He stood on the sidewalk as if waiting for an invitation to come along, hands deep in the front pockets of his jeans, shoulders hunched against the morning wind, his curly hair blowing over his eyes.

My heart softened.

What a cutie. Too cute. And too young. But he did seem older than seventeen. The way he looked people in the eye. The way he didn't glance down or away. He had a girlfriend who was out of the country. Why did that make him even more appealing? But it did. The challenge of the attached. The challenge of the celibate.

Sometimes I really hate myself.

"I could help," he offered when nobody acknowledged his presence. "Take you around town."

From the passenger seat of the van, Claire held up a piece of paper. "We have a map."

"Yeah, but do you know people? I know people."

"Don't you have school?" I asked.

Cruel to remind him that he was a kid, but it had to be done. We hadn't had sex last night, but I still felt weird about his staying the night. And the rest of them were acting as if they knew something. They knew nothing.

But he *was* a kid. Not that much younger than me, but still a kid. I didn't want to deal with this. Right now I just wanted to find something greasy to eat.

I sent brain waves in his direction. *Please leave.*

His black car was parked where he'd left it. He should get in and drive away. Better for him. Better for me.

Just drive.

Graham shrugged. "I don't always go to school. And I'd learn more spending the day with you."

Stewart sighed and drummed his fingers against the steering wheel.

"I know this old guy," Graham pitched. "He usually hangs out at a café by the river. He's always telling stories about Old Tuonela."

"I didn't think people talked about Old Tuonela." I tossed my pack in the backseat and slid in after it.

"Nobody talks about Old Tuonela. Some say the ancestors were sworn to secrecy or something. But this guy's mom was pretty crazy, and she used to tell him stuff. Stuff nobody else talks about."

We let him come.

He took us to a café by the river on a narrow, broken street filled with potholes. A locals' hangout. The kind of place where everybody stared at you when you stepped in the door.

It smelled like strong, bad coffee, scrambled eggs, and maple syrup. The tables dated back to the sixties or seventies. A lot of happy red and white. A plate-glass window faced the river. Big red letters said BETTY'S BREAKFAST. Next to the text was a poorly drawn coffee cup and a platter of pancakes.

The old guy wasn't there. That figured. Was the whole thing a ruse so we'd let Graham come with us? Annoying.

We sat down and ordered breakfast, hoping the old guy would show up. When we were done eating, I felt a little less awful, but there was still no sign of our man of secrets.

I got out my camera and took a few interior shots of the café before we left.

Outside Graham nudged me with his elbow. "There he is." I followed his pointing finger.

An old homeless man sat on a bench in the shade, watching sunlight dance on the river. It was the sign-carrying protester from the museum opening.

Claire introduced herself and told him about the documentary.

He was really old. Over eighty, I'd guess. He wore a heavy denim jacket. His liver-spotted hands rested on the handle of his wooden cane. He'd lost several teeth, and one of his eyes was cloudy. Perched on top of his head at a crooked angle was a filthy red cap advertising a local hardware store. The man's name was Harold.

I don't want to get old. I have a horrible fear of getting old.

It took less than a minute for him to agree to the videotaping. I worried that he didn't understand.

The man directed his gaze toward Claire. "Are you the one?" When she didn't answer, he moved to me. I wished he hadn't done that. "Are *you* the one?" Then to Graham: "You? Is it you?"

Graham uncrossed his arms and came closer to join in the conversation, picking up the slack, since nobody else seemed to know what to do with the old guy. "What are you talking about?"

A memory from last night came rushing into my brain. *I killed a man.*

"'He changed his shape and promptly became something else,'" Harold said. "'Went as something black to sea as an otter to the sedge; he crawled as an iron worm.'"

"He quotes the Kalevala," Graham explained. "It's kinda his thing."

Claire shot Graham an annoyed look and pulled me aside. Keeping her hand on my arm, she said, "Okay, this isn't going anywhere. The guy is obviously nuts. I don't want to hurt his feelings or set him off. Just pretend to videotape him for a minute or two; then catch up with us. I'll take Stewart and Ian and head down to the river. I want you to get some introductory shots and some presentation footage when you're done here." She jogged off across the grass, motioning for Stewart and Ian to follow, leaving Graham and me with the old guy.

I removed the lens cap and turned on the camera. "Guess we're on our own." Might as well actually record the interview. I could always tape over it if it wasn't anything I wanted to save.

Graham picked up a chair and placed it opposite the bench. He sat down, his body language relaxed, elbows on his knees, hands clasped. "What about the stories your mom used to tell you?" Graham asked. "About Old Tuonela?" Apparently he was used to dealing with people who were a little slanted.

"Tell us about the day before everybody left," Graham coaxed.

Harold seemed perplexed. "You want to know about that?" He put a couple of fingers to his bottom lip. "They weren't supposed to talk about that day, you know."

"That was a long time ago. You told me all about it. We were sitting right here."

"Did I? I don't remember."

"I could repeat what you said, but I'd rather hear it from you. You tell it better."

"They locked her up. The place on the outskirts of town. You know the one?"

"Tuonela Mental Hospital?"

"That's it. We used to go see her. Me and my sister when we were little. Our mother would be sitting in the garden, sun shining in her golden hair, looking so pretty, smelling like flowers. . . . But I think we reminded her of the past. Whenever me and my sister went there, our mother would get sad and mixed up and start talking about Old Tuonela. Like she couldn't stop herself. Like she just had to get it out."

I hadn't taken the time to set up my tripod. Kneeling on the ground, I tried to keep the camera steady.

"She told me they buried a buncha people in one grave," Harold said. "Mothers and kids. Just dug a big hole, threw them in, and covered it back up."

Graham glanced at the camera, then back to Harold. "What happened to the people in the grave? How did they die?"

"My mother was just a little girl. Maybe seven. Her friends were murdered. Mother hid under the bed, but she heard the whole thing." His mouth trembled. My eyes teared up, and I had to blink to clear my vision.

"Later she watched the burial." He let out a snort. "If you want to call it that. Guess nobody was really paying attention to a kid. She said they just dumped the bodies in a big hole.

"Right after that everybody moved. Everybody left Tuonela. Somebody killed Manchester. A woman, my mother said. Name was Florence. Whenever she told me that story, she had fear in her eyes. And what makes me *so mad* is that nobody believed her. Said she was crazy."

He got a faraway look on his face as he drifted off. "The youngsters rising. The folks coming up."

"What happened after?" Graham asked, bringing the old man back to the story.

"Her fear never went away. She died with it. With that fear. I had to go see her in the funeral home. She was cremated. She wanted to be cremated. 'Don't throw me in a hole,' she always said. But they still lay 'em out beforehand, you know? I had to lift her eyelids. I had to look at her eyes. Do you know they glue them shut? The eyelids? I didn't know that, and I tore the skin. But I had to know if the fear was gone."

I swallowed. *Jesus.*

"Was it?" Graham whispered.

Harold zeroed in on Graham. "No." His expression shifted as he thought of something else. "There aren't any records of those poor dead people in the hole." He became agitated. "They wanted to forget it ever happened. They wanted to move away and start over. Pretend those people never died. Pretend Old Tuonela never existed. But I can feel them out there; can't you?" He looked directly at me. "Rising up."

I could see him staring at me through the viewfinder.

There was something so wrong here, so skewed and wrong and off, like a digital image that had somehow picked up distortion. Video didn't tell the truth. A photo didn't tell the truth.

Could the truth be told in a fractured second? Could the truth be told in pixels?

And yet for all the weirdness, I couldn't help but feel a thrill of excitement over the footage I was getting. Footage Claire knew nothing about.

Would this be the year to unfuck my life? So far I hadn't had much luck with that. But was I on the threshold of something? Was the footage I was capturing a way to make my life happen?

"Like a buzz on your tongue," Harold insisted. "Like the wind creeping across the top of your skin, just skimming it." He hovered a palm over one arm to demonstrate. "Don't you feel them?"

"No." For a minute there he'd almost tricked me into thinking he was sane. That he was talking reality.

But what about the little girl? The little girl in the woods?

"I don't believe you," he said.

I raised my head to look him in the face without the interference of the camera. "Why would I lie?"

"Because this place was built on lies and deception. That sidewalk under your feet? A lie." He pointed to Graham. "Him? A lie."

"I'm not from here," I said. That should be

enough to protect me, to keep whatever it was away. "I don't live here."

"You don't have to be from Tuonela to hear the whispers. You don't have to be from here to be touched by what's out there. Was that woman who died the other day from here?"

"She was killed by animals."

"Was she now?"

How had it gone from an interview to this off-camera confrontation?

"You believe that? That's what they're telling people, sure. And maybe that's what they want to think, but it was something from Old Tuonela. Spirits who aren't happy about the Pale Immortal being given a place of honor in the town. You don't honor a mass murderer. You don't honor a man who killed innocent women and children."

"I don't think anybody is honoring him. He's just on display."

"When the people he killed weren't even given a decent burial? When nobody even made a record of their deaths?" He looked into the distance. "And what about that? If you think nothing's off-kilter."

With his cane, he pointed to a crowd gathering near the river. "Gloria Raymond was found floating facedown in the water this morning. People say she had a smile on her face. And that her eyes were wide open, staring at something in the next world."

He closed his eyes. "'Come by night all on its own and in the dark secretly unheard by the wicked one, by the bad one unspotted.'" Still quoting the Kalevala . . .

We left the old man and headed across a wide expanse of grass to find Claire and the others.

This trip was suddenly making sense to me, and my heartbeat quickened. Yesterday I had no future, but today I could see it. This was something I could do. This was something I could do well and right. My vision, not Claire's.

I grabbed Graham's arm. He stopped and turned, surprised.

I knew he liked me, even though he'd told me he had a girlfriend. I've never been one to use that kind of knowledge to get what I want. I hate girls who do that.

"You have to let me interview your dad."

He recoiled. I could see he was irritated that the subject had come up once more, disappointed that I was still using him after our bonding beerfest and bed snuggle.

"Please." I stared, trying to make him see how much I needed this.

You don't know how lost I've been. How unfocused.

I would grovel if I had to. I could do it. "Please." My grip tightened, the lock I had on his arm conveying my desperation . . . and maybe more. Maybe a promise.

He broke, defeated.

So that's how it was done. Just like that.

Yep, sometimes I really hate myself.

Chapter Fourteen

"I'd hate to see this road in the winter," Kristin said. "How do you get home when it snows?"

The car bottomed out, and Graham slowed to a crawl. "I don't know. I haven't lived here in the winter."

He suddenly found himself looking forward to introducing Kristin to Evan. After Evan's little trick the other morning, his father deserved a surprise guest. Let Kristin ask Evan for an interview. Graham was sick of protecting him. He could do his own talking. And company might not be a bad idea. Having someone else in the house might create a buffer and put Evan in a less hostile mood.

As the car crept up the rocky, rutted lane, Kristin ran the camera. It was early evening. Dark, but not the middle of the night.

Before they made the final turn, Graham stopped the car. "Shut it off, okay? I don't want you to film the house. Not without his permission."

She lowered the camera.

"Off," Graham said, recalling her bit of trickery at the museum.

She sighed and shut it off. "I'm putting the lens cap on too." He heard a snap. "See?"

He gave the car some gas. "No, but I believe you."

It had been raining off and on all afternoon, and now it was getting foggy. He put on the brights, but that made it harder to see, so he switched back to dim. They took a dip across a rocky, shallow stream, made a final turn, and headed up the hill, the engine struggling as he pulled to a stop in front of the sprawling house.

Not a single light.

Welcome home.

Every time he returned to the decaying mansion perched next to the border of Old Tuonela, he felt a dread that came from not knowing what the hell or who the hell he would find when he stepped in the door. Would Evan be the old Evan? Or would he be the exhausted, baffled, angry Evan?

And then there was the other stuff. The undefined and unexplained that was everywhere. In the walls, in the ground, but mostly emanating from the woods at the edge of the clearing, the woods that hid Old Tuonela and its secrets.

The secrets Evan was digging up.

In the old days with his mom Graham had learned that very often a cooling-off period was all it took for things to revert back to normal. Just stay away or lie low, be invisible, and by the time she noticed him again all the crap and tantrums would be forgotten.

A reset button.

He liked that button.

But Evan was a new mystery.

His dad hadn't even known of Graham's existence until recently, and Graham had been living with him only a short while. He didn't yet know how to play it. He didn't yet know what was needed to keep this particular adult pacified. Once he figured that out things would get better.

His cell phone beeped, indicating a text message. He fished the phone from his coat pocket and checked the readout screen.

Isobel.

Sometimes his cell worked here; sometimes it didn't. A text message got through easier than an actual call.

England is so cool! We visited the Tower of London today. Tomorrow we are going to the palace. We might even have tea with the queen.

Tea. With the queen. Could anything be more removed from Graham's current world of deep shit?

Proof that life went on outside Tuonela and Old Tuonela. Life went on without him.

When Isobel first left she'd text him several times a day. Now it was every few days. Soon it would be never.

Snap.

He pocketed the phone without replying.

"Who was that?" Kristin asked.

"A friend."

"Girlfriend?"

"No."

He didn't want to go into it with her. Being with Kristin made him feel guilty and good. Kinda like banging your head against the wall when you had a headache. The pain made you forget about the headache, at least for a while. Isobel was off munching on scones; he was hanging out with a strange girl named Kristin Blackmoore. Someone he wasn't even quite sure he liked.

"Wait here," he said. "I have to see if it's okay if you come in." He started to get out, then paused. "No filming."

"I won't."

"I mean it."

"Don't insult me. I'm a professional, not some paparazzi."

"We're all professionals."

When had he gotten so bitter? Even when his mother was alive and beating the crap out of him, he'd never been bitter. But at that point he'd still been able to delude himself into thinking things would get better once he met his dad. Once he met his dad, he'd have a normal life.

What a fucking moron he was.

His dad should be put in a straitjacket, and his girlfriend was halfway across the world having tea with the goddamn Queen of England.

And she wouldn't be back.

He refused to delude himself. He couldn't go through life being an idiot.

He got out of the car and approached the house, moving half-blindly, his eyes wide open but seeing nothing but the darker shapes of a few shrubs.

It was raining again.

Droplets fell so lightly they didn't make a sound. Instead their presence seemed to shrink his world even more, giving him the feeling that nothing existed beyond his immediate space.

He went around the back. The kitchen door was unlocked. He'd gotten after Evan about that.

He reached inside and turned on the light, his gaze immediately dropping to the floor where the eggs had been.

Cleaned up.

That was a good sign.

He tried to move quietly, but the house was old and the floors creaked. Upstairs, he found Evan's bedroom door ajar. He pushed it open, wincing at the noise.

"Evan?" he whispered into the blackness.

There was no answer, so he backtracked, turned on a hallway light, and rechecked the bedroom.

The bed was empty.

Sip, sip. Would you like another crumpet, my dear? Oh, thank you. Don't mind if I do.

When was he going to learn that his life was never going to be normal no matter how much he wished it? That no matter how many times he pushed the reset button, it would always default back to fucked-up?

He wanted to go to bed.

His muscles ached, and his skin felt tight the way it did when he hadn't gotten enough sleep. He *had* to go to school tomorrow. Couldn't slack off his last year. If he didn't do well he could kiss any chance of a scholarship good-bye. And the one thing he had to look forward to was college, because college was a way out.

And he was always looking for a way out.

He went back downstairs and found a flashlight in the kitchen. On the way to Old Tuonela, he stopped by the car.

She was smoking. In the car. Evan's car.

Graham could see the glowing tip of her cigarette illuminating her face when she took a drag. Evan had a nose like a dog; he would kill Graham. But Graham wasn't going to tell her to get out. He didn't want her roaming around.

He opened the door and bent forward. "I'll be back. Wait here." Then he headed for OT.

The gate was open just enough for a person to slip through.

Graham paused.

Could he do it?

He hadn't been this way since all the bad shit had happened. Maybe he should forget it. Maybe he should return to the car and take Kristin back to Tuonela.

The rain picked up, pattering against the fallen leaves. The volume increased until the sound almost seemed to be inside his head. Was Evan really down there doing whatever he did all night long? In the pouring rain?

Damn. Graham was sick of being the adult. Couldn't somebody else be the adult for a while? He wanted to be a kid while he was still a kid. Time was running out.

Deep inside he knew it was probably too late anyway, but that didn't keep him from embracing the resentment.

He took a deep breath and plunged forward through the gate. Willing his brain to shut off, he hurried down the muddy path, his feet slipping and sliding until he finally gained the cover of dense trees. Above his head a canopy of leaves that hadn't yet fallen created a roof and blocked out some of the rain and noise.

He should have forced himself to come down here before. Then maybe he'd have gotten desensitized and it would seem like nothing. Just the same as any other messed-up place. It was hard enough living on the edge of Old Tuonela, but this was too much.

His footsteps faltered. He paused to look over his shoulder, back in the direction of the car he could no longer see.

He also wanted to make sure *she* wasn't there.

His mother. He hadn't seen her for a long time. Long enough to make him hope he would never see her again.

He always smelled her first.

He would wake up from a deep sleep with the scent of rotting flesh in his nostrils. And there she'd be—perched on the end of his bed, yakking away about something.

He turned and continued down the path.

He pushed aside a branch of wet leaves. The flashlight beam reflected off the raindrops, creating a brilliant curtain that temporarily blinded him. He blinked, his eyes adjusting.

Christ.

Holes.

Everywhere.

How many were there? A hundred? More?

He'd known Evan was digging out here, but *damn.*

The flashlight was just some cheapie, the beam weak. He panned around, looking for signs of life. *Real* life. Not a rotten imitation of a living being his mother liked to emulate.

What am I doing here?

He had a sudden snapshot image of the man he'd killed. Of the way he'd looked at him right before he died. That utter disbelief.

"Leave. Get out of here."

Had that been his own voice in his head, or somebody else's?

"Shhhh. There you go."

Not in his head.

Evan? Was it Evan? Sounded a little like him, but not like him.

Graham's heart slammed in his chest, but he forced himself to move, navigating around the holes. Bent at the waist, he leaned forward while wanting to lean back. His voice, when he finally used it, came out a broken whisper. "Evan?"

Had someone answered? Was someone talking?

Mumbling. Coming from below. From the ground.

He wanted to turn and run like hell. Instead he slid one foot forward, then the other.

He directed the flashlight beam into the holes, left and right, sweeping until he found an occupied one.

He blinked the rain from his eyes.

What he saw made his leg muscles tighten as he braced himself for flight.

Evan.

Graham stared.

This hole was bigger than the others. Probably twelve feet wide and six feet deep. Evan just sat there as if it weren't raining. As if it weren't cold, his shirt and jeans splattered with mud.

Graham was careful to keep the flashlight beam directed away from Evan's face, but what the light fell on . . .

My God. Is that what I think it is?

Evan stared up at him without recognition.

Say something. "W-what are you doing?"

The rain channeled into the hole, collecting, creating a soup of mud.

A burial pit. Evan was sitting in the middle of a burial pit surrounded by the mummified remains of the dead.

The smell Graham associated with his mother wafted to him.

He was glad he hadn't brought Kristin. That's what he kept thinking, kept focusing on, his mind trying to distract himself from the immediate horror of the moment.

His fault. He should have gotten help. Instead, he'd been hiding Evan's problem, hoping he would get better on his own. Because if they took him away, if they locked him up in some nuthouse, what would happen to Graham? Would he be put in foster care? Because his grandfather sure as hell wasn't playing with a full deck either.

"Come on." He extended his hand toward his father. "You have to get out of there."

Evan stared up in baffled confusion.

Graham heard a sound behind him. He swung around, the flashlight beam swinging with him. Kristin stood there, mouth hanging open.

"Get away!" He shooed with his hand. "Get the hell out of here!"

She turned and ran.

Had she been holding a camera? Had she been filming? This freak show?

He looked back at Evan.

The man was oblivious.

Graham had to call somebody for help. But who? Did he even know a single sane person in Tuonela?

Chapter Fifteen

This was so normal. So nicely normal.

Rachel smiled at the man across the table.

David Spence.

She'd known him since high school. He was divorced, his marriage another casualty of Tuonela. He'd married an outsider, and his wife had never adjusted to the town. Few did. But there were some, like the mayor, who settled right in without even seeming to notice anything odd about the place.

David was still funny and charming. They'd even come up with some high school stories to relive. But he had a sadness around the edges that people from Tuonela had. The sadness that came once you finally acknowledged that this was something you couldn't fight. You couldn't change the past, and you couldn't pretend Tuonela didn't call to you. He *got* it. Which meant he already got her, to some extent. There was something comforting about that.

"I was glad to hear you'd moved back," David

told her. Embarrassment washed over him as he obviously recalled *why* she'd moved back.

"I'm sorry about your parents. That had to be tough, losing both of them so close together."

If she agreed, he would just feel worse. "I miss them."

"It hasn't been very long. It takes a while."

He wasn't just mouthing an empty, conditioned response. She could feel his concern, and sense the sorrow he felt. She found herself warming to him, to the idea of him. To the idea of having a guy in her life.

Maybe it wasn't so impossible. The promise of something normal within the confines of Tuonela. An intriguing concept.

But she was getting ahead of herself, ahead of the situation.

They ordered pizza.

She hadn't wanted to go anyplace fancy. She hadn't wanted to put that kind of real-date pressure on the evening. Just two friends out for pizza, reconnecting.

They talked some more, and for a short while she forgot they were sitting in a pizza joint in Tuonela. They could have been anywhere. They could have been in Iowa, or California.

Her cell phone rang.

She reached into her pocket and looked up at David with apology. "Sorry. I have to get this."

"No problem." He understood the responsibilities of her job.

She flipped open the phone and checked the display.

Evan Stroud.

Her heart raced.

No. Not here. Not now.

One more ring. Deep breath. Answer.

It took her a moment to recognize Graham's voice.

"Can you come out here?"

His words came fast and breathless.

"Here? Where's here?"

"To our place. Evan's."

To Old Tuonela.

The pizza shop and David tunneled away and she visualized herself at Evan's house. She hadn't been there since all the bad things had happened. She hadn't been there since her father's death.

"What's wrong?" Why didn't Graham call somebody else? He should know how hard a visit to Old Tuonela would be for her. But he was a kid. Kids didn't think about those things.

"It's Evan. He's acting weird. Doing weird stuff. I didn't know who to call. I didn't know what to do."

"I'll be there as soon as I can."

"When? How soon?"

She looked across the table at David. He was watching her with concerned eyes, clinging to her yet knowing she was already gone. But he still hoped.

"Twenty minutes."

"Okay. Good." So much relief conveyed in those two words. "Thanks."

She disconnected and pocketed the phone. "David, I'm so sorry. I'm going to have to go. An emergency has come up."

"That's okay."

But she could see he was disappointed. And maybe hurt. How could you hurt somebody you didn't really even know? But it happened all the time.

"Want me to come with you?"

What a perfectly horrendous thought. "No, but thanks. That's sweet of you to offer." She opened her wallet.

He shook his head. "What are you doing?" He looked horrified, so she put the wallet away.

"I'll get it next time." Why had she said that? A promise of next time? It had just come out.

He smiled and relaxed.

She reached behind her and slipped on her coat, buttoning it before getting up. To hide her stomach? Probably. Even though he knew about her pregnancy, she didn't want to flaunt it. "Thanks."

"I'll call you," he said.

David was wiped from her mind as soon as she stepped from the restaurant. She hurried to the van, shot out of the parking lot, and headed for Old Tuonela, her heart beating fast.

What was wrong?

What had happened?

When Evan had gone behind her back and purchased Old Tuonela, she'd vowed never to speak to him again. She'd felt betrayed. He could have at least told her. Coward. Maybe that was part of the reason she'd been so anxious to get away. There was too much pain here. The death of her parents. Then, at a time when she'd needed Evan; he wasn't there for her.

Now here she was, leaving a date to run out to the very place she'd sworn never to go again, to a man who'd betrayed her.

She pulled off the highway to take the narrow, twisting lane to Evan's house. Branches scraped the sides of the van and rubbed loudly against the undercarriage. She pulled up next to Evan's little black car, cut the engine, and jumped out.

Someone materialized from the darkness of the porch.

Graham. He ran across the yard to meet her.

"I tried to call you before you got here, but I just got your voice mail. Cell phones don't work here very well."

"It never rang."

She started walking toward the house. He reached out and put a hand on her arm, stopping her. "I don't think you should go in. He's better now. That's why I was trying to catch you. To tell you that you didn't need to come."

"Better?" She frowned.

"He's going to be mad that I called you. You should go. You should leave."

Graham was as skittish as a cat. He glanced at the house, then at the car. *He wants to jump in and get the hell out of here.*

"Graham, what's going on?"

"You didn't see anybody when you were driving up the lane, did you? A girl? With red hair?"

"No."

"I need to find her." He gave a little launching jump and ran for the car. "Go back home," he shouted over his shoulder. "You don't want to talk to him."

"Is he drunk?" That didn't seem like Evan. But then, a lot of things didn't seem like Evan anymore.

Graham paused in the open car door and let out a snort. "I wish. Then maybe he'd just pass out, like my mom used to." He shook his head. "He's nuts. That's what he is. Nuts. Go home. Please. Thanks for coming, but everything is fine. Or it will be when I get him to see a shrink."

"What about the girl?"

"She's a friend of mine. I'll find her."

"Nobody should be running around out here." She didn't have to state the obvious—that someone had been murdered just a few miles away.

He gave Rachel an impatient wave, started the car and took off.

With her hands in the pockets of her coat, she turned and looked at the house. A few lights on. One upstairs, one at the back of the building, maybe coming from the kitchen. She blew out a breath. She took a step.

I ran through the trees, small branches smacking me in the face. My breathing was loud, my lungs raw.

I stopped, hands braced on my knees.

Son of a bitch.

What the hell was *that*? What had I stumbled upon?

I pulled out my cell phone.

No signal.

My mind had been playing tricks on me, that's what it was. I hadn't really seen what I thought I'd seen. Had I? I'd been scared shitless, and it had been raining like hell. And dark.

But I'd had my camera running. When I got back to Tuonela I'd look at it. I'd see there was nothing there, that my mind had invented some crazy bullshit. Because minds did that. Filled in the blanks with nonsense.

Film might lie, but at the same time it told a certain amount of truth. It would tell if I really saw what I thought I'd seen.

Car lights.

The vehicle skidded to a stop. A door slammed.

I turned and ran.

My legs were shaking, and I was running with the additional weight of my camera.

As I ran I blindly felt across the tape compartment door. It was like some old Western where the cowboy reloaded his gun while running from the Indians. I would have laughed if I'd had any extra air. I did manage a laugh in my head, if only to help chase away the terror.

I popped open the camera door, pulled out the tape, shut the door, and shoved the tape inside my bra.

"Kristin! Stop!"

Graham.

Wow, had I ever been wrong about him. Thinking he was some sweet, naive kid.

He was part of that world back there, the world of his dad. A world that involved swimming around in a mud pit with bones and mummified corpses.

I killed a man.

Maybe he didn't mean he'd killed a man when the guy stepped off the curb in front of his car.

Maybe he was some evil spawn masquerading as something human.

Good job.

I heard him behind me, crashing through the brush, getting closer. I didn't have a prayer.

He tackled me. I catapulted forward. As the ground flew toward my face, I instinctively wrapped my arms around my camera, protecting it. I hit and rolled to my side with a loud *oomph.*

"I told you to stay in the car," Graham said.

"You'd better not have broken my camera."

"Give it to me."

I hugged it tighter. "No."

He shone the flashlight in my face. "Give me the damn camera."

"Go to hell."

He pried it from my hands. He turned it around, going over it like a damn monkey. "How do you open it?"

I smirked.

He popped open the tape door.

"Where's the cassette? What'd you do with it?"

"I threw it away."

"I don't believe you."

"Was that your dad back there? Was that Evan Stroud?"

I couldn't see his face. I wished I could see his face. He was just a murky, dark shape, backlit by fractured headlights.

"What did you see?"

"Nothing. It was dark."

"And you weren't filming either, right?"

"Right." I played along even though I knew he knew I was lying.

He shoved his hand into my coat pockets, one after the other. Then he patted down the pockets of my jeans, frisking me. "Where is it? I know you have it."

He wasn't going to give up. He was protecting his father. Protecting himself.

I struggled for breath. "I don't have it."

I tried to get away. I hit. I kicked. He was strong for a wormy kid. He held me down with his weight. I felt his hand go up my shirt, then into my bra, searching and finding the minicassette. He pulled it out, let me go, and jumped to his feet.

I followed. "I'm sure you'll want to view that on holidays. Maybe show it to your kids, if you ever have any."

"Come on. I'll give you a ride back to town."

I pulled out my phone.

"You won't get a signal out here."

He was right.

I could walk, but I didn't even know the way back to Tuonela. A woman had been murdered not that far away, and Evan Stroud was wandering around loose. What was a girl to do?

"I won't hurt you."

Graham may have been part of that other world, but he still seemed my safest choice. "Give me a ride then, asshole."

Chapter Sixteen

Rachel could have called David and told him to hang on—she'd be right back. Save her seat. Save her some pizza. Maybe save her a place in his life.

She didn't.

Instead she walked around to the back of Evan's house, where a dim light could be seen in the kitchen window. She knocked. When no one answered she pushed against the door. It wasn't latched, and swung open slowly.

Because of his illness Evan couldn't use regular bulbs. The kitchen was shrouded in a murky light that bathed the room in negatives, giving it a red-hued, darkroom appearance.

The place was in various stages of restoration and abandonment. Projects begun by previous owners, then forgotten. No doors on the cupboards. A wall that was in the early stages of demolition, slats and pieces of stained floral wallpaper showing.

She stepped inside—and let out a small gasp of alarm.

Evan sat on the floor, his back against the wall, legs outstretched and crossed at the ankles.

He was shirtless, his arms resting on his thighs, hands caked with what looked like mud. He didn't move. He didn't turn his head.

"Rachel." Her name floated across his lips in a whispered exhale.

He's lost so much weight.

Even in the dim light, she could see his ribs outlined against pale skin.

How long had it been since she'd last seen him?

She did some mental calculations. Months. Before she knew she was pregnant. He'd come to the morgue in what she later realized was a last good-bye before his betrayal.

Rachel had worked hard to convince the Tuonela city council to purchase Old Tuonela, bulldoze the buildings, and fence off the ground so that no one could go there again. No one could die there again . . . But Evan had come along and bought the ground from under them. He hadn't even told her he was thinking about it, and he didn't tell her he was the one behind the purchase once it was made. She'd read about it in the paper.

He was inviting trouble. He was putting everyone at risk. For what? A piece of dark history? The living were much more important than the dead.

He may not have been the vampire that half the people in Tuonela claimed him to be, but Evan couldn't be trusted.

He hurt you.

Yes.

Evan scrambled awkwardly to his feet and tried to stand up straight, one hand resting against the counter, one hand on his waist. On the right side of his chest, just above the nipple, was a red, raised scar that matched another one a few inches away on his arm.

Gunshot wounds.

She closed her eyes for a second and pulled in a deep breath, struggling to keep her distance. She'd always struggled to keep her distance when it came to Evan. But she didn't always succeed. . . .

It's so dark here. . . . So bleak . . .

Instability and confusion radiated from him, along with an attempt to cover it up.

Graham shouldn't be here.

It wasn't a healthy environment for a kid.

Evan didn't smell like alcohol. Graham had been right about that. "Have you been in the sun?" Was he suffering from light exposure? She knew how debilitating that was to him.

His hair was getting long and shaggy, and his jaw was covered with dark stubble—a contrast to the paleness of his face.

"I've been excavating."

"In Old Tuonela?"

"Yes."

"At night?"

"All night. Graham made me stop because of the rain. It wasn't raining that hard. It doesn't bother me."

Now she could see that his jeans were soaked.

She suddenly realized that he was staring at her

in an almost bemused way, with a sort of half smile, as if pleased she'd stopped by.

He was breaking her heart. He'd always broken her heart.

She'd loved him ever since she could remember. She'd loved him with a love that made no sense, that put her in danger's way, that left her exposed and vulnerable.

He could hurt her. He *had* hurt her.

The baby moved.

Jesus.

Like a somersault.

She felt something that may have been a small heel slide across her stomach. She put a hand to the top button of her coat, checking to make sure she was covered.

This was not good.

He's too fragile.

She was always thinking about other people. What about *her*?

"What are you doing here?" he asked.

"Graham called me. He was worried about you."

"I'm fine. Everything's fine."

Be the friend. Just be the concerned friend.

"I don't think so. What's going on, Evan? Besides the excavating? I think you need to move back to Tuonela. You and Graham."

"Everybody keeps saying that."

"Who?"

"My father. Graham."

"They're right."

"I have to be here."

She stepped closer. She reached up and touched his face, his jaw, made him look at her, listen to her. "This place is bad for you. It's bad for everybody."

He turned his face and touched his lips to her palm. He inhaled. "You smell different."

Her heart was hammering, and it took all of her willpower to keep from holding him close. "It's probably the new disinfectant I'm using in the morgue." She tried to pull her hand back, but he held on.

"It's you. There's something different about you. Your blood . . ." He paused for description. "It's singing."

Something's not right. Something's more wrong than usual.

She managed to tug her hand away. "What are you talking about?"

"I can hear it."

A strange sound of unease escaped her.

"And now you're afraid. I can smell your fear. I don't think you've ever been afraid of me. Don't be afraid of me." She could see his brain shift. "Don't tell me you suddenly believe that vampire nonsense."

"No. Of course not." But he was different, and he was making her nervous.

Something wrong.

She moved backward, away from him. She felt behind her for the door. "I have to go." Her cell phone was in her pocket. But would she get a signal? Probably not.

"You just got here."

"Take a shower, Evan. Take a shower and go to bed. You'll feel better tomorrow."

"Don't go."

"I'll call you." *Placate him.* "Tomorrow. We'll talk."

"Stay with me, Florence."

Time froze for a few beats.

"Did you just call me Florence?"

His eyes clouded and he seemed to briefly look inward. "Rachel," he corrected himself. "I meant Rachel."

"You said Florence. Who's Florence?"

He lashed out and grabbed her wrist. He pulled her against him so hard her breath skipped and their stomachs collided.

His eyes changed. His pupils dilated. "What?"

While keeping one hand on her wrist, he felt her stomach with the other. "Rachel?"

He released her and placed both hands on her belly.

The baby moved as it had earlier, a giant shift. She and Evan both inhaled sharply. She could see his focus narrow, his thoughts clarifying as he remembered and calculated. She could see his emotions come one on top of another, ranging from joy to despair.

"It's not yours," she said quickly.

Where had the denial come from? Certainly nothing she'd planned, but with his obvious instability it had just popped out.

Protect herself. Protect the baby.

"You never could lie worth a damn." With his hands still cradling her belly, his lips twisted into an odd smile. "What about my disease? Have you thought of that?"

"I've researched it—"

She stopped, immediately realizing she'd just admitted the child was his. Tears stung her eyes. Why? Because the truth was finally out and she wasn't carrying the secret alone? Or was it fear for her baby? Fear of Evan?

One night. They'd made love—or had sex—just one time. Her memory of the event was fuzzy, and later she'd wondered if it had really happened. Just a crazy dream, she'd told herself. Just a crazy Tuonela-induced dream. Until her periods stopped and the pregnancy test came out positive.

"Were you ever going to tell me?"

"Yes."

"When?"

"I tried. I left voice-mail messages." When he didn't respond, she thought it was all for the best. She would wait until she got to California. Distance would make it easier for both of them. She certainly hadn't meant for him to find out this way.

"Voice mail?" He snorted. "You didn't try very hard."

"No, I didn't. After all that happened, I wasn't sure you'd want to know."

"That hurts me."

"Evan, I'm sorry. But you've changed. Sometimes I don't think I know you at all." And she used to know him almost as well as she knew herself. "At one time I would have told you right away, but even now I question the wisdom of sharing such news."

He couldn't be trusted. "I think maybe I should never have told you. That nobody should know."

"I don't blame you. Poor thing will grow up being called the vampire's child."

"I've never been ashamed of you. You should know me better than that. But I have to protect the baby."

He nodded. "The baby."

She was beginning to relax when Evan's eyes changed. The pupils enlarged and became flat and black. He broke into a sweat, and he suddenly gave off a fevered heat.

He removed his hands and stepped back. "Go." There was confusion and terror in his voice that seemed to mirror her own earlier emotions. "Get out of here. Now."

"What's wrong?"

"Go!"

He was right; she'd never been afraid of him. Not even when the whole town believed he was capable of horrendous acts. But she was afraid of him now.

She turned.

She ran.

Chapter Seventeen

Standing in the middle of the parking lot in downtown Tuonela, I glanced up at the darkening sky, then back at Claire. I have a really readable face, so I had to consciously struggle to keep my expression neutral even though I was thinking, *See what I told you?*

"Well?" Ian asked me. "Should I finish setting up?"

"How quickly can you tear down if it starts to rain?"

"Ten minutes?"

Like most people who didn't actually deal with the day-to-day of filming, Claire had no concept of how much time they would waste if it rained. Not to mention the risk to expensive equipment. Yes, the interview with the psychic would have been better outside near the river, but sometimes you had to choose a backup location, which happened to be the Port of Tuonela building.

The psychic was driving in from Milwaukee.

Claire had wanted somebody from out of town. She'd also wanted somebody who was famous, although none of us had heard of Madame Sosostris. But I don't watch much television or read many newspapers.

Ian nudged me. "Check it out."

I followed the direction of his nod to see a red extended-cab pickup turning the corner. It was pulling a homemade ornate house on wheels. A gypsy trailer that was gaudy and tacky and ridiculously beautiful, with bright colors and a curved roof. We couldn't quit staring. Now I understood why Claire had wanted this particular person. *Let's add another nutcase to the project.*

I once had an instructor who used to rant about heavy-handed documentation. She called it creating a false reality.

"I have an aunt who reads tarot, so it's not like I'm trying to dispute its validity." I eyed the monstrosity in front of us. "Of course, my aunt looks like a regular person. And she drives a Chevy Malibu." *If you want to make fun of these people, you could be a little more subtle*, were the words I didn't speak but wanted to.

Minneapolis was known for its kitschy humor. It saturated everything from music to film. It was no accident that the Coen brothers were from Saint Louis Park, a first-ring suburb of Minneapolis.

You had to fight it. I'd been fighting it for years. Some people, like Claire, embraced it.

Claire rushed out to meet the driver, waving her arms and pointing to indicate where the vehicle should be positioned, with the river and lift bridge as backdrop. There was plenty of room, and it was just a matter of stopping.

The driver got out.

Madame Sosostris was what some people might call white trash. She'd probably been beautiful once, but cigarettes and alcohol had taken a toll. She looked the part of a fortune-teller: fried, curly red hair, a billowing skirt, and a wrinkled black T-shirt pulled down tight across a menopausal belly. Sandals plus lots of bracelets and bangles. God, she even had hoop earrings.

Ian smiled and rocked on his heels. "Trippy."

Madame glanced up at the sky, then hurried around to the back door of her trailer and began unloading and hanging and decorating the outdoors like an AARP member at a Winnebago camp.

An Oriental rug appeared. On top of the rug went a round table. Chimes were hung near a green door that looked like the entrance to a hobbit home.

"Cool," Stewart said.

I positioned the camera, framing the table in the foreground, the bridge and water as backdrop.

"Sorry I'm late," the woman said breathlessly as she dashed back around. "Had a flat."

Ian leaned close and mumbled, "More like a raging hangover, I'm guessing."

Stewart let out a snort and put a fist to his mouth.

The wind whipped up. The chimes clanged; the rug rippled and folded. Madame's skirt swirled, and she clutched at the fabric à la Marilyn Monroe.

Behind her the surface of the river turned black and choppy.

"Maybe we should wait," Claire offered with hesitation.

"We should hurry." I was suddenly intrigued by the juxtaposition of the weather and the cartoony trailer. Also the contrast in color. The wagon and woman were garish, the backdrop gray and colorless. This might work after all.

At least nature wasn't something Claire could manipulate.

"The cards will blow away," Madame said.

What was her real name? Were we supposed to call her Madame Sosostris?

"You're doing a card reading?" I asked.

"I do readings on towns. It's kind of my thing. But I always do intuitive readings without the cards. I can try that first."

"Why don't we capture some footage out here, then move inside if we have to," I said.

Townspeople were gathering.

Probably drawn by the trailer, but also by the camera and microphone boom.

I wished I had a dolly, but they were expensive and something Claire hadn't wanted to spend money on. I'd hoped we could at least grab a grocery cart somewhere, but they could be a noisy and rough ride. I'd always planned to make my own dolly, but had never gotten around to it. Lack of motivation? Yes. Because I knew I'd be using it for shit like this. If that wasn't a motivation killer, I don't know what was.

The camera was already rolling when Madame took her seat in a little parlor chair with ornately carved wood and a seat covered with deep red upholstery fabric. The kind that would leave a pattern on the backs of your legs if you sat on it too long.

The crowd grew. Probably thirty people now.

Madame closed her eyes and placed her hands in her lap. A few feet away the chimes raised all kinds of hell. I should have taken them down. They were going to overpower the audio.

With eyes closed and hair whipping around her head, Madame started muttering something about the town being dark. At that very moment, the sky got even blacker and the people behind me let out a collective gasp. I tried not to laugh, and I sure as hell didn't look at Stewart or Ian.

"They want something," Madame said.

Claire took a seat across the table from her. "Who?"

Madame frowned with closed eyes. "The strigoi."

"Strigoi?"

Claire glanced at us. We shrugged in silent unison.

"Strigoi are lost spirits looking for bodies to inhabit. These spirits can manifest themselves in various ways."

The wind died down; the chimes continued to chime, but not as madly. Now it was more of a steady beat. A *clang, clang, clang*. I could feel the rapt attention of the crowd behind us. And I'd be the first to admit the psychic was kind of freaking me out.

"The bait is your heart's desire," the woman

said. "They can imitate and tease you with your own longing. They tempt you with what you most crave. They find the tear in your soul, the source of your pain, and they torment you and tantalize you with it."

"They?" Claire asked.

"I feel many. Some aren't bad. Some are just mischievous and lost. It's the evil ones you have to watch out for. They'll draw you in. They'll trick you."

No gasp this time. Total silence except for the *clang, clang, clang*.

"I also feel the nearby presence of a revenant."

Revenant? A kind of vampire, if I remembered correctly. *Well, duh.*

"What's going on here?"

I turned to see a guy in a suit fighting his way through the crowd. I knew his type. We had a lot of young, successful businessmen in the city.

"Do you have a permit to film?"

The spell was broken. People began moving and talking. Someone mumbled something about the mayor.

"You can't just come into town and start filming," he said. "You have to fill out the proper paperwork. You have to have permission."

"I have release forms," Claire said.

"Do you have a permit?"

"No."

"Then move along."

Claire didn't let him intimidate her. *Go, Claire.* "I was under the impression that I needed a permit

only if we were blocking traffic or disrupting so...
thing," she said.

The mayor looked at the crowd, then back to Claire. "You *are* disrupting something. I want you to leave. Now."

"Who do we see about a permit?"

"You'll have to check with the Wisconsin Film Board."

He just wanted us out of there.

Claire held her ground. "I don't believe you."

"Look here. I worked too damn hard to bring tourism to this town. I'm not letting you come in and make us look like a bunch of idiots."

I could certainly see the validity in what he was saying. But that didn't keep me from enjoying the *Jerry Springer* aspect of the scene.

"Oh, I think you're doing a pretty good job of that by yourself." Claire might have said more, and weren't we all eager to see what transpired next? But the sky chose that particular moment to cut loose and dump on us.

Everybody scrambled. By the time Madame was back in her truck and we were in the van, rain was falling so hard we couldn't see two feet in front of us.

"We'll have to wait it out," Stewart said, not even bothering to turn the key and start the engine.

"That asshole." Claire swung around in the seat to look at me. Her hair hung in wet clumps on either side of her face. "Is that true? Do we need a permit?"

"Every town's different, although I think they would have a hard time enforcing anything unless they can prove you're making this for commercial reasons."

"He pissed off the wrong person." She held out her hand. "Give me that goddamn tape."

Everybody wanted my tapes.

I opened the camera and passed the cassette.

"Since he's so damn concerned about protecting the reputation of his weird-ass little town, I'm going to make sure a copy of this gets to the right people."

Ian leaned forward, both hands gripping the back of Stewart's seat. "WXOW in La Crosse?"

"Yes," Claire said.

We all whooped and laughed in delight. Seemed we'd finally united over something.

Chapter Eighteen

I couldn't believe we were drinking again, but if somebody else is buying it's hard for me to say no.

"Is it possible to be twenty-three and an alcoholic?" I asked Stewart, who was sitting on the bar stool next to mine. My fingers were greasy from the burrito basket I'd just consumed: one giant burrito, along with french fries served with hot sauce. Like visiting two countries in one.

Without removing his elbow from the bar top, Stewart lifted a brown beer bottle to his mouth. "Doesn't it take years?"

Ian wiped his hands on a napkin and shook his head. "No, man. I knew a kid in high school who got the DTs if he didn't drink."

"High school?" Stewart asked. "That's seriously fucked up."

"I've never known an alcoholic," Claire said from her seat next to Ian's. "Or a drug addict. Maybe I should make a film about that."

Hah. I'd suspected she was one of those sheltered

rich kids who'd never been exposed to the seedy side of life. Which explained why she always wanted to go to bars like the one we were now in. Dark little dives that smelled of stale beer and years of cigarette smoke.

I'd run into a lot of those kids in college. They came to the city from wealthy suburbs, wanting to experience the darkness they'd seen only in movies or read in books.

I looked around our little group and a realization hit me. *We* were the misfits. Claire was hanging around with *us* for the very reason the college kids searched out the seedy bars. We were *her* freaks. She got to spend all day and all night with us. But once this gig was over, she could go home.

I should have resented her, but I didn't. It actually made her more interesting in my eyes, because I'm curious about people too.

"I took one of those tests," I said. "The ones that ask questions like, 'Have you ever decided to quit drinking for a week or so, but only lasted a couple of days?' "

"And?" Stewart said.

"I think I answered yes to ten out of twelve questions."

"That calls for another drink."

We'd been there long enough for the faint odor of sewer gas to become unnoticeable. And long enough for suspicion to fade. We'd played darts and pool with the patrons.

It hadn't all been goofing off. We'd started with interviews.

Claire had wanted to interview some locals. The men warmed to her right off. Blond hair, big boobs, and red lipstick seemed to do that. They were more suspicious of the guys and me. But after a couple of hours and several drinks, we were all equals in fun and inebriation.

Booze, the great equalizer.

The bartender, a guy named Jake who reminded me of one of my overweight uncles, grabbed the remote and increased the volume of the television bolted high on the wall. That must have been the signal to shut up, because the noise level in the room was suddenly cut in half. Quite astonishing for a bunch of drunks. Jake ran the show. He was a congenial guy, but he didn't take any crap from anybody. You were a guest in his house and you played by his rules.

Earlier he'd told a couple of tourists to take a leak outside behind the tree if they weren't going to buy anything.

They left.

We bought another round of drinks to make sure our seats were safe and that we'd be able to use the restroom the next time the urge hit us.

Conversation dropped and heads politely turned toward the television. Somebody unplugged the jukebox, cutting off Tom Petty in midsong.

The news.

From station WXOW in La Crosse.

Now that the room was quiet I could hear the buzzing in my head. But beyond that my ears zeroed in on the upcoming story announcement. Something about Tuonela. I looked at the screen in time to see the teaser clip.

The psychic. Madame Sosostris. The tape Claire sent them had gotten picked up.

We whooped and waited.

"That's my footage." I kept my eyes on the screen along with everybody else in the place. "I filmed that. Well, not film. Video, but it's mine."

Claire sat at the bar with her hand over her mouth, her eyes big, trying to keep from laughing out loud.

The anchors came back.

A joke piece. That was immediately apparent. Well, that should please Claire. They were playing the same angle she'd been going for. Either way, it made the town look stupid.

They used only about fifteen seconds of tape. The part where the psychic mentioned revenants and said things called strigoi were looking for bodies to inhabit. Then they cut to a reporter ambushing the mayor outside his office. A microphone was jabbed in his face. I almost felt sorry for the guy.

Jake moved down the bar and collected our drinks.

"Hey, I haven't even started that." Stewart grabbed for one of the beers Jake was hauling away.

"You're done," Jake said.

Stewart blinked.

I looked around. Faces that had been friendly were now hostile. Ian grabbed my arm. "Come on," he whispered. "Let's get the hell out of here."

I slid off my stool and half expected somebody to

pick up a wooden chair and hit one of us over the head. They all just stared as we left.

Mayor McBride cursed under his breath, shut off the television, and tossed the remote down on the bed. *Goddamn them.* A minute later he picked up the phone and called his lawyer.

The owner and manager of the Tuonela Inn shut off the television.

She'd been nice to those kids. She'd fed them an inn favorite of apricot jam and cream-cheese French toast when she could easily have told them to go down the street and find something to eat.

You couldn't trust outsiders. That was what her mother had always said, but Annabel had never wanted to believe it. She'd even left Tuonela to go away to college. On campus she'd met a boy she thought was nice, only to have him and one of his buddies rape her at a frat party. She quit school shortly after that, but she never told anybody what had happened. Her fault for trusting the boy. Her fault for not listening to her mother.

No, you couldn't trust outsiders.

So what if the apricot jam came from the Dollar Store? It was the thought that counted. Those boys had seemed so happy to have a home-cooked meal. Just like that other boy had seemed so happy to have her come to his frat party.

It was Tuonela against the rest of the world; that's what it was.

Chapter Nineteen

Alastair didn't want to watch the news, but he was a cop. Cops watched the news.

He picked up the remote, turned on the television, and sank into the couch. His mind drifted from one topic to the next, until the word *Tuonela* got his attention and he straightened and focused on the screen.

The bit was one of those wink-wink things, half serious out of respect for the recent death of Brenda Flemming, but light, because who called in a psychic to do a tarot reading on a town?

He didn't know anything about art or film, but he immediately felt a visual draw to the piece. The psychic was a splash of brilliant color in the center of a gray landscape of black river and dark, roiling sky. The weather seemed the star until the woman started talking.

There was nothing exceptional about her voice. And the way she looked was just plain silly. But her words . . . She said something about spirits inhabiting the dead. And something else about a revenant.

Some would think the clip funny. The news crew certainly got a kick out of it, doing the usual good-natured chat once the story was over.

"That interesting little piece was courtesy of a group of University of Minnesota students who are in Tuonela working on a senior project."

"Wish I'd had that kind of senior project," the weatherman said.

Big chuckle for the camera.

Alastair shut off the television, tossed down the remote, rounded up his laptop, and took it to his bedroom, where he got ready for bed.

He balanced the laptop on the covers and did a quick search, surprised to actually find a page of links.

Strigoi are spirits that have returned from the dead. They pass through different stages after rising from the grave. Initially a strigoi might be an invisible poltergeist. After some time it can become visible, looking similar to the way the person looked in life. Strigoi feed on humans and can eventually inhabit the bodies of the living.

He clicked on another page.

Strigoi can slumber harmlessly for centuries as long as the grave remains undisturbed.

And a revenant . . . ?

An animated corpse that rises from the dead to torment the living. Those who returned from the dead were wrong-doers in their lifetime. A revenant must be destroyed by decapitation followed by incineration.

He didn't even bother to bookmark the pages. He powered down, shut his computer, and put it aside.

Strigoi.

Foolish nonsense . . . But a revenant . . . ? Maybe not so foolish.

Scratch, scratch.

With a gasp and a jerk, Alastair came awake, ears straining for a repeat of the noise. Strange that he was able to fall asleep, but he'd hardly slept the past several days, and he was so goddamn tired.

He grabbed his Smith & Wesson from the bedside drawer, turned on the light, and tossed back the covers. His heart was beating hard. Like he'd put away a pot of coffee.

Just a dream.

Silly old man. That's what he was. Some silly fool. Should have packed up his family years ago. Should have gotten out of Tuonela when Johanna was pregnant with Evan. But he'd been weak. And he'd had a great job offer. Yeah, he'd finally gotten out. Too late, but he'd needed to prove to himself that he could do it. That he could leave. He'd also hoped Evan would join him in Florida.

He should have known better.

He stuck his feet into slippers.

Such a normal thing for a man with a human skin in his freezer to do. What could be more normal and boring and mundane? *See, I'm a normal guy with a normal life. Nothing weird here.*

With his ears tuned for unnatural sounds, he made his way through the house, the night-lights weakly illuminating his path. This was the house he and Johanna had bought when they'd married. People did that back then. Marriage and a home. You settled in for the long haul.

They'd done a lot of work on the place. They refinished the hardwood floors, stripped and varnished the thick, heavy trim, and removed layers of wallpaper. A labor of love was what it had been.

That first year they planted a garden. A huge one. They'd packed the freezer with snap peas and green beans.

Who woulda thought . . .

The years had flown by, and lately he found himself thinking about the past more. It used to annoy him when geezers got nostalgic. *Look to the future, not the past.* But the past defined you. That's what he hadn't understood when he was young. You couldn't get away from it.

He was lonely.

He hadn't expected to live out his golden years by himself. His wife had never been a strong person, and news of Evan's terminal illness had been tough on her. Her heart just gave out one day. He missed her terribly, but he was glad she wasn't around to see this, to see what Evan had become. To see what he'd done . . .

Evan had gotten sick, and their world and focus had narrowed to a point. Find the right doctor. Find a cure. Save Evan's life.

Make a pact with the devil.

The front door was locked. The kitchen appeared undisturbed.

Alastair forced himself to go to the cellar, gun drawn. He'd gone without sleep for so long that his eyes were playing tricks on him. Shadows in his peripheral vision moved and shifted.

The earthy scent of damp stone and mildew hung in the air. He threw the freezer door open and jumped back, gun hand trembling. A moment later he dug down through the frozen deer meat.

Still there.

He let out a breath.

He slammed the lid and scrambled back upstairs.

Then he did what he'd been doing a lot lately.

He got drunk.

His goal was to drink himself into a stupor, to shut off his head.

But his head wouldn't shut off. And his thoughts kept going back to one thing, the same thing.

Evan.

Could Evan have murdered that poor woman? If so, could Alastair do what needed to be done?

He'd given his son a new life; could he take it away?

Evan couldn't focus on his digging. He finally gave up and went for a walk.

It felt good to move, to get out from under the trees of Old Tuonela, to see the stars. He picked up speed and his steps fell into a steady rhythm. He walked across cornfields that had been fall-plowed. Through pastures where cattle huddled and moved nervously as he passed. Before he knew it, his footsteps took him into the river valley and the heart of Tuonela.

The town slept a soft slumber.

Far off in the distance came the deep warning of a barge horn, the sound echoing off the river bluff and moving through the otherwise silent streets. For Evan the sound was a comforting reminder that other people also lived their lives at night.

Car lights approached, and he stepped into the shadows to wait for the vehicle to pass. Once it was gone, he resumed his journey.

To Rachel's.

He spotted a light in the turret window of her apartment. A faint glimmer of red framed in blue velvet. Maybe just a night-light.

He closed his eyes and inhaled.

She was there.

It had been hard to stay away before, but now that he knew about the baby . . .

He didn't blame her for not telling him and for not wanting anybody to know he was the father. *Christ.* He didn't want the kid growing up with that stigma either. What a life that would be. It would be no life. Hounded by the media, teased and feared at school. He wouldn't wish that on anybody, especially a child.

A shape passed in front of the turret window, blocking the light.

Rachel.

He stepped deeper into the shadows, but kept his vigil.

Could she feel him down here? Did she know he was but a shout away? He wanted to step into the middle of the street. Wouldn't that be romantic? Well, maybe not from her point of view. It seemed creepy, now that he thought about it. She would probably call the cops to tell them he was stalking her.

No, it was best if he left her alone and stayed away so no one would suspect he was the father of her baby.

He remained hidden until she moved from the window. Then he turned up his collar, stuck his hands in the pockets of his long wool coat, and walked home. But he couldn't shut off his head.

What about the baby?

What strange blood would move through the child's veins? At the same time Evan felt reassured by a basic knowledge of genetic code. Most likely both parents would have to be carriers of a recessive revenant gene—something they didn't need to worry about.

Chapter Twenty

"Slow down."

Gabriella Nelson let up on the gas pedal of her Ford Taurus.

Franklin bent forward in the passenger seat and strained to see through the darkness. "We're close."

"How close?" Gabriella asked. "Yards? Miles?"

"Stop."

She braked and the car lurched to a halt in the middle of the road.

"That's it." Franklin pointed. "The lane that leads to Old Tuonela."

"Oh, my God!" Millie shrieked from the backseat directly behind Gabriella's head. Hard to believe Millie was in her sixties.

"Should I turn?" Gabriella asked. "Should I go up there?"

"No!" Franklin's emphatic response wasn't as unexpected as it was cranky.

Gabriella had found him on the Internet. They were both members of a Yahoo! group called Weird

Wisconsin. She'd posted a question to the group, asking if anybody was familiar with Old Tuonela. Her post had generated a lot of interest and replies, and someone had finally told her about Franklin Trent.

At first the others in her group had been against the idea of contacting him—being on the Internet and all. They watched the news. They'd heard about the predators out there. But after asking around they'd made contact with someone who knew Franklin. "He's a little spooky but on the up and up."

He wouldn't take them into the woods and rape and kill them.

He was a ghost hunter, psychic, and urban explorer. More like unemployed stool warmer, Gabriella had decided. He'd been inside the Tuonela Mental Hospital, and the tunnels that ran below the streets of Milwaukee. He'd even been to the Ed Gein Farm more than once, but Old Tuonela was his specialty.

This would be his twelfth trip.

An even dozen, he'd told Gabriella in his e-mail.

Franklin had led a lot of people into Old Tuonela, but things were different now. Evan Stroud lived there. His presence on the outskirts of the abandoned town would make things much trickier.

A hundred bucks.

That didn't seem like much to pay the guy. Split three ways it was less than the cost of a fancy meal. Hell, Gabriella paid that much for a lot of things she hardly ever used, like her cell phone and gym membership.

There were three of them in their little group. Three was a good number when you were casting spells. They'd been witches for a couple of years. Ever since retiring. Gabriella had started it. She'd wanted a hobby, she'd wanted to expand her horizons, and she'd always been interested in the power of the unknown.

Millie had suggested they take a craft class together. Stained-glass making or some such crap. Shirley had wanted to start a book discussion group, but Gabriella had bigger things in mind.

They became members of Witch's Brew, a large group of practicing witches spread throughout Wisconsin.

They had witch coffee mugs and witch T-shirts. They went to Wicca meetings, where they talked about projects and fund-raisers. Where they discussed how to remove candle wax from a tablecloth, and what to do if a candle went out before the spell was completed. They collected herbs and even dried goat's blood—purchased from a supply shop.

But deep down Gabriella knew it wasn't real. And she suspected the rest of the girls felt the same way. Deep down this was playacting, something they were doing for fun.

"Where should I park?" she asked. There wasn't even a shoulder, just a weedy ditch.

"Pull forward." Franklin waved his hand. "You should come to a lane that leads into a neighbor's cornfield."

She accelerated, wishing Franklin had driven. Apparently his truck didn't always run, and all four of them wouldn't have been able to squeeze in anyway.

When she was young, Gabriella believed in many things. But as she'd aged, she'd become more skeptical. That didn't mean she voiced her doubts. It didn't mean she wasn't still looking for something that felt real and right. But at sixty-two she feared that would never happen. The time for believing was past and tied more to the path she'd already walked than the one ahead of her.

And so she'd decided to pursue this Wicca thing, hoping to find something. But all it turned out to be was a bunch of silly women doing silly things. But she liked silly things. Everybody liked silly things.

"Here." Franklin pointed in the green glow of the dashboard lights. "Take a right."

She turned and pulled to a stop in front of a metal farm gate. They all got out of the car. Shirley checked and worried over her denim fanny pack, verbally cataloging the contents for the third time. "Water. Camera. Flashlight. Hand gel."

"What about a container for the dirt?" Gabriella asked.

"I thought you were bringing it."

"Noooo."

Gabriella got back in the car and retrieved a Ziploc bag she carried for dog walks. It didn't seem the right thing for graveyard dirt, but she could shift it to something more suitable once she got home.

The women clustered and whispered.

Oh, the excitement! The darkness! The stealth!

They weren't doing anything illegal, Gabriella had told herself several times. Old Tuonela used to belong to everybody. It should still belong to everybody, and would if Evan Stroud hadn't purchased it out from under the city of Tuonela. Sneak.

It was just as much their place as anybody else's. That's the way she saw it.

"We walk single-file," Franklin told them. "Keep your flashlights pointed at your feet. Never shine it at the trees or parallel to the ground. We don't want to attract attention."

They nodded and clicked on their small flashlights, chosen for their very lack of candlepower.

"This is so exciting!" Millie said.

"Shhh!"

She dropped her voice. "This is so exciting."

Gabriella was excited too, but she hoped Millie exercised some self-control. Millie was a loud woman who liked to draw attention to herself, especially when out in public. Gabriella found it annoying. The last thing she wanted to be was part of a group of loud, obnoxious women.

They moved forward.

The first problem was finding the gate locked. They climbed it—not an easy thing for women their age. Franklin had to help Millie and Shirley. Hand on their waists, he guided them to the ground.

The day had been warm for late fall. Temperatures had dropped with the setting sun, but it wasn't horribly frigid. Gabriella wore a pair of cheap stretch gloves she'd picked up at the checkout counter of Tuonela Discount. Right now the gloves made it a little hard to grip the flashlight.

The ground was uneven and soft.

Gabriella hadn't been hiking in the woods since she was a young girl, and everything was much more difficult than she'd anticipated. There was a moment when she wondered if they should turn around.

"How much farther?" She gasped, one gloved hand clinging to a sapling, the flashlight hand braced against her knee.

Franklin surveyed their surroundings. "I think it's just over the next rise."

If it wasn't, they'd go back. This was getting ridiculous. Three old broads wandering around in the woods. One of them could break a neck, or at least an ankle. What had seemed like fun in the safety of Gabriella's living room was looking more foolish by the second.

On the crest of the next hill, they stopped to catch their breath. Franklin allowed the beam of his flashlight to move along the ground until it touched the foundation of a crumbling stone building. "There it is."

The article in the paper claimed Richard Manchester had been buried under an oak tree in the church graveyard. That's what they were after: dirt from the Pale Immortal's grave.

"I think I'll just wait here." The excitement was gone from Millie's voice.

"Me too," Shirley said.

Gabriella wanted to wait with them, but that

would be cowardly and senseless. "Let's go straight to the grave. I'll grab the dirt; then we'll hurry back."

She and Franklin moved forward.

The air seemed thicker, and their footsteps didn't make as much noise. It was too quiet, like being in some kind of vacuum. Her head felt funny: Pressure was building in her sinuses and ear canals. Her scalp tingled; her eyes watered. She put a hand to Franklin's arm for physical reassurance.

Franklin found a narrow path that led to a low stone wall. He stepped over and Gabriella followed. They paused in front of a rotting tree.

An oak tree had been planted over the grave of the Pale Immortal to keep him from rising up. A lot of people said the body should have been put back under the oak and not displayed in a museum. Gabriella hadn't really cared, but now that she was here, now that her head was buzzing in such a strange way, she wondered if maybe she'd finally found something that was real. Something to believe in.

Two massive tree roots as big around as a man straddled a dark pit where the coffin had most likely been. While Franklin shone his light at the base of the tree, Gabriella dug with her gloved hand, scooping loosened soil into the bag. She closed the plastic zipper, straightened, and tucked the dirt into her jacket pocket.

Something had changed.

She could feel Franklin's stillness.

It was too dark to read his expression, but there was no missing the clawed grip on her arm.

Did the simple act of believing change everything? Did it play an active role in an individual's reality?

A flashlight aimed at her face suddenly blinded her vision.

"Are you looking for Richard Manchester?" The voice beyond the flashlight resonated in her chest. It joined the weird sounds and thoughts going on between her ears, making her wonder if she'd heard the words only in her head.

Was he communicating telepathically?

She waited for Franklin to answer, but he seemed unable to speak.

"My boyfriend and I . . . we got a little lost," Gabriella stammered, her heart slamming. "Can you tell us how to get back to the highway from here?"

"If you're looking for Manchester," the man said, ignoring her lie, "he's no longer in his grave."

"Um . . . no. We aren't looking for . . . whoever you said. We just want to find our car."

"Would you like to meet him? Manchester?"

She frowned, perplexed. Was this Evan Stroud? Had to be. People said he was crazy. "I don't know what you're talking about."

"Right."

That was stupid of her.

"Everybody knows Richard Manchester. *Everybody.*"

"Oh, yes. Of course. The Pale Immortal. His body is at the museum in Tuonela."

"Would you like to meet him?" he repeated.

"I . . . we might go to the museum. Right, honey?" She gave Franklin a nudge.

He found his voice. "Yeah." He gripped her arm, and she could feel him shaking. "Tomorrow maybe."

"Not right now?"

Her small flashlight was still aimed at her feet. She lifted it and shone it at the mysterious speaker.

White skin.

Black hair.

Eyes like dark pits.

He took a stumbling step back.

She grabbed Franklin's arm and lifted it until his flashlight beam was parallel to hers, giving the man a double blast.

He dropped to his knees like somebody had kicked him in the belly.

Gabriella spun around, tugging at Franklin's jacket. "Come on!"

They ran.

They hauled ass as if the Pale Immortal himself were after them. Seconds later they caught up with Millie and Shirley. "Run!"

Crashing through the brush, tree branches smacking faces, lungs burning, with no thought to a broken neck or broken ankle, they ran. Until they were back at the car and Gabriella was sticking the key in the ignition, firing up the engine, slamming the car into gear.

Reverse. Drive. Tromp the gas pedal and roar away.

Sweet mercy.

"Oh, my God!" Franklin curled into the passenger seat, hands pressed to the sides of his face. "Oh, my God. I'm never going back there. Not as long as I live."

"What happened?" Millie said, leaning forward and grabbing Gabriella's headrest. "You have to tell us what happened!"

Gabriella gripped the steering wheel tighter. "I don't know."

"What do you mean, you don't know?"

"It was Evan Stroud." Franklin was out of breath. "We ran into Evan Stroud."

Gabriella wasn't so certain.

She replayed the event in her mind, but no matter how many times she viewed it her memory was the same. Yes, she'd been scared shitless. Yes, she knew her take was skewed.

She'd been to the museum to see the Pale Immortal. Who in the area hadn't? And now, when she pulled up the encounter in her head, she saw someone she swore was Richard Manchester standing there, not Evan Stroud.

But she wasn't going to say anything about it.

"Now what?" Millie asked. "Where are we going to find the right dirt?"

In all the excitement, Gabriella had completely forgotten about the bag of soil she'd collected. She tugged off her gloves and reached into her jacket pocket, her fingers coming in contact with the pouch.

They'd gotten what they'd come for: dirt from the grave of the Pale Immortal.

Chapter Twenty-one

We lost our room.

One day after the psychic clip aired on WXOW, the owner of Tuonela Inn told us she was over-booked and we had to leave.

Kicked out.

We could have argued, but Claire pointed out that we were quickly becoming too unpopular. Soon no-body would be talking to us if we continued to cause trouble. And we'd find another place to stay.

We didn't.

It might have been because of the whole tourist thing, but I had the feeling we wouldn't have found a room even if every room in town had been empty.

So we were going to camp out.

Camp! I hadn't been camping since I was a Girl Scout. And that was in somebody's backyard.

Normally I'd just pack up and leave. This was bullshit. But no way was I leaving now.

I'd screwed up some things in my life. My big one was dropping out of college, thinking I knew enough people in the business to make a living. But Tuonela was going to be a turning point. I sensed it. I felt it. Like a breeze blowing across the surface of my skin. Or the way skinny-dipping touched you in unfamiliar places. Places that had always been there but you hadn't noticed before. My blood was singing.

But we had to sleep in a tent. It was hard for me to hide my irritation.

We picked up two cheap pup tents at Target, along with camping supplies like lanterns, flashlights, and sleeping bags. "It's part of the adventure," Claire said.

I didn't want to spoil her delusion, so I just nodded and stared forlornly at my Barbie sleeping bag.

I hadn't told any of them about what had happened at Old Tuonela. That was my secret. My ticket to the future.

A guest appearance on *Geraldo* popped into my head. *Ick.* Erase that. Not *Geraldo*, although it's true my mother once thought he was hot when he was young. Now he was just strange. That happened to a lot of celebrities. They went from intriguing to just plain weird.

No, I was thinking *Oprah*, although the story was probably too offbeat for her. How many middle-aged women would relate to a guy who thought he was a vampire and spent his nights digging up graves? No, this would be something for one of those hour news shows. Something they could sensationalize.

"Do you have a five?"

I snapped to attention, and saw Claire standing at the checkout, palm extended.

"I thought you were paying."

"I'm five bucks short."

I dug around and pulled out a five-dollar bill.

Normally I would be irritated. It was her fault we had to buy the sleeping bags in the first place. Instead I was grateful to her for not seeing an obvious opportunity. Instead I was trying to keep my secret enthusiasm from showing.

The clerk, a bored high-school girl, ripped off the receipt and handed it to Claire. I grabbed a couple of bags and we headed out.

If Claire wanted to turn this gig into fiction while ignoring what was right in front of her face, let her do it. Because even if I pointed it out to her, she wouldn't see it or care. She wanted it her way and only her way.

"Why are you acting like that?" Claire asked as we headed for the van.

"Like what?"

"Pissed off. I can tell you're mad. You never seemed like somebody who expected to be put up in a luxury hotel."

"I didn't expect to have to sleep in a Barbie sleeping bag."

"It'll be fun. Oh, it might be physically unpleasant, but that will add to the documentary."

"You want to film our camping?"

"Yeah. Especially since none of us are seasoned campers. Could be funny as hell."

I made a sound of complaint.

Claire stopped. I stopped. "What the hell is your problem?" She was mad. "Do you know how many applications I got for this job?"

"Ten?"

"Close to thirty. And I'll bet most of them would be willing to drive here today if I called and asked them to."

I was sure she was exaggerating. "So why'd you pick me?"

"I liked your films. You were funny! I thought you would get what I'm trying to do."

"There's a difference between funny and making fun."

"I'm not making fun of anybody. These people are already what they are. Did I create a goddamn town where most of the people believe in vampires? Did I open a damn museum with a mummy called the Pale Immortal? How can you say I'm making fun of them?"

She had a point.

"You also seemed laid back. I thought you'd be able to shift gears pretty easily and not get bent out of shape if things didn't go as planned. I was really wrong about that."

I didn't want to go back to Minneapolis, that was for sure.

Normally I would argue and tell her I was better than those other videographers. And it would probably be the truth in most cases. Maybe all cases. "Sorry. You're right." It was her project, not mine. I was working for her. If she wanted funny, I could do funny. I could be a stand-up comic if she wanted.

And I knew what she was talking about. I did do some funny stuff in the past, but I grew out of it, thank God. I did the light stuff because I didn't want it to look like I was taking film too seriously. Nothing worse than some serious, black-turtlenecked asshole who made films. I never wanted to be one of those people. So I went the other way. *Ha-ha. Don't get too serious about this. I'm only kidding. If you don't like it, I won't be hurt.*

Art hurt.

That was the truth of it.

Nothing hurt so much as failing at your dream, which was why I'd given up before I could fail. Was there a psychological term for that? If not, I should make one up. Self sabotage? Fear-of-failure Syndrome?

We spotted Ian and Stewart at the same time. They were cutting across the parking lot, both clutching a paper bag.

Those two could smell a liquor store a mile away. Oh, and Ian appeared to have a huge crush on Claire. Poor guy.

"This is gonna be so cool!" Ian said. "I haven't slept outside since that time I passed out in the front yard." Pause for effect. "And I don't think that counts."

Stewart joined in the nonsense. "The *only* way to sleep outside is to get so drunk you pass out."

"Hmmm. I'm wondering what that merit badge looks like." I knew I was suddenly coming across as some sour old lady, but I couldn't help it. Becoming a crazy old lady with twenty cats wasn't a bad goal and had always been a secret although sarcastic dream of mine. But very often sarcasm is just a thin veil for the truth.

And yet I knew when they broke out the booze, I'd be first in line.

"Is this called making camp?" Ian asked.

"You're talking about breaking camp." Stewart opened another beer. Was that his fourth? Fifth? I'd lost count. I was on my fourth, but we'd started out with vodka. "You do that when you pack up and move on. Breaking camp."

"What about 'pitching a tent'?" Ian asked.

Both guys burst out laughing at that. *Ha-ha.* I knew I should be annoyed, but instead I found myself warming to them the way I always warmed to people once I got a few drinks in me.

And they'd impressed me with their wood-gathering skills and their ability to tend to the basics. With no knowledge of camping, they'd managed to get a fire going in the pit using several wadded-up newspapers and kindling.

We were in a designated camping area. We'd passed some vehicles on the way in, but they couldn't be seen from our location because the terrain was hilly and woody and twisted, with little knolls and valleys and tight clusters of dark trees.

At the pay booth we'd been handed a flyer that explained about the dangers of coyotes. It also explained that none had been spotted in the area, and the campground was patrolled and considered safe.

I'm not a big fan of uniforms, but I liked the idea

of rangers keeping an eye on the place. We were probably safer here than at the inn—what with pissing off half the people in Tuonela. I kind of liked the idea that nobody knew where we were staying.

The van doors were open, the CD player was on, the music cranked up. The human noise brought civilization to the woods; it made our little circle bigger, created a buffer behind our backs as we perched on logs arranged around the fire.

Claire was drunk too.

Just last night I swore I wouldn't drink for at least a week. Now here I was again. And there was no denying it felt good. To hell with everything else. What difference did it make? I needed to quit freaking out about things.

"I'm cold." Claire stood by the fire, hugging herself and bouncing.

"My coat's right there." I pointed. Like she'd wear my coat.

But she did. She put it on and checked the length of the sleeves. "I can't believe I've been making fun of this. It's so comfortable." She modeled it for us in front of the fire. We laughed our asses off. The more we laughed, the more she did the hilarious and awkward model walk. The stop, the turn, the bored and blank expression. She sucked in her cheeks and the guys almost wet their pants they laughed so hard.

Ian and Stewart jumped to their feet and began to prance around. Ian suddenly seemed extremely feminine—and also curiously attractive. I laughed at my own thoughts.

I could tell Ian liked that he was entertaining us.

He paced again, and we laughed some more. I got out my camera and turned it on. I was laughing so hard I could hardly focus.

"Dude, that's just too convincing!" Stewart was almost crying now.

Ian put his hands on his bent knees, then blew him a kiss. He crooked his finger at Claire.

Poor Ian. She was the rich socialite and he was the son of the poor gardener. Or something like that. People liked to pretend that kind of thing didn't matter in the twenty-first century, but that was bullshit. There was just as much class-consciousness going on now as there had been a hundred years ago. People were just better at hiding it.

Ian shifted gears and pretended to be a vampire, pulling out an imaginary cape, then hiding the lower half of his face.

Claire was still laughing, and the sound of it must have been an invitation to Ian. He swooped down, grabbed her, swung her around, and dipped her.

My breath caught.

Oh, he was going to be in so much trouble. And he was going to be so embarrassed tomorrow.

I felt even sorrier for him.

For a moment I thought he would kiss her, but he came to his senses. Maybe it was the sudden death of laughter. The music also stopped, calling attention to the awkwardness of the moment.

Ian let her go and stepped back into the darkness. For his sake, I was glad we couldn't see his face.

"I have to pee," Claire announced. "Where's a flashlight?"

Stewart produced one.

"I'll come with you," he volunteered.

There was a real restroom just over the knoll. I could even make out a faint glow from its light.

"Maybe we should all go," I suggested.

"I can pee by myself," Claire said.

She was mad at Ian, but also mad at herself for getting drunk and whooping it up with the help. Let her go by herself if she wanted to. I'd never been one of those girls who believed in peeing together.

I thought of the image I'd seen on my film that day . . . the day we'd arrived in town; then I abruptly pushed it from my mind.

Claire was already tromping off in the direction of the restroom.

"She'll be okay," Ian said. He got up and rummaged around in the van until he found another CD. He popped it in the player, and suddenly the night was once again filled with music.

Chapter Twenty-two

They were a little tipsy.

Last year Gabriella had joined a wine club before she realized she didn't even like wine. By the time she canceled her membership, she'd accumulated quite a few bottles of the nasty crap.

They'd dumped their guide off at his truck, then went back to Gabriella's place, where they'd opened a bottle.

"Here it is!" Gabriella waved the piece of paper in the air and wended her way through the piles of clutter in her living room. The lamps were turned down, candles were lit, and Shirley and Millie were sitting on pillows in front of the coffee table, the empty bottle of wine between them. At first the idea of continuing with their plan of a reanimation spell had given Gabriella a mild sense of unease, but now that they were safely home she could rationalize what had happened. What *had* happened?

Nothing.

Evan Stroud had found them digging on his

property and he'd chased them off. Pretty straightforward. She felt kind of silly about her reaction
now. Participating in the reanimation spell might be
a good way to redeem herself in the eyes of her fellow witches. And the wine didn't hurt.

"He was extremely good-looking." Shirley was
staring at an antique photo of Richard Manchester.
She'd been staring at it for ten minutes. "I mean, he
was *gorgeous*."

Gabriella dropped the bag of graveyard dirt on
the table and lowered herself to her pillow, legs
crossed as much as they could be crossed for someone of her age and physical shape. "It makes it easier to understand how so many people followed him
and did what he said, especially women."

"And a few men, I'll bet." Gabriella tried to take
the photo, but Shirley wasn't finished with it.
Gabriella shot her a look of annoyance. "A charis-
matic leader."

She'd found the photo on eBay. It hadn't been
cheap either.

"His eyes kind of follow you." Shirley moved the
heavy card left and right, let out a shudder, then
passed the photo to Gabriella.

Yes, he was a beautiful, beautiful man, with pale,
perfect skin and a sensuous mouth. Dark brows
above pale eyes that had probably been a brilliant
blue.

He stood posed with both hands on the hilt of a
long sword, the tip resting on the ground near his
feet. He wore a frock coat made of wool. It had a row
of buttons down the front, with matching buttons on

the sleeves, a bit of white cuff showing. Around his neck was a scarf with an embroidered crest.

It was hard to equate the mummy in the museum to this man. The mummy, while interesting, didn't seem to generate anything. It was just a shriveled crust of skin that had once held a man's soul.

"I would have followed him," Gabriella admitted.

She found herself fantasizing about his touch. Long, tapered fingers moved down her spine, pulling her close. . . .

She closed her eyes, and for a second she could have sworn she felt a soft flutter on her lips and even a little tingle—down there.

Millie reached for the green wine bottle and tipped it upside down over her glass, shaking out a few last drops. "Do you have the rest of the stuff?"

"And I have more wine. A lot more wine."

They opened another bottle and filled all three glasses—almost to the top, even though Gabriella had been told that wasn't the thing to do. She picked up the curled photo of the Pale Immortal and gave it a kiss. "I hate to see this go." The other two women mumbled their agreement. Gabriella placed the photo in the bottom of the bowl.

"Here's what Matthew gave me."

Her nephew was the night janitor at the Tuonela Museum. He'd been able to get them everything they needed.

Gabriella opened the lid of a metal cigarette tin. "Hair of the Pale Immortal." She placed the long, dark strands in a special spell bowl. "Button from his coat." She added that.

"Look!" Millie pointed to the photo. "It matches the buttons in the picture!"

Shirley nodded. "The real deal. No phony vampire buttons for us."

"Skin." Gabriella dropped the dried flakes with the rest of the items. "Matthew says the mummy sheds. He has to clean inside the case all the time." She dumped and tapped the rest of the contents into the bowl. Then she unzipped the plastic bag. "Goofer dust." About two spoonfuls.

She mixed it with the straight end of a crochet hook.

"Blood is the final ingredient," Millie said.

Gabriella was tempted to pretend with some of the red wine, but Shirley was already digging around in her purse and came up with three finger lancets. "Aren't you glad you have a diabetic in the bunch?" She passed out the lancets.

All three women pricked their fingers and squeezed blood into the bowl; then Gabriella stirred the contents once again.

"The powder," Shirley reminded her.

Many spells required a catalyst that was really no more than incense powder. Gabriella sprinkled the black powder over the top.

"Do you have the words? Who has the words?"

They'd gotten the words from a book of spells they'd found online, ordered from a place in Europe. A village with an exotic name that Gabriella had never heard before and couldn't remember. The spell was in another language. Someone thought perhaps it was ancient Finnish, but no one knew for sure.

"How do we know if we're even saying it right?" Millie asked.

"We don't."

It was short.

Gabriella sounded it out as best she could, ignoring the accent marks. The other women repeated the sounds. They were ready. Gabriella struck a match and tossed it into the bowl. The contents sparked and flashed, then began to slowly smolder. The women joined hands and spoke the words of the spell.

A good spell was based on repetition. They repeated the words, speaking in unison.

The incense powder couldn't cover the stench of burning hair and the melting shell button that had probably come from a clam found on the bottom of the Tuonela River. The ancient pressed-photo paper caught with a sudden flare that jumped from the bowl, then settled into a steady flame. The photo burned completely until the only thing left was a small pile of black ashes. The women released hands and blinked into the semidarkness.

"Well?" Shirley asked.

"I thought I felt something," Millie said. "But it might just be because I'm drunk."

They laughed.

"I wish we knew what we just said."

"Did you try Babel Fish? Enter it in Babel Fish and see what it says."

Gabriella grabbed her laptop, found the site, and typed the phrase into the box. "Finnish?" she asked.

"Try it."

"Nothing."

"How about an ancient language?"

She closed the Babel Fish page and did a search. "Here's something called Nostratic. Some believe it's the root language to many language families."

"Ooh, try that one."

There was a translation box. She entered the text and it gave her an answer.

" 'He who dies will live again. He who lives will die again.' "

Chapter Twenty-three

The wind blew out of the north, across and through Old Tuonela, bringing with it the scent of decay and the whisper of mingled voices. At first it was just a *sh-sh-sh.* But as he listened, he could make out a word here and there.

Come
back
to us.

Voices from the past, reaching into the present.

For so many years he'd felt trapped. Living in darkness, in a kind of limbo. Waiting. Always waiting.

Come back.

But limbo wasn't a bad place to be. No pain, no cravings.

Now he craved.

He had the notion that if he could somehow shed his shell the world would open up for him. But he couldn't sever the thread. It always pulled him back.

Wandering in his mind, he dreamed of the outside. The harder he concentrated, the more concrete and real it seemed.

It was possible to travel without a body. He had a vague memory of doing it before, but it took focus. Deep concentration. And it didn't last. He needed to find a way to make it last.

He concentrated . . . and suddenly soared upward.

He expected the display box to shatter. He expected to hit the ceiling. Instead, he shot through it to hover above the museum.

As he looked down, mesmerized, the wind caught him and gave him a push. He rode it, gliding along, floating over houses. And even though he couldn't see the people inside, he could sense them and smell them.

Especially the children and women.

Sh-sh-sh.

The voices held him up and carried him along. They were the breeze that lifted him over chimneys and treetops.

Sh-sh-sh.

They were familiar. Old friends. Family. Women he'd loved. Children he'd loved and killed.

Sh-sh-sh.

He drifted over the Tuonela Bridge.

The flowing freedom was sensual.

This place.

God, how many times had he wanted to leave it? How many times had he tried?

But suddenly whatever had tethered him was gone. For a hundred years he'd stood at the threshold of another existence, unable to move forward, unable to go back.

But something brought about his release.

Float away.

Just float away. All the way back to the mother country, to England.

Get away from this dark, vile place of memories best forgotten. Of traitorous, vile people.

What about revenge? For those who had tricked him and betrayed him? Especially one person . . .

If only he could truly inhabit his body again. If only he could be whole again.

He drifted over a sprawling Victorian house—and paused.

Something snagged at his mind. Something tugged at him.

And they whispered: *Yes, yes, yes.*

All he had to do was think of the direction he wanted to go, and suddenly he shifted and dropped.

He plunged straight down.

Instead of smashing against the roof, he moved silently through it. The shock and surprise caused his breath to catch, and it took him a moment to realize he'd passed the physical boundary of the roof.

He was in a chamber. The lights were off, and through the turret window he could see the Wisconsin River and the lift bridge.

She's down the hall.

Yes.

He could sense her presence and he moved toward it. He didn't have to worry about his feet making noise. He glided soundlessly inches above the floor.

He paused. To the left was a bathroom with a claw-foot tub. To the right, an open door.

He stopped in the doorway. He closed his eyes and inhaled.

Lavender. She'd always smelled like lavender.

Sweet girl. Sweet woman. Sweet love.

Oh, you hurt me. You hurt me so much.

Sh-sh-sh.

The whispers held him up. They'd brought him there.

True love.

That was what it had been. He would have done anything for her. She was his downfall. Some would argue he wasn't capable of love, but everyone was capable of love. Even the most evil, heartless of men loved in some form. Even if it was only for a fleeting second. Even if it was a twisted love.

And love blinded even the strongest.

She made a soft, restless sound and turned in the bed.

Could she sense him in the room? Invading her dreams?

Sweet, sweet girl.

He was both fearful and curious.

He moved closer, stopping at the edge of the bed.

She rolled to her back, arms above her head. He could see her breasts outlined against the white fabric of her T-shirt.

He remembered her. He remembered touching her and holding her and making love to her.

His gaze tracked down, and he let out an involuntary gasp. The sheet had slipped and he could see her belly. It was swollen, the skin tight.

Had he been here before? Done this before? It was hard for the dead to remember.

So familiar.

A baby.

He put out his hands . . . and placed his palms against her stomach. The baby kicked. And kicked again.

As if it knew he was there.

Interesting.

He loved children. If he were capable of smiling, he would have done so.

They were holding him up.

His followers.

With their whispers and their invisible hands.

He leaned closer; he brushed his lips against hers.

The woman in the bed awakened with a gasp. She sat upright, hands planted on each side of the mattress, eyes wide in the dark.

She shifted and touched her belly. He could almost feel her hands on top of his. The baby squirmed in protest, and she let out another gasp, this one sounding as if she were in pain.

Ah, my love.

He could almost taste her. The air suddenly seemed tainted with the sickeningly sweet scent of almonds.

How many ways did you try to kill me? First the poison, then—

Recalled agony ripped through his chest and he

jumped back. With dismay and regret, he felt himself dissolving and briefly wished he'd never come here, never floated through the roof to visit her room.

Don't think about that, the voices whispered. *Don't think about how she destroyed you. . . . You can be strong again. Stronger than before. We can help you. He can help you.*

The woman in the bed looked blindly about the room. "Where are you?"

Could she see him? What a delicious thought.

She turned slightly and reached into nothing. "*Who* are you?"

He felt himself fading.

One last sizzle before the spark went out.

She'd done it to him again. Killed him again.

He would answer if he could. He would tell her who he was, that he was her long-lost love, Richard Manchester.

Chapter Twenty-four

Evan dug.

He dug to find and forget. He dug to discover and escape.

The hole was so deep he had to toss dirt above his head. It spilled in his eyes and sifted into his hair. He could taste it on his lips.

He was driven by something internal and external; a sense of urgency overpowered his waking hours.

Hurry.

Dig.

Voices whispered to him, coaxed him, coached him. They felt it too. The urgency.

Hurry, hurry, hurry.

Over here. Dig over here.

He couldn't remember when he'd last eaten. Didn't matter. Food was unimportant. Sleep, when it came, wasn't sleep but collapse. His body giving up and tumbling into unconsciousness.

That was what he truly craved. Those few hours

when everything stopped. Those few hours of nothingness.

Don't think.

Somewhere beneath the turmoil in his head he felt he must find the secrets buried in the past and possibly, if not a solution to his situation, an answer. He needed to know who the Pale Immortal had really been, and why he'd done what he'd done. He needed to know what Evan Stroud had become and was becoming.

The shovel hit something solid.

He dragged the metal blade across a wooden surface, pushing dirt away until the object was revealed.

A child's coffin.

Working the shovel, he broke the box free, lifted and deposited it on the ground next to the hole, then climbed out.

It was held shut with a rusty metal lock.

He grasped the lock and tried to force it open. Pain lanced through the fleshy part of his palm. His fingers grew sticky. He raised the box to his shoulder and walked through the woods toward home.

Evan pushed open the kitchen door.

Someone sat at the table. Someone vaguely familiar. It took him a moment to remember the person's name.

Graham.

The kitchen was dark except for the light of a weak bulb above the sink.

"What are you doing back this time of the night?"

Graham asked. "It's not even close to morning." A nice combination of resentment and sarcasm in the kid's voice.

Evan lowered the box to the floor. It was a traditional shape. Not rectangular, but wide at the shoulders, narrow at the bottom.

Graham took note of what it was and jumped to his feet. "Is that a coffin?" He backed away.

"Find me a screwdriver."

"No."

Graham hovered in the doorway, looking as if he might bolt at any second, but unable to take his eyes off the wooden box. In the dim light, Evan could see that a cross had been carved on the top.

Evan pointed. "In that drawer."

"What'd you do? You're bleeding." Graham grabbed a kitchen towel and handed it to Evan. Evan stared at it.

Blood hit his boots and the floor. He wrapped the towel around his hand.

"You have to put that back." Graham pointed to the box. "You can't keep digging up dead people."

Evan crossed the room, jerked open a drawer, and pulled out a screwdriver. He held it to Graham. "Open it."

He shook his head. "That's desecration."

"Open it."

Graham moved reluctantly closer, his feet dragging. He crouched in front of the coffin and wedged the tip of the screwdriver under the metal latch.

"You should get a tetanus shot," he mumbled, "if you cut yourself on this rusty, dirty thing."

"I'll be okay."

It wasn't locked, but the rust had fused the metal.

Using the screwdriver, Graham broke the latch so nothing held the box closed but two hinges.

Evan moved closer, the bloody towel pressed to his injured hand. Graham looked up.

"Open it," Evan whispered.

Graham swallowed and shook his head.

"Do it."

In the end, the kid couldn't defy his father.

Using the fingers of both hands, Graham wiggled the lid until it loosened; then he swung it open, his feet sliding against the floor as he scrambled away like a spider. He stopped, the fear in his eyes changing to puzzlement.

Bent over like an old man, Evan shuffled closer to examine the contents.

No mummified baby. No body.

Books.

Not just any books—journals tucked among an infant's yellowed gown, a dagger, and what looked like the dust of crumbled flowers.

Evan lifted out one of the journals. Reverently and carefully, he opened it.

Feminine handwriting in faded black ink.

The brittle, brown pages smelled like a mixture of lavender and sage. He closed his eyes and inhaled.

"This is it," he whispered, his heart hammering. "What I've been searching for."

Graham crawled across the floor, stopping a foot from the box. "What is it?"

No records had been kept of Old Tuonela, and the

town's history was shrouded in mystery and folk-lore. Tall tales that continuously shifted and changed. Nobody knew what had happened one hundred years ago.

"A box of secrets." Evan clutched the leather-bound journal to his chest. They would finally know the truth.

He collapsed on the floor beside the coffin, reached inside, and picked up another journal, carefully turning the pages.

They'd been written by a woman named Florence.

Florence.

He'd heard someone whisper that name. . . .

Distantly he knew Graham was talking to him, saying something about leaving. About going to Tuonela and staying with his grandfather. Evan didn't answer.

A door slammed. A car started and drove away. . . .

He was lost in the words.

The earlier journals documented the arduous journey from the East to settle in what was now called Old Tuonela. At first it seemed simply a story of typical westward movement so prevalent at the time. Richard Manchester and his followers had settled in a beautiful and remote valley in western Wisconsin, where Manchester hoped they could live in isolation and peace without interruption or intrusion from the outside world.

But the story quickly grew strange as Evan continued to read:

The women sleep in one building, men in another. When a woman gives birth, the child is taken and raised in a nursery. My sister, Victoria, was heartbroken for the first several months. And now years have passed. . . .

Another entry, the tone changed:

The children are disappearing! Oh, my God! We fear Victoria's sweet darling could be next.

Manchester blamed the deaths on the coyote packs that could be heard howling just beyond the lights of the town.

The men began keeping nightly vigil. They organized a massive hunt and massacre, dragging dead coyote carcasses to the town square, where they set them on fire. But the human deaths didn't stop.

Some people began to suspect Manchester, but it was an unpopular theory. He was their leader. The suspicion created dissent, with a few unpopular thinkers becoming the outcasts—the others.

Some say he is a vampire. Some say that is why he is never about during the daylight hours, and why he insists upon public worship being held after dusk. I don't believe in such nonsense. My father was a physician, and I've seen diseases of the skin. Manchester has a disease of the skin. He also has a disease of the soul. The man is mad. As soon as the snow melts, my sister and I will leave this wretched place. We will steal away with her sweet daughter, return to Boston, and tell our story to whomever will listen. Victoria says no one will believe us. That we are the ones they will lock up and call mad. I fear she is right. For who in his right mind would believe that a man is drinking blood and devouring his own children?

There was a large gap of dates. Almost two months, followed by a brief entry:

Victoria is missing. Her daughter, Sarah, is missing. He's killed them. I'm certain of it.

Weeks later:

Manchester knows his life is in danger. I don't know how he knows, but he does. He told me he's worried someone will try to kill him. We are hardly ever alone, and guards remain in the room while I'm forced to tolerate his lovemaking. I would write more, I would tell you all about the poison that was put in his drink, but I don't dare.

He sleeps with guards in the room. They stand over him. But I will convince him of our need to be alone.

Another entry:

Oh, the death! Some brave souls joined to fight him and all were killed, mostly women and children. All dead. Sweet little lambs. His followers dug a pit, shoved the bodies over the edge like diseased cattle, and covered them with dirt. I know I should grieve, yet I feel nothing. Not even despair.

Two months passed:

I am pregnant. With his child. What will it look like? Will it be evil, like him? Should I drown it as soon as it takes a breath? Yes. His offspring cannot be allowed to live.

Another month:

He is dead.

I killed him with his own sword while he lay in bed. When the blade pierced his heart, I felt the babe move inside me.

Many of the people of the town have scattered. The

ones who remain buried Manchester in the church graveyard. As instructed, an oak tree was planted over his
grave to keep him from rising up.

We are the survivors. We don't talk about it. We know
we can't speak of this. We can never speak of this.

They must go first. Without me. They must leave and
never return. I will stay until the baby is born. I will finish my journal and I will kill the child. After that? Will I
follow them to the new place? Or remain here? To be close
to my poor dead darling sister, Victoria? Someone must
keep her company. Someone must stand guard over this
dark, evil place to make sure nothing escapes.

Chapter Twenty-five

I woke up to silence and realized I'd fallen asleep or passed out. The CD was no longer playing, my nose was cold, and the fire was a pile of moving, shifting embers.

Ian and Stewart were both asleep in their sleeping bags. Claire's bag was empty.

My heart began to thud as I tried to reconstruct the evening. That was hard to do, since I'd been drinking. Claire had gone to the restroom; Ian had put on a CD; then I'd apparently passed out. . . . I didn't have any memory of crawling into my sleeping bag, but here I was.

I tried to unzip the bag but couldn't get the zipper down. I wriggled out, kicking my legs free. I found my tennis shoes, slipped them on, and looked around for the flashlight.

Claire had it.

I wanted to wake up Ian and Stewart, but at the same time I knew I was being silly. Claire was probably either throwing up or working. The restroom had electricity and lights. She'd plugged in her laptop earlier. She was probably down there right now typing the voice-over for our camping footage.

Oh, man. I felt like crap.

I aimed myself in the direction of the restroom and stumbled through the dark toward the yellow glow put off by the light above the doors. I felt ashamed for getting drunk again, but I also felt too crappy to give it much thought.

Save it for morning.

Come morning, I'll hate myself more.

I was aware that I had to piss like a racehorse, and was glad to top the little hill and see the restroom down in a small valley. There were the two doors, and the single light above them.

So welcoming.

But the night brought with it a lack of color, washing the image in diluted shades, like a sixties television show. My vision wasn't that great, since I was still a little drunk, and my eyes seemed to have a haze over them, like a thin layer of Vaseline.

Unfuck my life.

When was I going to do that? Wasn't I supposed to be doing that right now?

I unbuttoned my pants as I hit the cement sidewalk. I was freezing my ass off, and I remembered Claire had borrowed my coat.

The restrooms had no doors. Just a turn to the left and a turn to the right.

"Claire?"

I took the final corner and recognized the pink-and-green tweed pattern of my coat lying in a pile on the floor under the sink. Just kind of shoved there.

I felt a strange mixture of anger and fear. Anger at Claire for tossing my coat in the corner, and fear because I knew there was something else going on. But I focused on my anger because that was the easiest thing to do.

A smell hit me.

I once walked in on my uncle when he was butchering a deer in the kitchen. If you've ever seen an animal butchered, you know that smell. It's raw and overpowering, like nothing you've ever encountered. I think humans are supposed to be repulsed by it.

That was the day I became a vegetarian. No more bloody carcasses for me.

Everybody said it wouldn't last. They were wrong.

The soles of my shoes stuck to the floor. I didn't look down. I didn't dare.

"Claire?" I whispered.

There were six stalls, all with gray doors.

I slowly pushed open the first door.

Empty.

The next.

When I hit the third door I felt the hair lift from my scalp. My mouth dropped open. At the same time, bile rose in my throat and I made a loud gagging sound.

It's just a deer carcass, I told myself while my eyes stung with fear. *Just a skinned deer.*

The blood on the soles of my shoes cemented me

to the floor. My eyes stared without blinking even as my mind was already running back to the camp, waking up Ian and Stewart, screaming at them to find the phone.

I don't know how long I stood there.

Seconds.

Hours.

It don't really matter, other than being long enough to forever embed the stench of blood and death in my sinuses, and forever tattoo what was left of Claire to my retinas. It would be there for the rest of my life. No matter where I looked, where I turned, it would be there.

I ran.

I wasn't aware of my feet moving, just the sensation of hurtling over the ground, a roar in my ears as big as the ocean. Somebody was screaming. She wouldn't stop.

Screaming my throat raw.

I flew into the campsite.

There were the remnants of our night. Beer bottles everywhere. Stupid kids. Stupid, stupid kids.

Ian and Stewart stood near their sleeping bags, hands hanging limply at their sides, both staring at me with terror in their eyes. Ian's mouth moved.

What's wrong? I think he said. But all I could hear was screaming.

He grabbed me by both arms and gave me a shake, making me look at his face, his eyes. I could see Claire's skinned body there.

I turned away.

The horror followed me.

It was like watching a silent movie. A silent movie with an orchestra that was playing too loud.

I couldn't tell Ian and Stewart; I couldn't communicate, but I could read them reading me.

Ian looked from me to the direction I'd come. He said something to Stewart. Stewart shook his head. Ian let go of me and ran for the restroom.

"*No!*" I was finally able to shout. "No, Ian!"

I ran after him. I grabbed him and knocked him down. He tried to push me away.

I remembered last night and how he'd dipped Claire. He'd always liked her, even though he knew he could never have her.

Never, never, never.

"Don't go," I sobbed.

I don't want him to see what I've seen. I don't want that to be his last memory of Claire. Let it be of her dancing by the fire.

He's no longer fighting me.

He knows. Of course he knows.

I'm crying, and he joins me. With fingers like claws, he pulls me close. He's holding me, but he isn't thinking of me; he's thinking of Claire.

Chapter Twenty-six

A policeman stood at the campground entrance directing traffic. The red light on his squad car turned slowly and soundlessly. When he spotted the coroner van, he motioned Rachel through with his flashlight.

As the van rolled slowly and awkwardly over the dirt lane buffered by pine needles, she caught glimpses of Lake Tuonela between clusters of trees.

If you didn't know it was out there, you might not notice; you might think the reflection was a flash of light from a house or outbuilding.

Repetition.

Everything was about repetition. Nature. Seasons. The patterns and arrangements of leaves and flowers.

Murder.

Murder would always happen, whether committed by the same person, or new crimes with all new players.

Sometimes Rachel wasn't sure she could continue

doing this. What about once the baby came? She'd have to hire help so she could leave in the middle of the night. The baby would be crying to be fed, and Rachel would come home smelling like death.

Lake Tuonela.

She and her parents used to fish there. Sometimes Evan and his family would come. That was when they were kids, before Evan got sick.

It had been updated since then with showers and electricity and actual flushing toilets.

It was easy to find the crime scene. Lights from several police cars lit up the night.

She pulled to the edge of the lane, shut off the ignition, and slid out of the van, her belly rubbing the steering wheel. She grabbed her evidence kit and walked toward the lights.

Outside the restroom Alastair Stroud stood talking to a red-haired girl with a Barbie sleeping bag wrapped around her shoulders. The girl's lips were blue, and she was shaking violently.

The blue lips and shaking were trauma-induced and had little to do with temperature. Not far away, sitting at a picnic table, were two guys who looked to be in their early twenties.

They were part of the documentary crew.

The town was buzzing about them. Rachel had been irritated by the little stunt they'd pulled with the psychic and the television station. On the other hand, Mayor McBride tended to piss people off and step on toes. Plus if he started tourism based on the Pale Immortal, he had to expect to be made fun of.

"This is Kristin Blackmoore," Alastair said.

"She's with the documentary crew, and she found the body."

The girl's eyes were swollen, her nose red. Her fingers clutched the sleeping bag under her chin while her lips trembled nonstop.

Rachel wanted to put her arms around her. If her dad had been alive, that was what he would have done. But it wasn't part of her job to soothe anybody, even though she'd sometimes fallen into that role since returning to Tuonela. Alastair didn't seem up for the task.

"Did you hear or see anything?" Rachel asked.

The girl shook her head.

"Said she woke up and her friend's sleeping bag was empty. She came down here and found the body."

"You came directly to the restroom?"

"Yes."

"Why here?" Alastair asked. "You didn't look around your camp first?"

"I don't know. I just figured she'd come down here." The girl frowned. "She was wearing my coat."

"What?"

"She was cold, so she borrowed my coat."

Those were the kinds of inane comments people in shock tended to make. But Rachel wondered if it was really as inane as it seemed.

"I'd better take a look at the body."

The girl blanched.

Rachel stepped forward and grabbed her. "Maybe you should sit down."

"I have blood on my shoes," Kristin said in a vague, breathless voice.

One of the young men got up from the table, came over, and took her other arm. "Come on," he coaxed. "Come and sit with me and Ian."

"We're taking them all downtown," Alastair said. "Interview them separately and see if their stories jibe."

They walked toward the restroom. Bloody shoe-prints led out of the women's room. The tread was from a sneaker, probably Kristin's. They would need a shoe imprint. "You think one of them may have committed the murder?" Rachel asked.

"Everybody's a suspect. She's almost too upset. The boy is almost too calm."

Rachel wasn't going to argue. She knew that even the most innocent-looking children could be guilty of murder, but these kids didn't seem likely suspects to her.

The body was just like the other one: skinned, the carcass curled into a fetal position.

"Coyotes?" Alastair asked.

She'd never believed coyotes had killed the last victim. It was just a case of Mayor McBride looking for a way to appease the fears of the town and the tourists.

"Don't look so skeptical," Alastair said. "They might look like scrawny dogs, but I've seen a coyote pack devour a calf as it was being born. Ate it before it could hit the ground."

"This is a restroom. I find it hard to believe wild animals would come into a place so saturated with the scent of humans." She scanned the floor. "No footprints." The only prints belonged to the same tread that had made the prints on the sidewalk.

"Maybe she was attacked outside, crawled in here and died. How long can a person live without skin?"

A horrid theory, but remotely possible.

Alastair pointed to smears of blood that led inside.

Dear God. He was right.

"Looks like the same MO as the girl in the woods," he said.

A wave of dizziness washed over her. She stepped outside and pulled in some deep breaths. Alastair followed.

"I'll know more after we get the body to the autopsy suite," she said. "When I do the exam, I'll try to find any anomalies."

"I'm not even sure it's who we think it is."

"It'll take dental records to make a positive ID."

"We can speculate all day, but it probably won't get us anywhere." He seemed preoccupied and distracted.

It had to be tough to have just returned to Tuonela, only to have two horrific deaths occur while you were in charge. He was acting almost as if it were somehow his fault. She didn't feel he'd been nearly aggressive enough in the first investigation, letting the mayor soften the severity of the case, but it would do no good for Rachel to point that out now.

"I dread calling the parents." He looked terrified

at the thought. Not cut out for this job. Too old, too softhearted.

"What about the skin?" Rachel asked.

A lot of people didn't know that Alastair had suffered a breakdown when Evan was ill. Rachel's father had told her about it, and told her not to mention it to anyone. Rachel was afraid that returning to his old job had been a bad idea. He should be golfing in Florida. He should be enjoying life.

"Officers are searching the area, hoping to find it."

"The last one was never found," she said. "Was information about the body being skinned released to the media?"

"Yeah, but we deliberately kept it vague."

"So would that rule out a copycat?"

"Not necessarily. Tuonela might have its secrets, but things get out. People talk. Especially when it comes to murder."

Chapter Twenty-seven

The gurney with the black body bag was slid into the coroner van. Alastair Stroud slammed the door and moments later Rachel pulled away.

This second death would bring state investigators, even the FBI if it made a big media splash.

Maybe it wasn't Evan. Maybe Evan hadn't done it.

For a brief second, Alastair considered framing the documentary crew. He was instantly mortified. *Jesus Christ.* He was one sick son of a bitch. He'd never as much as condoned white lies when Evan was growing up, and here he was toying with the idea of framing innocent kids.

But were they innocent?

Maybe not.

He wanted to hop in the car and drive directly to Evan's, but that would have been a strange thing for him to do when he had witnesses to question. Instead, on the way to the police station, he tried

Evan's number. Nobody answered. He tried Graham's cell phone. No response.

He met the kids at the police station, where he interviewed them separately. Their stories were all pretty much the same. They'd been partying, had gotten fairly drunk, probably passed out. The next thing they knew Claire was missing.

The girl—Kristin Blackmoore—was still shaking. And the kid Ian—he was in shock.

"I liked her," Ian said, not looking at Alastair.

Maybe he'd forgotten he was even in the room.

"Wish I'd told her that."

Poor kid.

Ian frowned in concentration, as if trying to tie events together. "We had fun last night. We laughed and played around." He shook his head. "That seems so wrong now."

"You didn't know." Alastair made his voice sound soothing and calm. "Did you?"

The kid looked up, hair hanging over his forehead, his eyes clearing. "What do you mean? Are you saying I did that to her?"

"I have to ask these questions. What about the others? Did she get along with Kristin?"

"Not really. But Kristin didn't do it. None of us did it."

Ian was coming around quickly. He jabbed his finger in Alastair's direction. "It wasn't any of us. You just want to be able to blame somebody else. You want to blame it on an outsider when it was somebody or some*thing* from your own town."

Alastair kept his expression neutral and felt

himself shut down a little. These were kids. They may have been from the outside, but they were still kids.

He continued with the interview and discovered that Claire and Stewart had dated a little.

Jealousy?

Grasping at straws. That's what he was doing. And Ian was right about his looking for a scapegoat. He needed a scapegoat.

Chapter Twenty-eight

"I wanna get the hell out of here," Stewart said.

He was leaning against the wall, arms crossed tightly over his chest, Ian beside him. Same pose, although Ian's head was down, his gaze directed at the floor.

I stood with my hands in my sweatshirt pockets, facing them. "They have to compare our stories. I've seen that on television." Since I was the one who'd found her, my interview had taken longer. "Is it cold in here? It's cold in here, isn't it?"

My words didn't register at first. After a second Ian looked up, stared, then said, "I don't think so."

"Who'd you get?" Stewart asked.

"The old guy." I tugged at my zipper, pulling it to my chin. "I think we all got him. Do you know he's Graham Stroud's grandfather?"

Without uncrossing his arms, Stewart pushed away from the wall. "Everybody in this town is related. It creeps me out."

Ian nodded but didn't say anything.

I felt like we were in some old movie.

The wall was cement block painted a glossy shade of cream. The acoustic tile ceilings were low, the yellowed squares repeating the pattern on the floor. Beneath an overpowering scent of pine cleaner was an odor that hinted of structural decay and urinal cake.

I automatically reached for my shoulder and the camera bag strap, then paused.

How could I be thinking about my camera at a time like this? But weren't these exactly the times when history was captured? When other bystanders simply watched, mouths agape?

"It's like some damn collective or something." Ian looked up. His eyes were bloodshot and not quite focused. Was he still drunk from last night?

I pulled out my camera and uncapped the lens.

"What are you doing?"

I pushed the power button. "What does it look like?"

Ian pulled his hands from his pockets and straightened away from the wall. "This isn't some goddamn photo op. Claire is dead. Claire just died."

"I know she did. I found her, remember?"

Ian shoved my shoulder. Not hard, but in a threatening way. "You parasite. You fucking opportunist."

He started to shove me again, but Stewart jumped between us. "Hey, come on."

"Did you film Claire's dead body, too?" Ian asked.

My face gave me away. While Stewart and Ian had been overcome by shock and grief, I'd gone back to the scene before the cops came.

"You bitch." He started swinging and floundering, trying to get around Stewart, who held him tightly. "You did! You bitch!" He quit fighting and collapsed against the wall.

I put the camera away.

I wanted to explain myself and defend myself, but maybe Ian was right. Maybe I was looking to exploit the situation while slapping a definition of gonzo journalism on it.

Unfortunately we all have some Jerry Springer in us.

Did I see the death of Claire as an opportunity to advance my nonexistent career? God, I hated to think I was that shallow, but at the same time I knew it was human nature to fool yourself. People wore public masks, but it was the private masks, the masks we wore to fool ourselves, that were the scariest and most disturbing.

"Don't worry," I said. "They confiscated the videotape." I had nothing left. All the footage I had shot was gone, and I'd probably never get it back.

Police Chief Stroud showed up. "You can go. We have phone numbers and addresses in case we need to contact you."

"We can leave town?" Stewart asked.

"I'd recommend it. You can pick up your belongings from the campsite. Investigators are done with it, since it wasn't part of the crime scene."

"I'm not going back there," Ian said.

Stewart shook his head. "Me either."

Stroud eyed us one at a time, his expression growing more sympathetic with each face. He reached into his back pocket, dug out a wallet, flipped it open, and extracted a twenty. "There's a truck stop five miles out of town. Cheap but good. Stop there and get yourselves some breakfast."

Ian stared at the money as if it were contaminated. Just the thought of food made me queasy, but we hadn't eaten in a long time.

Stewart must have been thinking the same thing. He grabbed the bill and stuck it in the front pocket of his jeans. But he didn't say thank-you. That would be letting him off the hook, when they all—Stroud included—knew Claire would still be alive if not for Tuonela.

We left the building.

"He may as well have said, 'Don't let the door hit you in the ass on the way out,'" Stewart said once we were outside and hurrying down the wide steps that led away from the police station. One half block and we were at the van.

Ian paused with his hand on the handle of the passenger door. "What about Claire?"

"What do you mean, what about Claire?" Stewart asked.

"We can't leave her here."

"Claire is dead," I said clearly.

He'd lost it. I remember when Grandpa died, they had to give Grandma something to knock her out because she couldn't stop screaming. Maybe Ian needed to be medicated.

He dropped limply against the van. "I know that."

I'd never noticed how fragile he was, with his thin wrists and bony elbows. Just a kid.

"We can't leave her." His mouth was all bent, and he wiped the back of his hand across his nose.

"The body has to stay here, at least for a while," I explained. "They want to do an autopsy."

He shook his head. "Here? With all these Stepford people? That isn't right. She should come back to Minnesota with us. She should be looked at by real fucking people, not a bunch of freaks who are probably trying to cover up shit anyway."

"They'll send the body home once they're done with it."

His shoulders began to shake, and pretty soon he was sobbing uncontrollably.

I'm not a physical kind of person. I don't like to be hugged, and I don't really even like kissing, but a surge of sympathy swept through me and I found myself wrapping my arms around him. He was taller, and he bent his head over me. All the pain and tension seemed to transfer to his hands as they clutched my arms. I immediately regretted my impulse, but I could hardly pull away. I patted his back, then rubbed like a mother might do with a child.

While human contact made me uncomfortable, it seemed to bring Ian something he needed. He began to calm down, and his shaking subsided.

We finally broke away from each other and automatically piled into the van. I sat in front in Claire's seat; Ian got in back.

That was when it hit me: I couldn't leave. Not yet.

Maybe I *was* a parasite; maybe I *was* just thinking of myself.

"We can't go."

They both stared in an are-you-fucking-kidding-me way. I wasn't going to convince them of anything.

"We're getting the hell out of here," Stewart said, obviously appointing himself group leader now that Claire was gone.

People were watching us.

They stood in groups on the sidewalk, huddled, talking, glancing our way, some staring, not even pretending to be doing anything else.

"Drive." I made a shooing motion with my hand.

"Gladly." Stewart put the van in gear and pulled away from the curb.

Heads swiveled. All the faces we passed held the same expression—or lack of expression—with a slightly slack jaw and unblinking gaze.

"Why are they looking at us like that?" Ian's voice was congested. "Like we did something bad."

"You were crying like a baby out there," Stewart said. "People stare. One time I saw a lady have a heart attack at a mall. People came and watched her blouse get ripped open and the paddles get slapped to her chest."

"We're their freak show," I said. "We came to watch them; now they're watching us."

We went a few blocks.

I pointed. "Pull over."

"No."

I had to raise my voice and get pissed off.

Stewart pulled over.

"We have to stay," I repeated, as if speaking to the village idiot.

He shook his head. Ian shook his head.

"If you cared that much about Claire, you'd agree with me." What was I talking about?

"This isn't about Claire." Stewart draped one arm over the steering wheel. "You just want to film some weird crap, put together a documentary, and raise your profile. You said it yourself—we came to make fun of the freaks. This was supposed to be funny. Well, it sure as hell isn't funny anymore. I'm going home."

He reached for the gearshift and I reached for the door release. "I'm staying."

"Kristin—no." He gave me a pleading look that said, *Don't do this. Don't make me feel like a jerk and a coward.* Because I could see he wasn't staying. And Ian . . . Well, Ian needed to go home.

I got out and went around back. I opened the rear door and dug out my equipment.

"Come on, Kristin," Ian begged. He was a wreck. I felt bad about leaving him, but I shook my head and took a couple of steps from the van.

"Wait." Stewart unbent himself and pulled out the twenty Stroud had given him. "Take this."

I waved a hand in refusal. "You need to eat. You'll need gas."

"I can get some money from a bank machine," Ian said, still sitting in the backseat. "Take it."

I took it.

"Are you sure you won't come with us?" Stewart asked.

"I'm sure. Go. You need to go."

I wanted them out of there before they started

asking obvious questions, like where would I stay and how would I eat once the twenty was gone. All the camping gear was still at the site. I wouldn't stay there, but I could get some fresh footage and pack up some stuff. My indecision must have shown on my face.

"Kristin?"

A car stopped behind the van.

Why didn't they just go around? Old people. Sitting there waiting like something was going to happen. Or not.

"Go." I waved them on. "I'll call you."

Stewart nodded. "You'd better."

He pulled away. I watched the van with the Minnesota plates until it crested a hill and disappeared.

What had I done? What was I doing?

The old people put their car in gear and puttered by. As if nothing in the world were wrong.

Chapter Twenty-nine

After Stewart and Ian left, I called Graham Stroud and asked for a ride back to the campground. It wasn't a rash decision. I thought about it quite a while, considering my options. I didn't have any, other than hitchhiking. And God, I didn't want to do that. I've hitchhiked before. It's humiliating, and there's always the chance of getting picked up by a serial killer. I also didn't want to do anything that would draw attention to myself.

So I called Graham.

I had no choice.

Of course I felt guilty. I was using him, but there were more important things going on here. I'm not a user. I hate users.

I asked him to pick me up downtown, in the grassy area between Betty's Breakfast and the river.

"I'm at school," Graham whispered. "I can't pick you up until after three."

"I'll be waiting."

I disconnected and looked at my watch. Almost

one. That gave me two hours to kill. I was tempted to go to the café and get something to eat, but somebody might recognize me. I went to a gas station instead, where I bought a bottle of orange juice and a box of cookies.

It cost more than I'd expected. How much was a bus ticket to Minneapolis? Without looking to the right or left, I paid, grabbed my stuff, and headed out the door.

People stared.

Bloody hell.

I'd never been paranoid about being stared at, but suddenly I felt exposed and threatened. I hurried across a grassy open area to a cluster of trees. Once there, I dropped my gear and sat down in the shade. I dug out my sunglasses and slipped them on. I instantly felt better, and could suddenly understand why movie stars wore big glasses and thought nobody would recognize them.

I fell asleep.

Don't ask me how I did it. How can a person sleep after witnessing what I'd witnessed? Sometimes I wonder about myself.

One minute I was watching for Graham's black car; the next someone was shaking me by the shoulder.

I snapped to attention, still on the ground but sitting up straight.

Graham Stroud stood over me.

My throat was dry. I swallowed a couple of times and wiped the back of my hand across my mouth. I got to my feet.

He picked up my empty juice bottle and tossed it in a nearby trash container. "What's up? You're the last person I expected to get a call from."

He wasn't the friendly Graham I'd known before our last encounter. This Graham was aloof and suspicious. He didn't want to be there.

"Claire . . ." That's as far as I got. I didn't think I'd have to tell anybody or talk about it. I figured the whole town knew. Wasn't that the way small towns worked?

My bottom lip began to tremble. Pretty soon my whole body would be joining in.

"*What?*" He was still annoyed, but the annoyance was tinged with a hint of concern.

I shook my head. Why had I called him? I needed time by myself. Time to let this settle. But I'd thought I was okay.

"Kristin?" The irritation was gone. Now he sounded worried, and he wasn't going to let it go.

I pulled in a deep breath and spit out the words: "Claire's dead."

I felt and saw his shock.

"When? How?"

Now that I'd gotten the news out, I felt a little more in control. "She was killed. Just like the other woman."

He frowned. "Coyotes . . . ?"

That brought me around. "Do you honestly think coyotes are doing this? That's bullshit." Then I remembered who his grandfather was. And his *dad. Jesus, his dad! Careful. Graham might know something. He might be in with the rest of them.*

What did that mean? Was I losing my mind? The whole damn town couldn't be involved in some huge cover-up and conspiracy. Could it?

Be careful. Don't say too much.

Yes. I had to be careful.

I glanced toward the street. Cars were driving past slowly. Watching me? A few people were milling about. Watching me?

"Can you give me a ride? To the campsite where we stayed last night?"

He glanced around. "What about Ian and Stewart?"

"Gone. Went home."

I could see him trying to figure out what I was still doing in town.

"I thought I'd stick around a little longer," I explained.

He knew I was up to something, but probably decided this might be a bad time to push it.

We got in his car and headed out of town, to the campground where the recent horror had taken place. We were approaching the last turn when I suddenly felt sick.

Could I do this? Could I go back there?

I pointed and gave him verbal directions. We didn't go near the restroom, but we could see a few cars in the distance. They weren't finished with the crime scene.

At the campsite I shot ten minutes of footage to replace some of what I'd lost. I could tell our stuff had been gone through; things weren't exactly where they should have been. The Barbie sleeping bag that I'd bitched about less than twenty-four hours ago was still there. I grabbed it. That was followed by Claire's bag. "Need one of these?"

Graham looked at it in horror. "Was that hers?"

"Yeah." I rolled it up, belted it, and handed it to Graham. He did the same to the other two. We collapsed the tents, then threw everything in the trunk of his car.

I took the camera and retraced the path I'd taken early that morning in the dark. Later I could make some adjustments so the footage would look like night and be a more accurate portrayal of the actual event. Or I could come back at night.

No.

Maybe.

No.

I held the camera low and moved through the dry grass. Dead leaves rustled under my feet. I was aware of Graham hanging back but following. Through a small valley, up the hillside, and there it was.

Close enough.

The body was probably gone by now, but a few cops were keeping an eye on the place.

I zoomed in.

Yellow tape was strung around the whole building. Television news teams were shooting an on-site report, using the brick restroom as their backdrop. A couple of men in dark suits wandered around the building, tablets and pens in hand.

"Detectives," Graham whispered, coming up behind me. "We should go. Before anybody sees us."

We backed up. Bent at the waist, we ran down the hill until we were out of sight.

My camera stopped. I checked the meter and realized I'd used the whole tape. And the battery was almost dead and had to be recharged.

"I need to go to a discount store or drugstore."

He checked his watch. "I have to be at work soon."

Graham knew Kristin was using him for transportation. At the same time, her friend had just died, so he could hardly be a jerk about it.

On the way back into town he stopped at a discount store called Big Bargains.

Inside, she quickly cruised the aisles. He watched her remove a three-pack of videotapes from the metal hanger and examine it.

"That what you're looking for?"

"Maybe." She grabbed another one, then cruised the aisles a little more, grabbing this, grabbing that. Reading the label on a pack of gum.

Graham had stolen a few things in his life and he knew what it looked like. That air of distraction. The pretense of being interested in something you had no interest in while your heart was hammering and your mind was in overdrive. But he didn't do that kind of crap anymore.

She wasn't even good at it.

He saw her slip one of the video packs under her shirt, tucking it into the waistband of her jeans. Didn't she see the damn cameras everywhere? And she was a cameraperson. Kinda funny, when he thought about it.

She returned the gum to its hanger, then retraced her steps to the videotape area. She put the remaining package back. "I can get them cheaper somewhere else. Let's go."

He glanced up and saw a man he figured was a store detective moving in their direction. The guy had that look about him: a hard jaw and a gaze that held no mercy. *This is just the way it is, kid.*

Graham grabbed Kristin and pulled her close so only a few inches separated them. He slipped his hand under her shirt, felt the crinkly edge of the wrapper, and pulled the tape package from her pants. "I think you forgot something."

The detective hovered in the distance. Now *he* was pretending acute interest in something he had no interest in.

Anger flashed in Kristin's eyes. She compressed her lips in a straight line. "You asshole."

"I think you mean ass-*saver.*"

He let go of her, grabbed the pack, strode to the checkout, and placed the tapes on the black belt. He normally didn't have money, but he'd cashed his museum paycheck last night. He wasn't going to have much left for gas and food now.

Kristin was pissed.

She left the store ahead of him. He wasn't worried about her taking off, because all of her stuff was in his car. That was where he found her: standing at the passenger door, arms crossed, glaring at him.

"You didn't have to do that."

"They were watching you, idiot. You'd be sitting in a back room waiting for the cops to come if I hadn't paid for this." He tossed the bag at her. She caught it.

"Nobody was watching me."

He let out a snort and shook his head. "Okay. If that's what you want to believe."

"I don't usually do stuff like that. I've never stolen anything before."

"No shit. That was pretty obvious. What the hell were you thinking?"

"I have to have videotape."

God, but he was sick of people dragging him into their bullshit.

"I know you're using me. I know you've done that from the beginning. To get to my dad. To get to Old Tuonela. A ride. What else do you want? My shirt? 'Cause I can give you that." He reached up and tugged his long-sleeved T-shirt over his head. He threw it at her. It hit her in the chest and dropped to the ground at her feet.

"My car keys?" He dug around in his pocket and made contact. He tossed the keys. She didn't catch, and they went skittering across the blacktop to vanish under a car.

Oh, shit. She was crying. Not making a sound, just standing there while tears tracked down her cheeks.

"I saved your ass in there." He jabbed a finger in the direction of the store, but his words were hesitant. He didn't know that much about girls. There had been his crazy, nutty mother and the calm and level Isobel. "I saved your ass in there," he mumbled.

She bent and picked up his shirt, clutching it to her in a ball. Then she turned and haltingly looked around for the keys, her movements jerky and awkward.

"I'll get them." He dropped to his stomach and reached under the car, stretching until his fingers snagged the metal loop of the key chain. Above him, he heard her gasp.

He reversed and shoved himself to his feet.

Her eyes were wide. "What happened to your back?"

He grabbed his shirt. "Don't you know it's not polite to ask those kinds of questions?"

"Somebody beat you."

He turned his shirt the right way, stuck his arms in the sleeves, then tugged the neck opening over his head and pulled down.

"Your dad?" She looked extremely worried about that. "It was your dad, wasn't it?"

"No." He smoothed his shirt, wondering at the burst of adrenaline and anger that had driven him to remove it. He never let anybody see him with his shirt off. "Evan would never do anything like that."

But he thought about the other morning when Evan had tossed the food on the floor, when he'd grabbed him by the throat. For a second Graham had thought his father was going to kill him. His uncertainty must have shown on his face.

"Did he?"

"No."

"Swear?"

"I swear."

"Because if he did, you can't protect him. Physical abuse is unacceptable."

"I know, I know. It wasn't him, okay? It happened a long time ago."

Everything had shifted. He hardly knew her, yet they always seemed to climb on some emotional teeter-totter whenever they were together. This weird, volatile shift and trade-off. *Your turn to lose it. No yours. After you, please. I insist. You lose it first. I'll lose it second.*

He tried to remember what Isobel looked like and sounded like and smelled like. It was hard.

Chapter Thirty

Kristin had no place to stay. Taking her to Old Tuonela was out of the question after what she'd witnessed there, so Graham took her to his grandfather's house. Not the best arrangement, but better than her sleeping in the park or on the street or in the woods.

While Alastair was at work, Graham and Kristin cooked scrambled eggs and toast. Scrambled eggs were Graham's specialty.

"This is a bad idea," Kristin said between bites of food. "My staying here."

Graham popped open a can of diet cola and slid it across the table to her. "He never goes in the basement. I swear. You can sleep down there tonight, then use my car tomorrow after you drop me off at school. You'll at least be safe here."

"Just one night." She took a drink of cola. "Then I'll figure something else out."

"What?"

"I don't know." She shrugged. "Something."

They finished eating.

"Do I have time to take a shower?" she asked.

"If you hurry."

While Kristin showered, Graham paced and kept peeking out the front curtains, hoping Alastair didn't come home early. Once Kristin was finished he took her down to the basement and helped her roll out her sleeping bag in the corner near the freezer.

"He won't come downstairs," Graham told her again. "If he does, hide here." He opened a door to show her a small closet lined with shelves that had probably held jelly and canned stuff at one time.

It smelled like damp cement and rotting wood. Cobwebs clung to rafters and lights. He was sure she'd rather sleep in a tent if it weren't for a murdering psycho roaming the streets.

Kristin looked at the sleeping bag without enthusiasm. "Thanks." She sounded exhausted. Now that she'd showered, her hair was darker and her skin seemed paler. Her eyes were puffy, with circles under them.

"I'm going to go back upstairs," he said.

She grabbed his arm. "Stay here until your grandfather gets home."

She tugged him down until they both sat on the sleeping bag, cross-legged, face-to-face. She was wearing a different shirt: a thin black T-shirt with really short sleeves. He could see part of a tattoo poking out. Red and black.

"Stay and talk to me for a while. Tell me what's going on with your dad."

"There's nothing going on."

"How did you get those scars on your back? Why are you staying here? With your grandfather?"

"Is this going to be part of your movie? Is that why you want to know?"

"I want to know because I like you. It has nothing to do with the film."

"Oh, film. Sorry. Film." He got sarcastic sometimes. "It's just easier to live here." He shrugged as if that would drive home the lie. "With school and all."

"Come on, Graham. I saw your dad out there."

"Digging. So he digs. He's like an archeologist. He writes about Old Tuonela. Why wouldn't he want to find out as much as he can about it?"

She touched the side of his face.

He almost closed his eyes.

Stupid, but the feel of her fingers against his skin made him weak and fluttery. Her hand dropped. "You're a sweet kid."

"I'm not really a kid, you know. Not here . . ." He put a hand to his chest, then instantly wished he could erase that bit of drama.

"You killed a man," she stated. "How did it happen? Was it a car accident?"

She so obviously wanted it to be a car accident, and for a moment he was tempted to say yes. "No."

"Some other kind of accident?"

"It was intentional." He suddenly just wanted to shut her up. Just wanted her to stop talking about it. "I stabbed him, okay?"

That surprised her. He could see the *whoa* in her

expression. And now she was afraid of him again. *Shit.*

"Self-defense?" The question was tentative.

He had no choice but to elaborate. "Look, he was going to kill my dad. He was going to kill Evan."

"You saved your father's life?" She eyed him with renewed curiosity.

"Yeah. I guess so." He shrugged. It was just something that happened. Something he had to do. "Don't put that in your movie." Pause. "Film."

Chapter Thirty-one

A skinned squirrel. That's what Rachel thought whenever she looked at the carcass on the autopsy table. Unprofessional of her, but there it was.

She'd waited for rigor mortis to reverse. Night arrived and she was finally able to straighten the bent limbs, but even straightened, the body had lost much of what made it appear human.

She turned on the voice-activated minirecorder.

What made a person human? How strange that skin seemed to play such an important role in who we were.

It's what's inside that counts.

But maybe it was really what was outside that counted.

Skin cloaked and wrapped and contained. It held and exposed our vanities. It carried expressions of individualism, like tattoos. Ed Gein of Plainfield, Wisconsin, had worn suits of human skin. When he was finally caught and his house searched, they found lamp shades and furniture made from his murder victims.

The ancient exhaust fan created a hum in her head, reminding her that she'd forgotten her earplugs. A recent test put the noise level of the industrial fan above seventy decibels—leaf blower range.

Sh,sh,sh.

She hated the fan.

Sometimes when it ran she heard voices buried below the din. Like a roomful of people talking and mumbling, their words indistinct. Just an audio illusion that had to do with the unnatural harmonics and white noise.

You let us in.

That's what the people seemed to be saying. Or had those faraway voices always existed, and the continuous roar and hum of the fan somehow opened a door?

Hearing was often about perception and not about what was really there. Lyrics played backward could sound like, "Paul is dead." Or "There's a devil in the toolshed." The mind turned random, meaningless sounds into words in much the same way the eye detected faces where there were none.

Making order from chaos; that's what people did.

Later, when she played back the recording, she was certain she would hear nothing but her own voice.

Sh,sh,sh.

Rachel forced her thoughts away from the fan and the murmur.

She heard a movement behind her, but when she looked nothing was there.

With each swing of her head the roar of the fan shifted and changed, seeming to come from different directions. She picked up a scalpel.

The overhead lights clicked off. She dropped the scalpel and swung around.

Evan stood in the doorway, a hand on the wall switch. "Rachel."

"Goddamn!" She took a deep breath, closed then opened her eyes. "What are you doing here? How did you get in?"

He pulled a key from his pocket and held it up with long pale fingers. His skin was ashen, his jaw dark with stubble. Was that gray at his temples?

"I came across it a few days ago." He placed the key on a stainless steel countertop. "I forgot I had it."

She thought about the handprints on her belly, and the times she'd felt she wasn't alone in her apartment. Could Evan have come in when she was asleep?

"This is the second body you've found like this?" He indicated the corpse on the table.

He shouldn't be in the room with the body. She quickly covered it with a sheet.

"It looks more human now," he observed.

He was right. The sheet was lying against muscle, outlining. Even the face suddenly appeared feminine, whereas it hadn't before.

"Any suspects?" He stayed back, clinging to the shadows. "Other than coyotes?"

She adjusted the swing arm so light shot in the

opposite direction. "I shouldn't be talking to you about this. Once again people seem to be whispering your name."

"No surprise there. And the skin?" he asked. "Did you find the skin?"

"No. Not yet."

"What about the first victim? Was her skin ever found?"

She looked at him closely. "Wait." She shut off the exhaust fan. "You know something, don't you?" The sudden silence made her ears ring.

His brows lifted.

He was unwell. Such dark bruises under his eyes, and he'd lost so much weight. Now that the fan was off, the air in the room settled and she could smell him. He smelled of soil and decaying plants.

"I . . ." he began. His voice dropped and adjusted to the lack of sound and the echo. "I hate for you to think badly of me."

He was a lost soul, confused and tormented. But she couldn't be his stability. She couldn't be anybody's stability. She had let him go.

Yeah, like she'd let Tuonela go.

"What are you doing here?"

"I have something to show you."

She fought the urge to touch him. And she suddenly forgot why she was angry with him.

Old Tuonela.

Yes, that was it. He'd gone behind her back and bought it out from under the city. They'd had plans to bury what was left and fence it. Put up KEEP OUT signs.

"That place will drive you mad," she said. "You know that, don't you?"

"I'm fine. Things are fine."

So sad. Like talking to a drug addict or an alcoholic. "You've lost weight."

"I've been doing more physical work than I'm used to. Burning a lot of calories. I know I look different. On the outside. But what about me?" He put a hand to his chest. His nails were caked with dirt. "Do I still seem different?"

She considered him. "Not today." She could swear she heard the pounding of his heart. The steady, *lub, lub, lub*. It soothed her.

"Sometimes I feel like . . . I'm fading," he admitted after some consideration. "I forget what I'm like and who I am."

"You're exhausted."

"I've been thinking. About you. Me. The baby. Could we have a normal life? Could we rent movies and eat popcorn together? Could we plant a garden? With flowers that would bloom at night?"

"Night-blooming jasmine."

"Yes."

"We would grow tomatoes. Better Boys. I love those."

"You could pick them at the hottest part of the day, and they would taste like sunshine."

All dreams. Sad and impossible.

"I wonder if there's some way I can be in your life. Somehow. But I know that's impossible. For so many reasons . . ."

She wanted to tell him he'd betrayed her; she

wanted him to admit to it, but at the same time she didn't want to start an argument that would go nowhere.

He passed a hand over his face. "I'm living in two worlds."

"Move back to Tuonela."

He let out a snort of shock and shook his head in disbelief. *You don't get it.*

But she was trying to. "I have a lot to deal with myself right now." Did she always have to be the wise, stable one? The person others came to with their problems? What about *her*? Wasn't she allowed to fall apart?

Both of her parents were dead. Evan had his father. He had Graham. Who could she count on? Who would she call if she needed help? Who would come? David Spence? Yes. David would come.

Not Evan.

She loved him. There was no doubt in her mind about that. But love didn't always mean a future together. That's what kids didn't get. You could love someone from afar. You could even love someone close. But it didn't always mean a life together. It didn't mean you were good for each other.

She snapped off her gloves and tossed them in a nearby hazardous waste container. She reached behind her back and untied her gown as she walked toward him. "Let's step out of here."

She tried not to think about what had happened in this very room last spring. Sex in the morgue. *My God.* That was the kind of thing that made a person question her own sanity.

Heat shot up her neck and crawled into her cheeks. She hardly remembered it, and yet she had proof it had happened. But it all came back to her when she slept. She would wake up consumed by a sweet ache, a sweet yearning, missing what she didn't even remember.

A faint illumination came from the emergency bulb near the elevator; Evan had turned off the hall lights when he'd come in.

She crossed her arms and leaned against the wall. "What are you doing here?"

A shadow fell across his face, and she could barely make out his features. He fiddled with a button on his long wool coat.

Fingernails caked with earth. The nails themselves were pale and smooth. Did they look slightly like the nails of a cadaver?

What a cruel thought.

I'm so sorry, Evan.

"Was your grandmother's name Emily Florence?"

"Yes." She frowned. "Why?"

"What was her mother's name?"

"Florence Elizabeth. Florence Elizabeth Cray."

"Born in 1906?"

"I'm not sure."

"Florence had a sister named Victoria. Victoria was one of the women murdered by Richard Manchester."

Victoria. How did he know about Victoria? She didn't want to hear about Victoria.

She glanced over her shoulder in the direction of

the skinned corpse. Victoria hadn't visited Rachel in months.

"I don't want to talk about her," she whispered. Talking about her, thinking about her, might bring her back.

But Evan was suddenly animated.

"Remember the photo at my house on Benefit Street? The photo of the woman in the tub? I think that's Victoria."

Rachel swallowed. "Yes. I know it is. I've known for a long time."

"What you didn't know is that Victoria was your great-aunt."

"You can't know that. My ancestral line was lost in the big move."

"Not lost." He unbuttoned his coat and reached inside. "Just left behind." He pulled out a book. A leather-bound book in faded red, the page edges yellow and uneven. "A journal," he explained.

The book smelled of damp earth, mildew, and ancient paper.

He wanted her to take it.

She didn't want to touch it.

Yet in her mind she could already imagine how the embossed floral design would feel against her fingertips.

He brought the book close, opened it, and reverently searched the pages until he found what he was looking for. Then he turned the journal around so she could read it.

"This is why I'm staying out there. *This* is why I saved Old Tuonela from being destroyed."

"It's too dark." She took a step back. "I can't see." But she could make out strong cursive letters that had been written with a sharp quill pen.

"Florence Elizabeth Cray and Victoria were sisters. Victoria was killed by the Pale Immortal."

"You already said that."

"Florence plotted her revenge. She tried to poison Richard Manchester, but succeeded only in making him temporarily ill and extremely pissed off. So she got back at him in the best way she could. She made him fall in love with her."

Rachel stared at the book, intrigued now.

"Do you want to read it?"

"No, you tell me." She was only remotely aware of her hushed voice and the hand she held to her throat.

"She gained his trust, and when she was finally alone with him she killed him with a dagger. Your great-grandmother put an end to the Pale Immortal's reign of terror. I thought you would want to know that. I thought you should know."

She smiled, and a lightness fluttered inside her.

"You come from a line of strong, tough women. You should be proud." Evan's heart was beating loudly again.

"That's not all, is it? That's not everything."

"No." That single syllable carried so much weight. "Maybe that's enough for now."

"Tell me. You might as well tell me everything."

"Before Florence killed Richard Manchester . . . Before she killed him, she seduced him and slept with him. And when she killed him, she was pregnant with his baby." Evan watched her with an intense, unreadable expression.

Her eyes stung. "No." Her chest suddenly felt hollow, and she realized fear was really the absence of something, not the addition.

Why was he telling her this? It was cruel. "I was right. You should have left Old Tuonela alone. What good can come of such information?"

"We all deserve to know the truth."

She shook her head and pressed a palm to her trembling lips, then a hand to her swollen belly. This was where they clashed. This was where she couldn't begin to understand Evan Stroud. "You're cruel."

"I'm sorry. I thought you should know. I thought you would want to know."

"Did you think it would make me happy? Did you think this was somehow going to add something to my life? To know that my great-grandfather was the Pale Immortal?"

Why had he really been so eager to share such awful news? Because he thought this made her more like him? Had he wanted to hurt her? Was he so caught up in Old Tuonela that it hadn't occurred to him that she would find such information devastating? Or was it to deliberately drive an even bigger wedge between them?

For a second he seemed poised to open up; then she saw his brain shift. "Are you okay?" Not what he'd originally intended to say.

"I was fine until a few minutes ago."

"I'm sorry. I thought you should know. If not for yourself, for the baby."

For the baby? "What are you saying?"

Once again he seemed to be struggling with a decision, and seemed reluctant to speak his mind.

"Are you trying to tell me I might give birth to a vampire? My God, Evan. Not you, of all people. Is that what you really think?"

"Of course not, but that's what people will say. That's what the child will have to deal with."

"Have you mentioned the contents of the journal to anyone else?"

"No."

"Evan, nobody can know about this. About the journal."

He looked dismayed. "We can't keep it to ourselves. This is history. Not just your history, but the history of most of the residents of Tuonela."

"I understand, but you're talking about ruining a child's life, a child's future. *Our* child."

"We will never see eye to eye on this, will we?"

"What difference does it make if people never know what happened?" She couldn't keep the anguish from her voice. "Oh, why did you go out there? Why did you buy that damn place? Sometimes I think you did it to hurt me. What have I ever done to you other than love you?"

He flinched as if she'd confessed hatred rather than love. He flinched at words that brought most people joy.

She held out her hand. "Give me the journal."

He didn't move.

"Give it to me." She was crying.

He tucked it in his coat. "I'm sorry, Rachel." He turned and left.

Thirty minutes later Rachel finally managed to pull herself together enough to return to the autopsy suite, where she realized she hadn't turned off the handheld recorder. She picked it up, rewound, then pushed play.

The constant roar of the fan.

Expected.

Sh, sh, sh.

She held the device close to her ear—and could detect the murmur of voices beneath the roar of the exhaust fan.

Like the wind the other night.

The audio documented Evan's arrival, and she heard his voice softly speaking her name. That was followed by her exclamation of surprise. The roar stopped; she'd turned off the fan. Then came conversation, followed by the snap of her gloves and their footsteps as they left the room.

Sh,sh,sh.

Whispers.

More than one voice, continuing even after the sound of the fan ceased.

Rachel shut off the recorder. The click of the stop button was deafening.

Oh, Jesus.

She moved to the door and hit the wall switch, flooding the room with light.

The body looked the same.

She stepped close enough to grab one corner of the sheet and jerk it free.

She was a coroner. A medical examiner.

But sometimes the dead talked to her. It was why she'd become a coroner. Facing her fears. Subconsciously she'd thought she'd dig deep into death until it finally left her alone.

The great-granddaughter of the Pale Immortal . . .

Did she finally have an answer to a question that had haunted her most of her life? Was that why death followed her? Because she came from a lineage that had somehow traversed death?

No! Those were crazy thoughts. *Crazy, crazy!*

Richard Manchester had been human. A human who had done some very sick and evil things.

Stop thinking these thoughts right now.

Nonsense. Total nonsense.

She inserted a fresh tape and pushed the record button. She turned on the exhaust fan and snapped on a new pair of latex gloves. She opened a clean set of instruments.

She did her job.

When she was finished, she wheeled and slid the body into the cooler.

Without replaying the audio track, she placed the recorder on her office desk. She would type up her notes tomorrow.

She took a shower in the claw-foot tub, washing with lavender soap. After drying off she slipped on a pair of jogging pants and an oversize white T-shirt. She opened the refrigerator and stared at the transparent container of liver.

So why did she crave raw meat if she wasn't the pregnant great-granddaughter of a vampire?

Iron deficiency. Easily explained. It certainly made more sense than being the descendant of a vampire.

The phone rang.

David Spence.

"How about I bring something by? Chinese. How does that sound?"

She didn't want to be alone. Did he sense that about her? Her loneliness? But she couldn't be with David Spence. She'd been fooling herself about that. He wasn't the one she wanted. And being with David would be worse than being alone, because now she had so much more to hide.

She told him she was tired and was going to bed. She hung up and drank the blood from the liver container. With her bare hands, she ate the raw meat.

Then she went to bed.

Daughter of darkness.

Chapter Thirty-two

A scraping sound woke her. Rachel looked at the window above her head and saw the shadow of a bare branch.

Only the wind.

The sound came again. Not from the window, but from inside her apartment.

Someone in the hall.

She groped for her portable phone. Touched it. Grabbed it.

Scrape.

Moving closer.

A kind of dragging and a *thunk*, combined with a rustle—like dry leaves or the hem of a taffeta gown.

A fetid odor drifted nearer. Probably her clothes or shoes, she reasoned. That went with the job.

She moved from the bed, the noise of the shifting mattress magnified a hundred times. A night-light, plugged into a low hallway socket, illuminated the path to the bedroom. A shadow crept across the floor.

With her heart hammering, head roaring, Rachel tried to dial 911. Wrong buttons, then a dial tone that filled the room. She tried again and failed.

She watched the open doorway. Up, back down at the phone. Hands shaking, breathing labored, fingers blindly hitting numbers.

The smell getting stronger.

Coming from whoever—whatever—was in the hall.

And then there it was.

Standing in the doorway, blocking the light. Maybe five feet tall, with an indistinguishable shape. Narrow at the top, wider at the floor, with trailing, draping pieces that had the appearance of wrinkled fabric.

Not Victoria.

And not Evan.

She did something you're never supposed to do when faced with an intruder: She reached for the bedside lamp and turned on the light.

Oh, my God.

The dangling bits of fabric were shriveled fingers tipped with curved nails. Blond hair hung down each side of the face. Instead of eyes, two opaque black pits stared back at her. The mouth was a gaping hole.

She knew what she was looking at, although her mind refused to believe it: a human skin.

Standing.

Moving toward her.

Chapter Thirty-three

The skin moved deeper into the room.

Rachel stared, her body and mind frozen.

It came closer, nails clicking and scraping against the wooden floor.

Move.

Without taking her eyes from the wrinkled flesh, Rachel dragged the quilt from the bed.

The skin moved closer, a heavy stench wafting with it.

Click, click, click.

Blond hair.

It was the girl's skin. The dead girl's skin. Claire's skin.

Dear God.

No.

Impossible.

When the skin was a couple of yards away, Rachel gripped the quilt with both hands—and tossed.

Cotton print sailed over the nasty mess, covering it, knocking it to the floor.

Rachel ran.

With bare feet she shot around the blanket and bolted from the room. Halfway down the hall, she skidded to a stop.

Go back. Shut the door. Lock it in there.

Couldn't do it.

She ran from her apartment. She took the stairs to the basement and morgue. In her office she called 911.

It seemed like hours, but it was probably only ten minutes before she heard sirens outside. She met a police officer at the delivery door.

"An intruder?" he asked. "Where?"

"Upstairs."

Another officer pulled up and stepped from his patrol car. They went ahead of Rachel, weapons drawn.

Up two flights of stairs to the third story and her apartment.

"Wait here," the first officer whispered over his shoulder.

"In the bedroom," she told them.

He nodded and they moved forward.

She put a hand to her heart. Some people said that intense fear could harm an unborn baby.

I have to get out of here.

One of the officers returned. He shook his head. "Nothing. Nobody."

She pushed past him. "I'll show you."

In the bedroom she grabbed one corner of the quilt and gave it a tug, then quickly dropped it. The officer strode across the floor. She let out a shriek of alarm as he scooped up the blanket.

He shook it. "Nothing." He brought the quilt to his face and sniffed. "It is a little rank, though. You might want to toss it in the wash."

"Did you get a look at the intruder?" the other officer asked. "Enough for us to put together a composite?"

She glanced around the room. Was it under the bed?

The officer saw her concern, got down on his knees, and checked. "Nothing." He straightened and walked to the closet. He shoved the hangers of clothes back and forth. "Nothing."

But a skin . . . A skin could make itself very flat. It could hide a lot of places. Maybe even a crack or a seam in the wall. Maybe even under a layer of wallpaper.

The house was old. There were a lot of places for a skin to hide.

"Did you get a look at him?" the first officer on the scene coaxed.

She shook her head. "No. It was dark."

"But the light was on when we came in."

"I ran. I didn't look."

Had she really seen anything?

She *had* been asleep. And she *had* just autopsied the body of Claire Francis. And she *had* just eaten a container of raw meat.

Pregnancy did strange things to a person. She'd never been one to have night terrors, but that must be what had happened. Dreams that were so lucid and so frightening that the dreamer insisted they were real.

The officers went over the building thoroughly, from the attic to the coolers in the morgue. "He's long gone," the younger cop said, sliding his weapon into his belt holster. "But I'll have someone keep an eye on the place, at least until morning."

She walked him downstairs so she could lock the dead bolt once he was gone. At the door, he bent and picked up something. "This yours?"

The journal.

Florence Elizabeth Cray's journal.

Evan must have changed his mind. *Thank you, Evan.* She tried not to appear too eager as she took the book. "Yes, it's mine. Thanks."

She bolted the door behind him.

The journal in her hands felt familiar.

It smelled old. Like leather and paper and damp earth.

She would put it away. She would lock it in the safe in her office, where no one would ever find it.

Something slipped out and hit her foot. A photo. Old, on heavy cardboard. She picked it up.

A young girl with blond hair wearing a low-waisted dress with a dark bow on the hip that matched her Mary Jane shoes. The child's eyes held a look of death and defeat.

Rachel turned the photo over.

Our sweet, darling Sarah.

Chapter Thirty-four

Ever since the night he thought the Pale Immortal had been trying to get out of the display case, Matthew Torrance had been a little spooked. Sometimes when he had his iPod going and his headphones on, he heard strange sounds. Like whispering. Like a lot of people whispering. Like some kind of gathering was going on in the museum basement. He couldn't make out what anybody was saying; he just picked up the roar.

Now, as he ran the buffer across the entry hall of the museum, the whispers started again.

Sh, sh, sh.

He who dies will live again. He who lives will die again.

He tugged the headphones from his ears, letting them loop around his neck. He shut off the buffer and surveyed the room.

Nothing.

Nobody.

Fuck. He was so paranoid. And he hadn't even smoked anything yet. Maybe his friends were right;

maybe he needed to cut back. But every time he thought about it, he panicked. What the hell would he live for if he didn't have his weed?

Sh, sh, sh.

In case he was picking up sounds from a distance, he reached down and paused his iPod.

He who dies will live again. He who lives will die again.

The voice was in his head. Coming from inside him. He smacked a palm against the side of his face. *Shut up in there.*

More chanting.

He was losing his goddamn mind.

He pulled out his cell phone. Should he call his brother? Just for the human contact? What would he say? He and his brother didn't chat. They didn't have that kind of relationship.

He scrolled down the list of names, then punched the dial button.

Voice mail. Then came his brother's recorded message, followed by the *beep.*

Matthew opened his mouth to leave a general reply like, *This is Matt. Not calling for any reason.* Instead, he said, "*He who dies will live again.*"

He shut the flip phone and looked around, mouth hanging open.

He wanted to toss the phone to the floor, but restrained himself, gripping it tightly instead.

O-kay.

Take a deep breath.

There you go.

He ran to the stairs and took them two and three

at a time. Up to the roof, the metal door clanging, then slamming shut behind him. Outside he gulped in frigid air. In the glow of security lights, he could see his breath.

He wanted to smoke a joint.

But the thought of going back into the museum when he was stoned . . . bad idea. He paced the roof, hands in the pockets of his work pants. He wasn't wearing a coat, and pretty soon he started to shiver.

He caught a glimpse of something beyond the edge of the roof, low, on the ground in the grassy area between the sidewalk and street. A dark form moving out of the corner of his eye. He stepped closer to the ledge. The brick street was deserted. Something fluttered—a small shape—maybe a night bird. It moved skyward and vanished.

He went back inside. Back to work.

He grabbed the buffer handle and prepared to start the machine up again. Dirt and debris were scattered across the floor. He'd vacuumed already. He didn't buff unless the floor was clean; otherwise the grit would scratch the surface. Some people thought he was a slacker, but he was conscientious.

He followed the trail, losing it a few times.

Downstairs. In the basement, the room with the Pale Immortal.

He reached into his pocket for the comfort of his cell phone. A half hour ago he'd wanted to toss it away; now it was his friend.

He rounded the corner, following the sepia glow

of lights meant to add mystery and creepiness to the display.

The Pale Immortal was there, staring at him with black pits, smiling at him with a black mouth.

Alastair's phone rang, waking him from a deep sleep. The first deep sleep he'd had in days.

Another problem at the museum. The night janitor saw something or heard something. Again.

"I think you can handle it," Alastair told the officer.

"Uh, you might want to get down here for this."

"Just write it up like the last time."

"This isn't exactly the same as last time."

Alastair struggled to focus and wake up. "What do you mean?"

"They claim to have something strange on videotape."

Alastair was dressed and at the museum in under fifteen minutes. He went directly to the case. The Pale Immortal was there, looking as normal as a mummy behind Plexiglas could look.

"Who called it in?"

"Same guy as before. Said he'd taken a break and had stepped outside on the roof for some fresh air and a smoke. Came back in to finish buffing the floor and said the Pale Immortal made a face at him."

They went to the security room to view the video footage.

The museum director sat in the control chair going through the different cameras. He clicked some keys and pointed to one of the screens. "Front doors." He hit the fast-forward button. "Back and side doors. Pale Immortal chamber." He clicked more keys. "Now watch this." He pointed to a screen.

"Did that thing smile?" Alastair asked.

A titter of nervous laughter erupted from the officers near the door.

"Can you go back?"

The director stopped the tape, reversed, then played it again. It definitely looked like the Pale Immortal smiled.

"How long does a single tape run?" Alastair asked.

"Twenty-four hours."

"And you use the same tape over and over?"

"Yeah."

"How old is this tape?"

"I don't know. Close to a year, maybe. The system is antiquated, and we didn't invest in new tapes when we opened the new exhibit because we're hoping to eventually go digital."

"It's a ghost image," Alastair said. "I've seen it before with recyled tape."

One of the officers nodded. "Remember the tape from that car lot? Where there was supposed to be a ghost running around the cars? But it ended up being a partial image of a customer who'd been in the lot that day. The tape hadn't completely erased."

Everybody relaxed. "Ghost hunters got a lot of mileage out of that before it was debunked."

Alastair stared at the frozen image on the screen. "For some reason people want to believe that kind of nonsense." And he needed to believe the opposite.

Chapter Thirty-five

Something cold and wet woke him. Evan blinked.

It took him a few moments to figure out where he was. In Old Tuonela, lying on his back on the ground. He'd been digging. . . .

He must have blacked out.

Where does the wind begin?

His eyes were open and he could see stars. He stared at them, feeling strangely removed from his own body. He lifted a stiff hand to touch his jaw, fingers coming in contact with abrasive stubble. His skin was damp and cold.

He rolled forward until he sat up. His lantern was dead, and he could make out vague, huddled shapes of low shrubs and the towering blackness of tree trunks.

He felt so strange.

Light and heavy and filled with observation rather than participation.

Get up.

He shoved himself to his feet and stood there,

sensing his weakness. His knees wanted to give out, but he forced himself to place one foot in front of the other and move forward, toward home.

Whispering.

Were they talking to him? Or did they even know he was there? Were they talking to themselves?

Soft voices coming from everywhere, as if a million fireflies carried the sound on their wings. He could see them, moving through the vegetation and thick air. Yellow dancing lights.

When their lights turn green, it means they're dying. It means they don't have much time left.

What did you do when you knew your days were numbered? When you saw your light had turned from yellow to green? Go to Disney World? Go on a cruise? Take a hot-air-balloon ride?

Rachel.

He would go see Rachel if he were dying. That's what he'd do. Even if she was mad at him. Even if she hated him, he would go to her.

What about Graham? What about your father?

He felt bad about them, but if he had to choose one person . . . if he had one last visit to make, one last person to touch and gaze upon, it would be Rachel.

Sorry, Graham. Sorry, Dad. He loved them both, but he would have to see Rachel.

The gate was in front of him, blocking his way.

Somehow he'd reached it even though he hadn't been aware of the journey. It wasn't latched, and he scraped through the opening.

Up through the madly dancing fireflies, around

the back of the house, over the broken flagstones to the kitchen. Never pausing, he continued down the hall that led to the stairway that would take him to his room.

A man with a purpose.

The cellar. We're in the cellar.

Evan paused with his hand on the banister. Who was that? Who was talking to him?

Then another voice, masculine, insistent: *No. Stay away.*

That voice held persuasive power. Richard Manchester's voice.

Up the stairs, turn on the landing. To his bedroom. To the dresser.

Open the drawer and feel inside, all the way to the back.

He found the silk scarf and wrapped it around his neck. A scarf that had belonged to the Pale Immortal.

He reached deep into the drawer and pulled out a silver tin. He removed the lid and lifted the container to his face. He closed his eyes and inhaled.

It smelled like black earth and musty leaves. Of wet, moss-covered rocks, mushrooms, and the bark of a hemlock tree. And, of course, something else. Something darker and more forbidding and compelling than all of those things.

The heart of the Pale Immortal.

The heart of a vampire.

He'd already drunk a broth made from a portion of the tin's contents. What would happen if he finished it? Would he be stronger? Would he become immortal? These were questions that had no answers.

The only way to know is to do it.

True.

Consume the entire contents. What more could it hurt? You're halfway there already.

Halfway to what?

He was neither one thing nor the other. He had a foot in both worlds: the world of the living, which he could never be a part of, and the world of the dead.

Land of the dead.

He wanted to embrace it. He wouldn't be here otherwise. Deep down in his soul, he knew it was true. He could tell Graham and Alastair and Rachel he was here to preserve history. That was part of it, but as time passed he realized this was really a selfish endeavor.

Old Tuonela spoke to him. Old Tuonela defined him.

And if he finished the contents of the tin maybe he would be whole.

He couldn't go back. There was no way to go back to who he'd been before. The old Evan was still inside him, but he would never be as solid as he once was. Now he was half human and half something else.

He wanted to be a whole something else.

Do it.

What about Rachel?

What about Graham?

They don't matter. Neither of them matter. This is about you, not them. And are either of them here? Are they with you now? No. You've been deserted and aban-doned by the people you love. Take the step. Consume the broth. Finish the tea.

Sometimes he thought the loneliness of his exis-tence was driving him mad. Would he feel less lonely if he drank the tea?

Yes. You'll have me. You'll have us. All of us.

Who were they? Who was talking to him? Who was in his head?

The dead. The dead of Old Tuonela. They wanted him. They needed him.

He took a pinch from the dark contents of the tin and placed it on his tongue. Bitter longing filled his mouth, warm and seductive.

Sweet, sweet ache of death.

Evan.

They were calling to him. He had to stop them. Had to make them shut up.

He closed the tin and shoved it away, then dove for the window that towered from ceiling to floor. He ripped away the cloth. With his fingernails, he scratched at the black paint until morning sunlight streamed through the glass, piercing his retinas. He stumbled back, crashing to the floor.

The cellar. We're in the cellar.

Chapter Thirty-six

Shotguns were the weapon of choice.

"No rifles," Alastair Stroud had told them when he was presented with the idea of a killing spree. People were afraid, and fear made people do crazy, nutty things. No one knew that better than he did. The last thing he wanted was a bunch of angry men running around with rifles that could shoot a distance of two miles.

One of the twenty hunters tucked his box of shells into his orange vest pocket. "I never miss."

Just the stupid kind of mentality Alastair was trying to avoid. "Wisconsin DNR hunting regulations apply." And it was always open season on coyotes. "Didn't you read the rules I posted?"

One hundred men and a handful of women had signed up to thin the coyote population. Out of those one hundred, Alastair had chosen twenty men, hoping to keep the chaos level down. They hadn't wanted the press getting hold of the story. They didn't want PETA on their asses, at least not until this was over.

Mayor McBride loaded his shotgun and snapped it closed.

Did he know anything about firearms? Alastair wondered.

McBride would have been one of his top eliminations, but the hunt had been his idea, and he was the mayor, after all. Alastair just hoped to hell he didn't kill somebody.

Twenty antsy, serious, important men, dressed in canvas jackets and orange vests, waiting for the sun to appear over the horizon. The air was crisp, the ground covered with a layer of frost. Shoulders were hunched, shotguns braced under arms, and hands tucked into pockets.

Men with a purpose. Men defending their children and wives against an enemy they could now understand. Know your enemy; find your enemy; kill your enemy. Hopelessness and lack of control were gone. They were in charge.

When bad things happen the fear comes, followed by a need for action. And it didn't matter if the action was right or wrong, just so it happened. Because there was nothing humans hated more than being helpless. Even if Alastair disapproved of what was about to take place, he understood it.

He'd tried to talk the mayor out of a massacre, but once he saw that the roundup would take place regardless of his involvement, he agreed to put together a plan. Nothing worse than a bunch of pissed-off men with shotguns running rampant through the countryside.

The sun came up.

The men of Tuonela moved in for the kill. Alastair slipped on a pair of leather gloves and went with them.

The most active areas of coyote movement had been staked out earlier. The grove where the body of Brenda Flemming had been found was a myriad of dirt paths, footprints, and droppings. Coyotes weren't scared of humans the way deer were. Coyotes liked to lurk at the edges and watch you. And even when you spotted one, it might not run off.

Alastair deliberately broke away from the rest of the hunters. He followed a narrow path that led to a den dug into the hillside and under tree roots. The dirt showed signs of having been recently disturbed, and it was just a matter of waiting for a coyote to step into the sunlight.

Alastair lifted the shotgun to his shoulder and waited, keeping the barrel and sight trained on the hole. When the animal appeared, he squeezed the trigger. It dropped without a sound.

He lowered the barrel and approached.

Dead. A clean shot.

He hadn't wanted it to suffer.

In the distance he heard the report of guns. A couple of blasts were followed by yelps of pain. He glanced around. Seeing no one, he knelt by the dead coyote, reached into his coat pocket, and pulled out several strands of long blond hair. He pried open the coyote's mouth and wound the hair around two back teeth.

Alastair experienced a wave of self-loathing. He'd been feeling that a lot lately. He hated what he'd become, and yet he couldn't see a way out, so he just kept digging himself deeper.

Rachel flushed the toilet, leaned over the sink, and cupped cold water to her face. Why was it called morning sickness when it hit at any hour of the day or night? And why was it getting bad now, when she was in the third trimester?

The first three months had been easy. She hadn't even known she was pregnant, blaming the skipped periods on stress, but now the baby seemed to be draining the life out of her.

Her cell phone rang.

Alastair Stroud, calling to tell her the coyote slaughter was over. "We're in the square."

"I'll be down in a few minutes." She flipped the phone shut. Sometimes she hated men. A lot of times she hated men.

In the kitchen she took a few sips of a protein drink, hoping it would settle her stomach; then she headed to the square.

It looked like half the town had turned out.

Dead coyotes had been removed from truck beds and were on display, lined up ten wide and three deep.

Cameras were clicking.

News teams had set up in a grassy area on the opposite side of the street. The mayor, dressed in his

Day-Glo hunting vest and cap, was being interviewed by television stations. He hadn't wanted news of the hunt to leak out before the event, but he sure as hell wanted the press here now, once it was over. He was bent on bringing tourists back, even if it meant the slaughter of innocent animals.

When the mayor's interview was over, he spotted her and made his way over. "Quite a success, I'd say."

Rachel stared at him. "If you're talking about creating your own reality, I agree."

She'd shocked him, but he quickly recovered. "I'm surprised by you. Somebody who sees so much death."

She let out a little sound of protest. "That doesn't mean I like it or embrace it."

"I never said that. And nobody likes it. This was something that had to be done."

She'd always resented the way he'd come in and just taken over, and it had surprised her that he'd beaten out two locals for the position of mayor. It seemed people were ready for guidance and big ideas. She could understand that, since nothing up until this point had really worked for them. Tuonela had been in a state of decay and decline ever since she could remember.

Alastair Stroud appeared. "We'd like for you to autopsy a random sampling of animals."

That veiled demand didn't improve her mood. "Animal autopsies aren't in my job description."

"Come on, Rachel. Just do a cursory exam. Maybe

check stomach contents. Look for signs of human remains."

"If that's what it will take to prove that this slaughter was completely uncalled-for and that these animals are innocent, I'll do it. Pick out the three most likely suspects and bring them to the autopsy suite." She turned and strode away, quickening her pace and making it inside the morgue just in time to throw up again.

Rachel followed standard autopsy procedure, beginning by dictating the basics into a small recorder. That led to the external exam of the first animal's fur and paws. She pried open the mouth and brought the swing arm close, all the while aware of Alastair Stroud standing a few feet away.

"You could have stood up to the mayor."

"I tried."

"I can see that." She picked up a pair of tweezers from the instrument tray.

"I can only do so much."

"I'm beginning to think that's a problem with everybody in this town, me included. An inability to take action." With a gloved hand, she held the animal's jaw open and extracted long pale threads from between the back teeth.

Jesus. Now, that was totally unexpected.

She held the strands under the light.

Alastair stepped forward. "Is that what I think it is?"

"Forget everything I just said," she mumbled with distraction. "Hair. *Human* hair."

Alastair let out a low whistle.

Rachel tucked the strands into an evidence bag and plopped down on a nearby stool, stunned. It could take a while to shift gears. "I'll see if we can get the crime lab to put a rush on this."

"Now we know the perpetrator."

She looked up at him. "Do we?"

This was too easy. Too obvious, the hair strands appearing to have been freshly introduced rather than packed and matted with oral debris. She started to voice her suspicions, but caught herself at the last second.

Alastair was standing there looking like an anxious trick-or-treater. Rachel thought about how odd he'd been acting lately.

What the hell was he up to?

Chapter Thirty-seven

It didn't seem like I slept at all, but I must have, because the creak of floorboards above my head jerked me awake. Weak light filtered through the small ground-level, block-glass window, indicating that morning had arrived.

Graham really should have warned me about the mice.

I'd heard them scratching, the sound coming from the vicinity of the freezer. Sometimes I swore it seemed like they were *inside* the freezer.

At one point I'd gotten up and opened the freezer lid, then quickly hid when I heard footsteps on the floor above my head.

I rubbed my face, braided my hair, and wished I had a drink of water. I looked up at the wooden rafters and wondered what I was doing. How did I constantly get myself into these situations? Why hadn't I just gone back to Minneapolis with Ian and Stewart?

Was I fooling myself? Convincing myself I could

make a documentary that would have some impact and meaning either socially or artistically? I mean, I'd worked with a lot of people who thought they had talent when they really didn't. Was I just another one of those delusional fools? How did a person know? That was the problem with delusion.

I heard a door slam, then heavy footsteps. A minute later the basement door opened. I jumped to my feet and grabbed the sleeping bag.

"Just me," Graham whispered. He jogged down the steps. "He's gone. He left really early. I gotta get going. I have a big test today. It's worth half my grade, and I'm already late." He glanced at the freezer. "Hey, why's this open?" He closed the lid.

"There were mice trapped inside."

"Mice?"

"Yeah. Inside the freezer."

"So you let them *out*?"

"Yeah."

He laughed and we left.

I dropped Graham off at school. He got out of the car, pausing and leaning in the open door. "Pick me up right here at three thirty."

I was fiddling with the radio. "Yep."

I headed downtown to see if anything was going on. A press conference was in progress on the courthouse lawn. I dug out my camera and kept a low profile while inching my way through the crowd of bystanders, reporters, and newspeople.

Mayor McBride was going through his spiel, an obviously prepared speech, talking about how they'd get to the bottom of the deaths. He went off on a coyote tangent again. Apparently they'd had some huge coyote roundup that had ended in a massive kill.

Buncha lunatics.

I got it on tape. I might use it; might not.

I shut off the camera and looked up from the viewfinder. A guy in a dark suit was watching me. *Crap.* I got the feeling he was with the mayor. One of his thugs. Did people really have thugs, or was that just on TV?

I capped the camera lens.

The guy in the suit began wending his way toward me, cutting through the clumps of people. I jumped, turned, and began walking away quickly. I broke out of the crowd and chanced a look over my shoulder.

He was still coming, faster now.

I ran.

I didn't really know why. I hadn't done anything wrong, but something about a big guy in a suit just made me haul ass.

Graham's car was nearby, but I didn't want the guy to see me getting in it. I cut down an alley, through a yard, down another alley. Glanced over my shoulder. Not there. Circled back to the car, jumped inside, started the engine, pulled away.

Checked the rearview mirror.

There he was. Standing in the middle of the street.

I headed out of town, to the place I'd wanted to visit again since day one. The scene of the original crime. The place where the little girl had appeared, then disappeared.

A few heavy frosts and the trees had lost most of their leaves. Now, rather than a repeated pattern of yellow, the repeat was dark, symmetrical trunks under a gray sky.

I began filming as soon as I stepped from the car. Keeping the camera low, I walked slowly toward the grove of trees. The leaves were thick and buoyant under my feet. They absorbed sound and created heaviness around my ankles that weighed me down. My body seemed closer to the ground, and my legs weren't as light as they'd been on the road.

I could see a few birds clinging to tree branches, but they were silent, watchful. The area felt lifeless and hollow.

Before entering the trees I paused and kept the camera focused on the spot where I thought the little girl had appeared. I panned to the right and left, bringing the camera back to the beginning.

Nothing unusual in the viewfinder.

But then, I hadn't seen anything in the viewfinder last time.

I glanced up and checked the path. The sky was a slate gray, distant and cold and talking of snow. My fingers were turning red, and I felt a chill wrap around my ankles and creep up my pant legs. Why hadn't I worn socks? Why hadn't I borrowed some heavier clothes from Graham?

Foolish and unprepared. Story of my life.

I moved forward and tried to ignore my physical discomfort.

Into the woods.

Even though most of the leaves had fallen, a few

clung stubbornly to branches, twirling as if trying to break away and drop to the ground. It was even quieter here.

The trees had been planted by a human hand, unnaturally close together. The artist in me appreciated the way the trunks lined up from every angle, all paths leading into black infinity.

Should I have come here by myself?

I'd thought it would be okay, since it was daylight. Both of the murders had happened at night. But now, with the sky turning so dark, and with the woods so isolated . . .

It was like night.

I paused and looked behind me.

I'd come farther than I'd thought. I could see Graham's car, but it was small and undefined. When I swung back around, the other side of the woods didn't seem any nearer. The entire place created an optical illusion.

Should I stop? Go back?

I'd gotten footage. Maybe not everything I'd wanted, but probably enough. I always shot too much anyway.

But I wanted to get to the other side.

I walked faster; to hell with the jerkiness of the camera. It might add a little something.

Five more minutes and the view ahead hadn't changed.

I paused to check behind me.

I couldn't see the car anymore. I lifted the camera to shoulder level and did a slow 360-degree pan, the black trunks nearest me blurry while the distance was in sharp focus.

This was going to be some of the coolest stuff I'd ever shot.

For a moment I forgot about my plan to make a documentary on Tuonela. I was just excited about what I was capturing.

I heard a rustle. I lowered the camera and visually scanned my surroundings. Dark trees. Standing. Watching. A flutter of a leaf, then hollow air.

A movement. Something black. A shift of bark. Was that a head? Someone looking from around a tree? And another? Was that another someone?

Like a kaleidoscope, black objects seemed to ooze from the tree trunks, moving in unison. I gasped and took a step back.

The sky was darker now, and I blinked, trying to make out what I was seeing.

Shapes moved toward me.

I tried to scream, but the air swallowed the sound as soon as it left my mouth. I ran. The wrong way. Away from the car, but it was my only choice because it was also away from the dark shapes coming after me.

Chapter Thirty-eight

As soon as the bell rang, Graham was out of the school building, looking up and down the street. No sign of Kristin or his dad's black car. *Great.* Where was she?

He waited while the buses pulled away. Pretty soon everybody was gone, and still no sign of his ride.

He walked home.

It wasn't far.

Was he the worst judge of character in the world? Kristin was a flake, but had he misread her? He'd known she was using him, but he'd felt that at her core she was all right. He certainly didn't think she'd do something like steal his dad's car. Was that possible? No, she wouldn't do that.

Would she?

She wasn't at his grandfather's house. He'd half thought maybe she'd be there. Nobody was home. After an hour he called Alastair and told him at least part of the story.

Never tell them the whole story.

"Kristin Blackmoore was supposed to leave town yesterday," Alastair said. "What was she doing with your car? Your dad's car?"

"I let her borrow it. She wanted to get some video before she left. It didn't seem like a big deal."

"I'll see what I can find out." Alastair disconnected.

An hour later he called back and Graham answered the phone before the second ring.

"We found the car," Alastair said. "At Aspen Grove."

Graham swallowed. "Kristin?"

"Her belongings were inside, but no sign of her. I have some officers searching the area right now."

"She's there. Somewhere. She has to be somewhere. Or maybe Ian and Stewart came back and she left with them." But would she have abandoned the car? With her stuff in it?

"That went through my mind," Alastair said. "But we found something that led us to believe otherwise. Something that led us to believe she might be in trouble."

Surely Alastair wasn't talking about skin. Graham hoped to God he wasn't talking about skin.

"We found her camera and bag in the middle of Aspen Grove."

Kristin might leave a lot of things behind, but she would never leave her camera. "What about videotape? Maybe that will tell you something."

"We're looking into that right now."

Chapter Thirty-nine

The metal shovel hit stone; sparks flew, and Evan flinched in the darkness. In the glow of the lantern, he leaned close and dragged the shovel across the rounded rock of the foundation.

The foundation of the Manchester house, where the voices had told him to dig.

He could feel himself fading again. As his body weakened, so did his resolve. Richard Manchester was taking over.

His thoughts were jumbled and confused. Was this new Tuonela? Or old? Old, right? Or was it Tuonela before it became Old Tuonela?

If he walked upstairs, would he find a magnificent house that hadn't been a victim of time and neglect?

I'm losing my mind.

No, you're coming home.

Sometimes, when he finally fell into an exhausted slumber, a hushed roar of a hundred distant voices whispered to him. And he would find himself reaching for the oil lamp near his bed where no oil lamp existed. He would look at the floor and instead of seeing black stains left from a leaking roof, he would see a thick Oriental carpet in hues of rich burgundy and blue.

The walls were painted in beautiful shades of green, the woodwork brought over from England by ship, then train, then wagon. Stained glass imported from the finest Boston glassmakers.

I could have been so happy here.

I should have been so happy here.

If only he could go back. Do it all over again.

He'd been brought down by love. Weakened and tricked by love.

Oh, the shame.

He repositioned his grip on the shovel. His palms were raw, the blisters peeled and bleeding. But it wasn't his body. This body was expendable.

Evan paused and frowned and listened.

Had someone said something?

Were they whispering again?

You had to listen hard. You had to tune yourself in to them, open up to them; otherwise you would mistake the voices for the wind.

Where does the wind begin?

In Old Tuonela.

He'd brought support beams from the condemned area of the mansion to use as braces. But one man could do only so much, and if the earth decided to shift and breathe the braces wouldn't hold.

They'd filled it in when they'd left. His followers.

His mutinous followers. If he'd lived, it wouldn't have happened.

People were so fickle.

Love of his life.

Hate of his life.

Bitch. He'd been brought down by a woman.

The shovel hit something new, making a hollow sound, sending a shuddering impact up his arm.

A door.

He dug faster, but soon came to realize that the entrance had sunk and shifted too much ever to open.

Holding the shovel above his shoulder like a javelin, he beat at the rotten wood. Little by little it gave way until he was able to put the shovel aside and rip a section free with his hands.

He grabbed the lantern, ducked, and squeezed his body through the narrow opening.

Once inside the inner chamber, he lifted the muted light.

Another section of cellar with a foundation made of stones collected from the nearby hills, valleys, and riverbeds.

This part of the cellar was unchanged and untouched. As if she'd wanted it that way. As if she'd somehow been able to keep the tons of dirt from breaking down the door and swallowing her.

Victoria.

There she was. Where he'd left her over a hundred years ago, never to be found by anyone, not even Florence.

That knowledge gave him a small flicker of

sinister comfort. To know that when he and Florence had been upstairs fucking, Victoria had been down here, chained to the wall.

He laughed, and the sound echoed in the small chamber.

He would make sure she knew this time.

He frowned. She? But she was dead.

Florence was dead? Wasn't she?

No, he'd seen her. Seen her sleeping, her belly swollen with pregnancy.

Bring her here. Show her Victoria; then kill her and cut the baby from her womb.

He stared at the skeleton shackled to the wall. At the strands of hair and clothes and mummified skin. Next to it was a smaller corpse, Victoria's child.

A girl?

He couldn't remember.

He lifted the lantern higher and stepped closer.

Cobwebs and a layer of dust covered both mummies. The child wore a dress. A cotton sleeping gown with embroidery and lace trim. He closed his eyes; he could see her. A blush to her cheeks, dimpled fingers, long blond hair, and blue eyes.

Sweet, sweet girl.

Smelling of life.

Now a shriveled corpse.

Leaning against the wall was the sword he'd eventually planned to use to end their lives. He'd meant for them to die; but this hadn't been his plan. Not this abandonment. But they'd gotten what they deserved. He'd been jealous of Victoria and the bond she and Florence had shared. His plan had been to remove her from the equation. Get her out of the way; then Florence would turn to him for comfort.

The alarm was raised. Victoria and the child went missing. After two weeks they were presumed dead. But they'd been here. In the catacombs beneath the mansion. Richard had been able to smell them even when he was in the solarium.

Especially at night. Always at night, the humid air a carrier of sound and scent.

Babies always smelled so sweet.

And yes, he took a perverse pleasure in setting the trap for Florence, knowing all the while that the two she longed for were such a short distance away.

She came to him easily.

Too easily.

He should have been suspicious, but infatuation clouded his judgment and reason.

He comforted her in her loss. She clung to him, sobbing, distraught, beside herself with sorrow. But not so distraught that she was unable to plot and plan. Not so distraught that she was unable to bring about the downfall of him and his kingdom. His beautiful Tuonela.

Bitch.

Making love to him. Whispering sweet words in his ear. Speaking of tomorrows together. Oh, his memories were thick with dark nights of sweet, sweating flesh and tangled bedsheets. Of candles burned to the quick and penetration so deep his soul left his body.

Never turn your back to a woman.

Never close your eyes and smile with her name on your

lips. Because when you do, she'll stab you. She'll pierce your heart with your own blade.

He'd made but one gasp. His eyes had opened and he'd looked at her with bafflement and disbelief and hurt. He tried to question her, but blood clotted his throat and filled his mouth.

She was smiling.

The witch was smiling.

Standing there naked, draped in dark hair, a dripping blade in her hand.

Oh, the actress! Never had he seen such acting in all of his life. He'd been convinced that she'd loved him above all others. That she'd worshiped him and would die for him.

"That's for my sister," she'd said. "And my niece." She'd stared at him unblinking, as if unwilling to miss a single second of his pain and death. "And for all the other sweet innocents you've killed."

Then it was his turn to smile.

Because her sister and niece had still been alive, chained to the cellar wall, out of earshot. If he'd been able to speak, he wouldn't have spoken a word.

Her cockiness faded. "Why are you smiling? What do you know?"

He'd taken his last breath knowing she had not only killed him, but her sister and niece as well. Sweet revenge, but in no way complete.

Now, in the depths of the cellar, he picked up the sword and tested its weight.

Chapter Forty

Alastair leaned over the workstation and peered at the screen. "So, what do you think?"

Eric Fontaine rewound the tape and pushed play.

Alastair had driven two hours to get the footage to Eric. He hadn't wanted to risk the mail, and he hadn't wanted to send it over the Internet. They were in the basement of Eric's suburban home located outside Madison. Alastair could hear the television upstairs, and occasionally the wheels of some plastic riding toy directly above his head. He could smell dinner being cooked. Something Italian. Maybe spaghetti.

Eric hit the pause button. "It looks real."

They both stared at the monitor and the image of a young girl standing at the edge of Aspen Grove. Alastair knew when and where the video had been taken, because he'd been there. He'd even spotted himself in some of the footage.

"But it isn't real," Alastair said with conviction

while still managing a question. "I was there that day. There was no little girl roaming around."

"Oh, yeah." Eric leaned back in his swivel chair so far Alastair thought he might tumble over backward. "I said it *looked* real. I didn't say it *was* real. It's relatively easy to do this kind of thing. Probably done in Final Cut or something like that. Good job, though."

The chair squeaked and he leaned forward. "Notice the girl's skirt? You can see through it. I mean, you can see the trees on the other side. Pretty cool, but not that hard to do."

"So it's fake." Again the question combined with a statement of fact.

Eric looked up, and Alastair could tell he was trying to figure out if he was serious. Or crazy. Of course it was fake. Cops didn't ask if a ghost was real. You didn't do that kind of thing.

"I'm only asking because of the seriousness of the case," Alastair explained. "A person is missing, and I need a statement from a specialist so we can move the investigation forward."

"I get it." Eric relaxed. "I'm guessing an old still was put over the top of the original footage. How about I send this to a buddy of mine? Get his opinion?"

"No." Alastair had specifically brought the footage because he didn't want any copies getting out. "This is evidence. I came to you because I knew you were one of the best, and I hope you can be discreet. I don't want anybody knowing about this."

"Okay." Eric popped out the minicassette and handed it to Alastair.

Eric's evaluation was what Alastair had hoped for. He thanked the younger man, pocketed the cassette, and left the basement through a side door. Outside he pulled out his cell phone, called the mayor, and gave him the report.

"That's good news," the mayor said. "I'll call a press conference."

"That seems a bit premature."

"Have you found any evidence of foul play?"

"No."

"It's a scam. I think that's fairly obvious by now. Kristin Blackmoore wanted someone to find the camera and the footage. She wanted it to make local and national news."

Maybe. Very possible.

In his mind's eye, Alastair saw the image of the little girl in the transparent nightgown. He felt sick and confused. He thought about the skin in his freezer. He thought about Evan. More than anything, he thought about Evan.

In the basement, Eric Fontaine opened the door to his dubbing room, ejected the fresh DV copy, returned to his chair, and popped the tape into his workstation deck. He played it through, rewound, paused. Then he captured a screen image of the girl and made a JPEG.

Yes, he was discreet. But a guy had to share something like this with his best buddy and fellow media tech. He dragged the image into the body of an e-mail, wrote a short note, and pressed send.

• • •

James took a long swallow of beer, then lowered the bottle to glance at the computer screen. An e-mail was trying to come through. Something fairly big, because it was taking a while to download. The program chirped and he opened the mail.

From Eric Fontaine.

James scanned the attached text, picking out a few words, enough to know Eric wanted his opinion. Of course the image was fake, but what did he think of it?

He leaned closer and peered at the screen. He could see through the girl's dress. Not only through her dress, but also through her.

Pretty cheesy.

Oh, Eric, Eric, Eric.

The kid was always sending him shit. It was nice to be look : up to, but James was getting tired of pretending .. was impressed.

Had Eric made this himself?

Probably. He'd done that a couple of times before. Sent him something and pretended someone else had done it, hoping to get a truthful response from him. Why not just come out and ask?

James scanned the text again.

Aspen Grove. Outside Tuonela.

Oh, yeah. Tuonela.

Eric lived in Wisconsin. James was from California and had a hard time visualizing the Midwest. In a lot of ways it didn't exist and didn't matter to him. He couldn't help it. That was just the way it was.

He put the image in a new e-mail and titled the e-mail *Aspen Grove Ghost*. He went through his address book, clicked on the group file of over a thousand names, and sent the image to everybody on his list. Once James accidentally sent a nude photo of his ex-girlfriend to three hundred people. These things happened.

Maybe if he hadn't had so many beers he would have exercised some restraint, but he got his kicks tormenting amateurs like Eric Fontaine. James was looking forward to sitting back and watching the furor and speculation once the image made its way around the globe.

Chapter Forty-one

Graham heard the sound of a key turning in the lock. He shut off the television, tossed down the remote, and jumped to his feet as Alastair stepped inside the house.

"I just saw the mayor on the news," Graham told him. "He's saying there's no evidence of foul play and that people suspect Kristin staged her disappearance."

Alastair sighed and tossed his hat on the couch. "I'd hoped the mayor wouldn't go public with that statement yet. It's a little premature."

"No shit!"

"Watch your mouth."

Graham didn't care. "Does this mean nobody's looking for her anymore?"

"People are still looking."

His grandfather sounded calm. Too calm, which stirred Graham up even more. "Who? How many?"

"We don't want men endangering their lives to find someone who isn't even lost or missing. Someone who's trying to pull something over on us and the media."

"That's bullshit. Are they afraid to go out there? That's what I think."

"Of course they're afraid. Two people have died in the area. We don't have the perpetrator—whether it's animal or human. This isn't just a missing-persons case. We can't allow innocent people with no police or tracking experience to wander around in the kill zone. That would be irresponsible."

"But Kristin could be out there. She *is* out there."

"You don't know that."

"You don't know she isn't."

Where was the logic in his grandfather's thinking?

Graham looked at him closely, trying to read his expression. "Are *you* afraid?"

Yes. Something like queasiness—and even guilt—flickered across Alastair's face. "You are, aren't you?"

"Everybody's afraid," Alastair said. "I wouldn't let that keep me from trying to find someone if they were lost and needed help. I hope you don't think that poorly of me."

"She's been gone for two days."

"Graham, I don't think she's out there. We're going to keep looking until we have proof otherwise, but we don't want the whole community traipsing around in those woods. Come morning we'll start looking again. We can't search for her at night."

Maybe they couldn't, but Graham knew somebody who could. He grabbed his car keys and headed for the door.

"Where are you going?"

"Nowhere. Just out for a while."

"I don't want you to miss any more school. This is an important year."

How could he even think about that? College had been a pipe dream anyway. He wasn't getting out of here. He was going to be stuck in Tuonela forever, like everybody else.

It was getting cold; he grabbed his jacket.

How long could a person survive when temperatures were close to freezing? Had she worn any winter clothing? Probably not. She hadn't struck him as the type to think ahead. She was spontaneous, with no caution in her.

"I'll be back in a little while."

He hated lying to his grandfather, but lying had been a big part of his life back when his mother was still alive. It came naturally. You did what you had to do.

For a moment he thought Alastair was going to physically restrain him. He took a step toward him; Graham flinched and raised his arm.

He'd had quite a few years of practicing that move too.

Alastair didn't hit him or grab him. He suddenly looked sad and old.

Graham didn't feel connected to his grandfather the way he felt connected to Evan. Even taking into consideration Evan's weirdness and his new and strange persona. Maybe Graham would eventually connect with Alastair. Of course, if he kept lying to him that would never happen.

"Ten o'clock," Alastair said. "Be back by ten."

Graham could see Alastair was just playing along. Pretending life was normal, like everybody else. That back-by-ten kind of stuff didn't belong in this world. The world of skinned bodies and crazy moms and dads. Tuonela just couldn't get away from the past. That's what it was. The whole town was trying to pretend bad things hadn't really happened, that it was really just a silly, zany carnival ride. Would people ever admit otherwise?

"I'll be back by ten."

He left and got in his dad's returned car.

Low on gas. And he was broke because he'd spent a large chunk of his check on videotape for Kristin.

Would she do that? Fake her own disappearance to create a media buzz? He had to admit the idea was kinda cool.

Fifteen minutes later he pulled up in front of the Manchester house.

He slipped from the car, then paused at the narrow path that led to Old Tuonela.

Was his dad out there excavating like a crazy man? Graham decided to check the house first, circling around back to the kitchen.

He hadn't seen Evan since the whole baby coffin incident. The impact of that memory brought along a giant wave of doubt. This was probably a bad idea. He had a lot of those.

Inside the house he flipped the wall switch, dowsing the room in a faint red light. "Evan?"

He shouted into the depths of the house: "Evan!"

He heard a crash—like the sound of someone stumbling and blundering around, then heavy footfalls coming from the bowels of the building.

Graham had never been in the basement. He'd opened the door and looked once, but it smelled like mildew and age. Nothing he wanted anything to do with.

Evan appeared at the top of the steps. In his hands he held a dirt-encrusted sword that he leaned in the corner, near the basement door. He paused and blinked owlishly against the dim light, then surged forward to grab Graham by both arms. "Hey, I'm glad to see you."

Graham was shocked by his father's appearance. He shouldn't have left him out here by himself.

"You've lost more weight," Graham said. "Haven't you been eating?"

Evan let him go and waved his words away with a weak hand.

He was dirty. His hair looked as if it hadn't been washed in weeks. He needed to shave, and his eyes were bloodshot.

"What are you doing here?" Evan asked. "I thought you were staying with your grandfather."

Should he even mention Kristin? Evan wasn't in any shape to help look for her; that was for damn sure.

"What's wrong?" Evan prodded.

Graham could see his father's mind jump ahead, see the panic set in. "Rachel? Is Rachel okay?"

"She's fine. Or at least, I think she's fine."

"Your grandfather?"

"He's okay."

"But something isn't right. I can tell."

"Yeah, well . . . A friend of mine is in trouble."

'What kind of trouble?"

"She disappeared. Vanished into thin air, if you listen to the cops."

Evan was immediately alert. More like the old Evan. "Where?"

"Aspen Grove."

"She was a friend of yours?" Evan frowned. "I thought she was from Minneapolis. Some officers were here asking if I'd seen anything. Of course, I'm going to be the first person they suspect." Just stating a fact.

"I met her at the museum."

Evan nodded as if to say, *These things happen.* Girls happened in a guy's life.

There had been a very brief period of time when Graham thought Evan and Rachel would *happen.* But apparently he'd been wrong about that, and now Rachel was going to have a kid.

"There were no signs of foul play," Graham said.

"But her camera was found, isn't that right?"

"Yeah. Some people think it's a scam. A publicity stunt."

"You don't?"

Graham shook his head. "I don't know her very well, but I don't think she'd do that." He thought about how she'd almost stolen the videotapes. He hadn't thought she'd do that either. "I don't think anybody's trying very hard to find her. It's really cold out. And people have been killed. Skinned . . ."

Evan was already moving. Opening drawers, grabbing things like flashlights, a backpack, blankets. He seemed taller and stronger.

The old Evan.

And not.

Because the old Evan had sometimes seemed like two people: one, a quiet and reclusive writer; the other . . . someone forceful and dynamic and frighteningly intense.

Graham experienced mixed emotions. He was glad somebody was doing something, but he wondered if Evan was the right guy for the job. Evan Stroud in any form didn't exactly instill confidence.

Graham moved toward the door.

"Stay here," Evan commanded.

What? *Now* he decided to play dad?

"We could be gone for hours." He gave Graham a level look. "There's no telling what we'll find."

A skinned body.

That's what he meant. "I don't care. I want to come. If you find her, if she's still alive . . ." His words trailed off.

Evan smiled.

When had Graham last seen him smile? "It wouldn't be good for her to see a vampire looming over her?"

"Yeah. That's right. And a familiar face might not hurt either."

"You'll need warmer clothes."

Graham spun around and darted upstairs.

"Gloves! A hat!" Evan shouted from below.

Underneath his concern for Kristin, Graham felt a strange thrum of excitement put in motion by his father's sudden clarity and the fact that they were doing something massively important together. Father and son.

He forced those selfish emotions down, but they wouldn't stay.

Was he an adrenaline junkie? He'd heard of people who, after making it through some traumatic event, were unable to live a normal life. They started doing risky things so they could experience that high again.

Downstairs Evan was waiting.

"Aren't you wearing a hat and gloves?" Graham asked, annoyed that he'd told Graham to dress warmly when he wasn't doing the same.

"I don't get cold easily."

They left the house.

Other than running around the track at school, Graham wasn't used to doing anything physical. But Evan, for all his weight loss and the dark circles under his eyes, seemed powered by something unknown. They took a straight path to the grove of trees where the first murder had occurred. They made a circle, then stopped in the center of the grove.

Silent.

Still.

Evan made an intense visual sweep of the area. "She's not here."

They headed back toward the Manchester house

and Old Tuonela. Graham checked his watch. A little after one.

"Are you sure you don't want to go inside?" Evan asked once they reached the starting point.

Graham was exhausted. His feet and fingers were frozen.

Something brushed his cheek, and it took him a second to realize it was snow. Just a few random flakes.

Graham shook his head. "No. I want to come."

They went through the gate, then down the narrow path that led to Old Tuonela. Graham's heart began to slam in his chest, but Evan was in his comfort zone, moving forward as if it were broad daylight.

The flashlight was deliberately dim, and Graham stumbled along behind, determined to keep up.

They walked. Up and down hills. Over streams, ripping their way through dense, tangled vines.

Graham lost track of time and direction, and he began to think Evan had been right: He should have stayed at the house. His legs grew weak, and he trembled inside from cold and exhaustion. Another hour and he wouldn't make it out under his own steam.

There seemed to be no pattern to Evan's approach.

Graham had seen stuff on TV about search teams. He knew they were methodical. What his father was doing was totally random, with no plan, no purpose except to walk and keep walking.

There had been many times, as Evan spent the

nights digging away for what seemed no real reason other than to keep moving, when Graham had wondered if his dad had obsessive-compulsive disorder. Now he found himself wondering that again. Had his sudden concentrated energy simply been because he now had yet another project he could manically throw himself into?

Graham turned away from his thoughts to focus once more on the physical. In his state of fatigue, his ears were doing weird things.

Whispering. A constant *sh,sh,sh* that sounded like a thousand voices. Like faraway conversation. Like being in a crowded train station or theater where you were unaware of the noise until it stopped.

Sh, sh, sh.

He needed to get home. Get some rest. Get warm. Get some sleep.

Had he ever had a good idea in his life? Maybe from now on he should take every idea and do the opposite. Maybe that would work for him.

Graham opened his mouth to say they should go back when Evan stopped dead and put a hand to Graham's chest. In silent communication, Graham strained to make out the area illuminated by Evan's dim flashlight.

A splash of color embedded within the gray landscape.

Fabric.

Clothing.

Chapter Forty-two

They hurried toward the splash of color, Evan in the lead and moving surely. Graham followed behind, his legs weak, this time from fear of what they would find.

He wanted to call her name, but the sound caught in his throat.

Evan reached her first. Graham hung back, unable to make himself step closer.

And then came Evan's next words: "She's alive."

Graham let out a weird, shuddering sob and ran to join his father, crashing to his knees beside him.

In the back of his mind, he questioned how Evan had found her when teams of searchers hadn't been able to. Some kind of primal intuition? He seemed to be plugged into a network the rest of them couldn't see or feel. Or was it something more sinister? Had he known because he'd been involved in her disappearance?

Graham pushed those thoughts away. Kristin was here. They'd found her. She was alive.

Graham looked at her and recoiled.

Dead.

She was dead.

But then her head turned very slowly.

"What's wrong with her eyes?"

They looked so weird. Empty. Completely empty.

"Slow pulse. Breathing is shallow," Evan said. "She's suffering from hypothermia."

It was like staring at something dead that was somehow still moving. There was no consciousness behind her eyes. The skin on her cheeks looked like mottled marble. Her lips were blue.

"She isn't shivering. That's good, isn't it?"

"She's beyond shivering. We have to get her to a hospital so her core temperature can be brought back up."

Graham pulled out the quilt and they wrapped her in it. How could it possibly help? "She's frozen. I mean, I think she's actually frozen."

"Hypothermia makes the muscles lock up. Can you find your way back to the house? So you can call for an ambulance?"

"No." He was worthless. "I can try."

"I don't want you getting lost too."

"How far is it?" Graham checked his watch. Four-thirty.

"Two miles at least." Evan handed his flashlight to Graham. Then he crouched down and picked up Kristin. Or the body of Kristin, because Graham couldn't quite think of it as a person.

Graham led the way, with Evan following behind, giving him verbal directions.

Kristin wasn't a small girl. She couldn't have been light, even if she'd lost weight. Yet Evan, as emaciated as he was, didn't seem to have trouble carrying her.

Sh, sh, sh.

"Don't look at them," Evan commanded. "Keep your head down and keep moving."

What was he talking about?

Graham glanced up.

In the blackness, he could make out the darker outline of towering tree trunks silhouetted against gray clouds that reflected light back at the ground. The image reminded him of the construction-paper silhouettes he used to make in grade school.

But then the branches moved and shifted, shapes breaking away to float above them.

Graham stopped and blinked.

"*Go,*" Evan commanded from behind.

"What *is* that?"

"Nothing. Just go."

But Graham knew. *The dead of Tuonela.* "Christ," he breathed.

People had reported seeing strange shadows and shapes in town. And then there was the museum janitor who said the Pale Immortal had moved. "They've gotten out, haven't they?"

"They can't hurt you. Just keep going."

But they *could* hurt him. The psychic had claimed they were looking for bodies to inhabit. She'd been right all along. It was probably one of these things that had skinned Claire and the other woman. And maybe even coaxed the old lady into the river. "Why didn't they take Kristin?"

They drew closer. He couldn't see them, but he could feel them.

The air in front of him changed. It became heavy and dense; then it seemed to retreat, to get sucked away. Graham tried to inhale, but nothing happened. There was nothing to inhale.

Panic.

Evan appeared beside him.

The shadows retreated and the air returned. Graham gasped and dropped to his knees, pulling in deep breaths.

Whatever was out there had been afraid of Evan.

Join the club.

Chapter Forty-three

The way to unfuck your life is to die. That's the big mystery I finally figured out.

Now that I knew the answer, I couldn't believe I'd missed it for so many years. It had been right in front of me all along. Right in front of everybody.

Some religions claimed the secret to life was really death, but that's not what I'm talking about.

Dying feels good. The right kind of dying, anyway. Nobody tells you that. I suppose if the secret got out people would be jumping from bridges shouting, *Yee-haw!*

It's the best feeling. The best high I've ever experienced. I'll even admit right here that I tried heroin once. I liked it so much it scared me, and I never did it again. But this is better. Who would have thought death was like heroin, only better?

The way it embraces you. The way it takes away pain and regret and sorrow. I don't need anything. It doesn't matter if I make the best documentary in the world. Or the worst.

I don't care.

That's the high. The complete absence of caring. It's beautiful and amazing and wonderful.

Peace.

I'm finally at peace with myself and the world. I no longer hate myself. I'm no longer disappointed in myself. I've lived the best life I could live, and that's all anybody can do.

"Did she say something?" the kid asked, his voice coming out of the darkness.

We're moving. Going somewhere.

What's his name?

Graham. That's right. Nice kid. But I've gone beyond him and his world.

"No," the father replied.

Maybe it's them. Yeah, I'll bet it is.

Whispering all around me.

Sh, sh, sh.

When I open my eyes I can see them watching me. Am I already dead? Is this hell? Because I could swear I am being carried through the woods by the vampire known as Evan Stroud.

Oh, well.

No big deal.

Hard to believe I'd been afraid of him. Now he seems . . . Well, he seems like one of *them.* Like the others who are watching me and whispering. Waiting for me.

You're already dead, one of them whispers. And the rest join in, taking up the chant: *Already dead. Already dead.*

Why are they saying that? I haven't crossed the

threshold yet. I'm still trapped by the weight of my body, the confinement of my skin.

Skin is the largest organ.

You've been dead a long time. Ever since that day you fell through the ice.

No.

The heroin haze began to lift and I didn't like what I saw.

I opened my mouth.

"She *did* say something."

Graham swung around to hover over me. "What is it?"

"Am . . . I . . . dead?" The words came out as a funny croak. I don't think I've talked in a long time.

"No!"

He sounded upset. *Don't be upset.*

"Are *you* dead?" I asked. Because wasn't this the land of the dead?

"No!" Even more upset.

"But they're dead." I pointed above us. "And I'm pretty sure he's dead." I pointed to Evan Stroud. "So I thought I must be dead."

Graham made a strange sound. Kind of a terrified sob. The kind of whimper people make when they know things are definitely not okay.

"Don't worry. I don't mind being dead," I said. "Really I don't."

"She's delirious," the vampire told the kid.

Didn't they get it? I was the opposite of delirious. Every kind of delusion and self-deception had fallen from my eyes. My mind was clear, and I was connecting with the truths of the universe in ways I'd never come close to before.

We walked and the sky swirled and the voices whispered until we arrived at the Manchester house.

Things became a jumble, and I kept dropping away into unconsciousness. I think Graham called an ambulance, but there seemed to be some problem. Nobody came. Maybe nobody would come. Maybe there was no ambulance to come. Whatever the reason, the two men argued briefly.

My next awareness was that of bouncing roughly down a road. I had the vague idea that I was in a backseat, being held against someone's chest. Arms around me, cradling me.

I couldn't keep my eyes open. When I did manage to open them slightly, I couldn't focus.

"Should I rub her hands? They're like ice."

Yes, it was Graham. Graham was holding me like a baby.

"No, she might have frostbite. Best to just leave her hands and feet alone." We hit another bump. "Goddamn rural ambulance service," the father muttered under his breath. "What good are they if they can't get here in under an hour? I can get pizza delivery in less than that."

He ate pizza? A vampire?

I wanted to laugh.

Instead, I began to slide. Down a black pit that had no bottom. Down, down, down where the dead people were.

How many times can a person die? I wondered.
Only once, the voices answer.

Maybe I should rephrase my question. *How many times can a person come back from the dead?*

They took her to Tuonela Medical Center.

Evan pulled up to the emergency room entrance, his eyes protected from the glare of streetlights by dark glasses. "Sorry, I can't get out of the car."

"I can handle it." Graham wished Evan could have come in, but the sun would be up soon. He had to haul ass.

Three people in scrubs shot out the emergency room door. They placed Kristin on a gurney, but couldn't straighten her arms or legs. "Go," one of the nurses said. They wheeled her up the ramp. Graham followed, and Evan drove away.

They started an IV.

"Are you family?" someone asked.

"No."

"You'll have to stay in the waiting area."

Graham didn't argue. He wasn't sure he wanted to be in there anyway.

In the waiting area, the chairs were hard and the ceiling was low. He walked down the hallway and looked out a big window. The sun was coming up, and he could see downtown Tuonela and the pattern of light on the river.

His heart swelled and he knew it was too late for him.

Maybe he would leave this place, but he would always come back.

His eyes felt gritty and his stomach felt weird, the way it did when he hadn't slept for a long time. He suddenly became aware of himself. His boots were muddy; his wool coat was littered with burrs and twigs. He reached up and pulled some leaves from his hair.

He walked back into the waiting room, sat down, and fell asleep.

"Graham?"

He turned to see one of the nurses standing over him. He shot to his feet. Was Kristin dead?

"Your friend would like to see you."

He almost ran.

Kristin was in an emergency bay behind a blue curtain. She looked tired, but her eyes were lucid.

She plucked at the blanket. "Guess I'm going to live."

He stared at the IV needle in the back of her hand. "That's good." But she seemed sad about not dying.

"What happened out there?"

He could see her searching her memory. She frowned in concentration. "I wanted to get some footage of the grove. . . . I was walking around, and I saw something. Something that scared me, so I ran. And I got lost."

"What did you see?"

She shook her head. "I don't know." She looked up at him. "I don't remember."

Her gaze suddenly shot to his left.

He turned, expecting to see someone behind him.

Nothing.

Nobody.

When he swung back around, she was still staring at the spot. And he knew she saw something he couldn't see. The dead Evan had let out. The dead who whispered in the dark.

Chapter Forty-four

Downstairs in the morgue office Rachel checked her e-mail while outside a front moved in and the wind made the building creak.

A friend in California had sent her a JPEG. The title of the e-mail was: *Anybody you know?*

She scrolled down.

A photo.

She immediately recognized the location. Aspen Grove. One corner of the shot just caught the end of her van with the letters COR visible. She was in the picture.

She could feel the way the air had felt that day, she could smell the way it had smelled. She recalled the brush of something against her arm. A slight turn, expecting to see someone.

Nothing.

Now she stared at a child in a nightgown. Long blond hair. Standing to Rachel's right and back a few steps. She felt herself sinking, felt herself slipping into something she wanted no knowledge of.

Numbly, she let her eyes shift and she read the rest of the e-mail.

This has been traveling around the Internet. Thought you might find it interesting, or at least get a good laugh out of it. Hope all is well in spooky Tuonela. Come back to California, where you belong. Love, Zak.

Which world was real? California or Tuonela?

Even if Tuonela didn't exist on the outside, it was real to her.

She looked at the image again.

Little blond child.

She slipped a sheet of photo paper in her printer and pressed the print button. While the image was processing, she crossed the room to the fireproof filing cabinet. She opened the drawer and pulled out the journal Evan had brought.

She'd put it away that night, and hadn't looked at it since.

She opened it to the page where the photo had been tucked by the hand of a woman who'd been dead a hundred years.

Little blond girl.

The printer shut off.

She held the two images side by side.

The same child.

She turned the photo over.

Our sweet, darling Sarah.

She pressed a hand to her mouth.

Dear God.

What did this mean?

What conclusion could a logical person draw? A doctor of medicine? A medical examiner?

The image was fake. Something made in Photoshop.

No. The time for denial was over. She'd been in denial for too long. The entire town of Tuonela was in denial.

Why had Evan done it? Why had he insisted upon digging out there? The ground. It was the ground. Couldn't he see that? Didn't he understand?

Maybe it wasn't his fault. All along she'd blamed him, but maybe he had no control over his actions. Maybe instead of avoiding him, she should have been helping him.

She put a hand to her stomach.

How many times had she made that protective gesture in the past few months? Maternal instinct had engaged long ago. She wasn't abandoning Evan; she was protecting her baby. Mothers did what they had to do. Parents did what they had to do.

She looked at the photo again.

Sarah. Victoria's daughter.

Murdered by Richard Manchester, the Pale Immortal.

The words of the psychic came back to her: *They are spirits looking for bodies to inhabit.*

Was Sarah caught between two worlds? The world of the living and the dead? In her confusion, was she seeking human form? Had she skinned the two women?

This can't be. This is impossible.

Whatever was going on, Evan was somehow involved. Even if he didn't know it.

She locked the journal back in the safe, put on her

jacket, and hurried to the morgue's delivery entrance. A turn of the knob and the tongue slipped from the catch plate. The door was ripped from her hand, smacking against the wall. Her hair shot straight up. A nearby tree creaked and bent; electrical lines snapped against the sky.

The temperature had plunged since she'd last been outside—she checked her watch to be sure—an hour ago.

All her life she'd lived with an urgency, a slow *drip, drip* she'd always chalked up to her need to be anywhere but where she was. Her own internal warning system. But what if the warning wasn't coming from inside? What if it was coming from somewhere else? And nobody was paying attention, so accustomed were they to tuning it out.

While her hair whipped and stung her cheeks, she turned her face to the northwest. Buildings and roads and hills and bluffs stood in the way, but she could feel it out there.

Old Tuonela.

It's so strong.

Why hadn't she noticed the growing strength before?

Where does the wind begin?

Out there. In Old Tuonela. In the Driftless Area, beyond the plains and hills, beyond the chasms and the roads that turned back on themselves. The wind began in Old Tuonela.

Evan.

She struggled to close the door, shutting and latching and locking.

She stepped from the protection of the building.

The force of the wind took her breath away, and shoved her to the side. Above her the sky was a slate gray, but below clouds moved rapidly, racing and changing, with no order or pattern, unlike any clouds she'd ever seen.

Leaves swirled and circled up into the sky, while others marched across the street like a row of soldiers being called into service.

She got in the van, started the engine, and headed north, toward Evan, toward the land of the dead.

Chapter Forty-five

There were many doors between the land of the living and the land of the dead. Dreams were just one of those doors, and Richard Manchester used the dark, lonely hours before dawn to visit Gabriella Nelson.

The wind blew south out of Old Tuonela. It circled to follow the flow of the river and the bend of tree branches as they reached and pointed toward the new town.

This is the way. This is where life dwells. This is where our sorrow and our children have gone and where we must follow.

Because the ties of past generations could not be forgotten, and there was no such thing as starting over. Time meant nothing to the dead, and a sleep of a hundred years was but a single sigh.

Gabriella's dreams were more real than real life, and every morning when she awoke she thought Manchester was still with her. She would reach for him and find the spot beside her empty and cold. The loss brought about a grief that swamped her and held on so tightly that not a morsel of food had passed her lips for days.

But night brought about his return.

As she slept, Manchester held her in his arms and brushed his lips against her neck and breathed in her ear.

He told her things.

Never had she felt so wanted or so loved.

She craved him. Every waking thought was consumed by him.

She stopped answering the phone. Knocks at the door were ignored. She shut out the world.

Nobody else existed. Nobody else mattered.

She spent her days at the museum. Oh, she tried to be subtle, but when you hung around a mummy for hours on end people tended to notice. So she tried to disguise herself. And tried not to linger too long. Tried not to let anybody see her pressing her face to the glass of the mummy case.

Richard told her what she must do so they could be together forever.

A very simple plan. . . .

The museum was closed when she pulled into the parking lot. Earlier she'd called her nephew and explained that she was going to lay down a containment spell so the Pale Immortal couldn't walk around the museum anymore.

Matthew had humored her.

Two weeks ago she would have thought that

sweet of him. Now she saw him as simply a way to get what she needed. He meant nothing to her.

While the wind blew violently from the north, Matthew met her at the back door and let her in. He smelled like pot and his eyes were bloodshot. "So, you think this will work," he said with a silly grin.

"It won't hurt anything." Her voice was just right. Kind of teasing but serious.

He nodded. "That's what I said. What can it hurt? But we put a heavy-duty latch on the case. I don't think he's going anywhere."

"I have to do this alone."

He stared. "You want to go down there by yourself?"

"Do you have a problem with that?"

"No, but . . . Wow. Okay."

If he'd argued, she'd come prepared to kill him with the knife hidden in her coat pocket. That was how it would have had to be. That's what she'd been told to do.

In the basement, she unlatched the case. And even though it probably wasn't necessary, she got out her goofer dust and performed a quick spell. Then she waited and watched as Richard Manchester slowly came to life.

She wasn't sure how long it took. Time was strange, more like a dream where a few seconds seemed like hours.

Should she say anything?

Did she need to? After what they'd shared?

He moved toward her. He came straight for her. When she looked into his eyes, she saw nothing.

Not even pupils, but black holes she sensed went deeper than his body, something connecting to a world she didn't yet understand.

"I'm here," she whispered. "I came for you."

She waited for him to respond, to say something, to embrace her the way he'd embraced her in the dreams. Instead he grabbed her, sliced her throat with her own knife, and drank her blood.

She watched him in horror, unable to speak. She felt the life draining from her body, felt the blood soak into the sweatshirt that said, I BRAKE FOR COVENS. He pulled away, his hands still gripping her, his face, from lips to chin, covered with blood, while his flat button eyes continued to look at her with nothing.

He'd tricked her. He'd used her.

There are so many of them. An army of his followers.

She understood that now.

They were everywhere. In the leaves that marched across the street, in the wind that came from Old Tuonela. Why hadn't she seen them before?

Everywhere. Talking. Whispering. Living inside her, under her skin.

She felt that skin slip from her body as they fought over her.

They'd tricked her.

Oh, they were smart.

But there were others. Watching, sad and silent.

Chapter Forty-six

Rachel drove slowly up the lane to Evan's house, careful of the deep ruts and pits. Small bits of ice hit the glass, sounding like tapping fingernails. Buildup on the wipers scraped and scratched.

She set the fan speed to high, the air blowing hot in her face. Gripping the steering wheel with both hands, she peered through a small, clear area of the windshield.

Whispers were carried by the sound of the fan, mixing with the white noise.

Stay away.

She took the final curve and the van lunged forward, settling into the gravel parking area. She shut off the engine and left the keys in the ignition.

Out of the van, she circled around to the back of the house, the stone walk icy and slick underfoot, the force of the wind pushing her sideways. When her knock went unanswered, she stepped into the kitchen and shouted Evan's name.

The floor above her head creaked, but no one responded.

Upstairs she checked vacant rooms until reaching a door that was partially ajar. She peered through the opening. The room was wrapped in darkness, but she was able to make out a darker shape hovering in the corner.

Evan?

She pushed the door open, allowing dim light to find its way inside. Yes, it was Evan.

He held an ornate silver tin, one finger poised above it as if he'd been sampling the contents. Shirtless, a white scarf wrapped around his neck, his skin almost iridescent in the gray twilight.

She'd practiced in the van. She would be firm. "Evan, you have to come with me. Right now. You can't stay here a minute longer."

He said nothing.

"Get a shirt. Get a coat."

When he didn't respond, she charged into the room.

The bed was a rumpled mess, dirty clothes everywhere. Books were stacked along one wall; some of the stacks had tumbled to the floor. It didn't look like a place where a person actually lived. It was more like an abandoned building taken over by a homeless person. How had she let this go on so long? Maybe if she hadn't been grieving over the loss of her father she would have exhibited more clarity.

From behind her came the sound of metal on metal as Evan snapped the lid to the tin in place.

She found a shirt and brought it to him. She tried to take the tin away, but he wouldn't let go.

"You wanted to give that to me once, remember?" she asked.

He turned, tucked the tin in the dresser, then closed the drawer. "That would have been a shame."

"W-what?" The question was a half laugh in response to his odd statement.

He took the shirt and slipped it on, but made no effort to button the buttons.

She reached up and began to do it for him.

His hand wrapped around her wrist. It hurt. She tried to pull free, but couldn't. "What are you doing?" She tugged. "Let go."

"Ah, Rachel. Sweet, sweet Rachel." He leaned close and inhaled. "Sometimes I get confused. Sometimes I get you mixed up with somebody else."

"Who?"

"Florence."

"The woman in the journal." She couldn't bring herself to say *my great-grandmother*. Not yet.

Until recently she'd never been afraid of Evan, and she was having a hard time thinking of him as someone she should fear. And yet if anybody else were holding her like this, she would be fighting him.

"You should never have dug up that journal," she told him. "You should have left it where it was. We need to put everything back. Everything you've uncovered. It all needs to be returned to the ground."

"Too late."

"No." She shook her head. "We can do it together."

He pulled her close, until she was near enough that he let go of her wrist and wrapped his arms around her. He dug his fingers into her hair.

He means you harm. You and the baby.

Her breathing and heartbeat quickened.

It was too dark to see his face. "Ah, Florence."

"Rachel. I'm Rachel."

"The same."

"Who are *you*?"

"Don't you know me? Father of your child? I'm Evan."

"What happened to you? Sometimes you don't seem like Evan at all. Sometimes you seem like somebody else entirely."

He laughed. "Do you want to know what happened to me? I'll tell you. My father, my very own father, fed me a broth made from the heart of the Pale Immortal."

The tin.

"He did it to save my life, or so he says."

"When you were so sick. When you were a teenager."

"But he chickened out before giving me very much. And then when I moved into his house in Tuonela, I found the tin. And you know how I have a penchant for exotic tea. . . ."

"You drank it."

"Not all of it."

"Throw the rest away. Get rid of it."

"I was thinking you and I could share a cup. And the baby. We can't forget about the baby."

"I would have helped you. Why did you push me away?"

"I didn't want you to see what I'd become."

"Mental illness holds no shame."

"No, you don't understand."

"The tea is nothing. Nonsense. You've convinced yourself it has power. Don't you see that? You're trapped by your illness, and this gives you the illusion of strength, but it's not real."

"It's real."

There was no use arguing. "You have to leave here. This place is bad for you."

Her words made sense, and she tried not to think about the whispering voices and the skin that had crawled across her floor, and her earlier resolve to finally see what had been in front of her all along.

He pressed his face to her scalp and inhaled deeply. "I can smell him. The baby. The boy. I can smell his blood. Sweet little baby. Sweet, sweet, infant."

Evil, dark and dank, flowed from him.

Real or not, Evan thought the tea had changed him. He thought he was possessed by the Pale Immortal. The danger to her and her baby was real. And immediate. There was no time to reason, no time to try to reach him.

She wrenched herself away.

He was fast. Right on her heels.

He caught her arm. With her free hand she flailed,

fingers stretching and reaching for the wall switch, finding it, flipping it on.

A dull red light barely penetrated the gloom.

Evan laughed and pulled her closer, pushing her to the wall at the same time.

She jabbed her knee into his crotch.

That was all it took to drop him.

She ran.

Her feet pounded down the stairs.

Hit the landing, another flight to the first floor. Through the kitchen to the back door. Turn the knob and pull.

The door moved a few inches back and forth—a vacuum created by the storm.

Evan. Right behind her.

With a burst of adrenaline, she tugged and the door flew open, shuddering against the wall.

Out into the darkness, into the night, hands stretched blindly. Snow fell, deep and thick and wet. The wind roared. Ice pellets hit her face. Wind snatched her breath away.

She put a hand to her mouth and nose and leaned into the storm, visualizing the path that would return her to the van.

Freezing rain followed by snow had created a deadly combination. Her feet touched a stepping-stone and shot out from under her. She slammed to the ground so hard it took her breath away. An explosion of pain ripped through her.

Evan was coming.

She rolled to her knees and pushed herself to her feet. The van was there.

She opened the door.

Sobbing in pain, she grasped the steering wheel to pull herself in.

Shouldn't have come. Should have stayed away.

Across from her, the passenger door flew open and Evan dove inside. He grabbed the keys from the ignition and tossed them over his shoulder into the darkness behind him. Then he made a fist, broke the dome light, and crawled across the seat.

Rachel stepped back, slammed the door, turned, and ran—this time for the house.

With a hand cradling her stomach, her breathing ragged, she raced back the way she'd come, reaching the refuge of the kitchen, slamming the door, locking it.

She pulled out her cell phone even though she knew it was pointless. No signal. She stuck it back in her pocket.

The door shuddered as the weight of Evan's body slammed against it.

He pounded and shouted.

Snow shot through cracks in the walls, and wind shrieked around windows. Glass shattered and something thundered against the table.

A massive stone.

Evan followed, tumbling through the window, crashing to the floor. Without stopping, he rolled and jumped to his feet.

Rachel spotted a cordless phone on the kitchen counter. She grabbed it and began dialing 911.

Evan swept up the base, tugged it from the jack, and smashed it against the wall.

The handset went dead.

Always run out, never in.

No choice.

She dropped the phone, grabbed the nearest door, and wrenched it open. Dark stairs.

No. Go another direction. She looked over her shoulder.

Too late.

She hurried down the uneven, ancient stairs.

Darkness swallowed her.

Her palms moved over stone and dust and dirt.

Her feet made contact with the ground. She lurched forward, hands outstretched.

Some sort of tunnel.

She smacked her head, then ducked.

Turning, winding, until she came to a solid wall. Frantic, she felt for a door, an opening.

And found one.

It was small and broken, but she managed to squeeze through.

A room. Damp and cold. Blindly, she found a notch in the wall and tucked herself inside and waited.

He would find her.

Like an animal, he would sniff her out and find her.

She heard him.

Moving closer, his feet shuffling over the dirt

floor. She saw a faint light bobbing and moving in her direction.

There was no escape.

She turned, her eyes seeking something, anything. If not a way out then a weapon.

In the darkness she caught the dull glint of metal. She moved for it, her hand wrapping around a wooden handle.

A shovel.

She lifted it high and faced the entrance. Evan burst through the opening. She started to bring down the weapon, then hesitated.

She couldn't do it. She couldn't hit him.

He grabbed the shovel and tossed it aside. He held a lantern that gave off a muted light. Dust particles curled and drifted.

Sh, sh, sh.

"I see you found them."

She didn't understand.

He lifted the lantern higher, the weak light penetrating the deep crevices.

And then she saw the mummified remains.

"Victoria and her daughter."

The girl in the photo. The poor little blond girl.

"When they were down here dying, you and I were upstairs making love. How does that make you feel?"

He'd read the journal; he was living in Richard Manchester's house, drinking a tea he thought contained the heart of the Pale Immortal.

Oh, Evan.

"This is what I wanted to show you. This is what I've waited a hundred years for you to see. By killing me, you caused their deaths." He stood in front of her, pressing her to the wall, too close for her to knee him.

"Ah, sweetheart. I loved you. But you knew that, didn't you?"

Parallel lives. It was easy to see how someone who'd lost touch with reality might be confused.

"I'm Rachel."

He smiled crookedly. "Ah, but you are also Florence. Florence is in your veins, and in your voice, and in your slightest gesture. Can't you feel her? Reaching through time and seasons and heavy winters? You are Florence. Your blood will be the sweetest blood I've ever tasted."

She caught his face between her hands and held on tightly, forcing him to look at her. "Evan!" She gave him a wake-up shake. "Evan! Look! It's me. Rachel."

His eyes closed and she shouted at him again. "Damn you, Evan Stroud!" She slapped him hard. Once. Twice.

His eyes opened and flared in anger, but she saw recognition in their depths. He stared, his breathing harsh and ragged.

"I'm sorry I didn't help you sooner, but I'm here now, and you're stuck with me. Do you hear? I'm not going anywhere, and I'm not letting you walk away from me again."

Her words reached him.

He let out a sob and collapsed, dropping to his knees. He wrapped his arms around her legs and pressed a cheek against her thigh.

"Rachel." Her name was muffled, his mouth against the fabric of her jeans, the words spoken with a kind of baffled wonderment. "Don't leave." He clung to her. "Even if you aren't really here, don't leave."

She was thinking everything was going to be okay when she felt her water break.

Chapter Forty-seven

Graham handed the cash to the parking attendant. The wooden arm lifted; he stepped on the gas and the car shot out of the hospital ramp.

Kristin leaned forward in the passenger seat and looked up at the sky. "Whoa."

Graham gripped the steering wheel tighter. "This is freaking awesome." He'd never driven in snow.

His cell phone rang. Alastair.

"Where are you?" his grandfather asked.

"Ready to head to Old Tuonela."

It would take only ten minutes to get there. He didn't want Evan to be alone. And Kristin . . . Well, that had just happened. She would be leaving for Minneapolis once the storm passed, but in the meantime she needed a place to stay.

Pretty simple.

"Better come to my house," his grandfather said. "The weather is nasty. Visibility is bad, and some north-south roads are already drifting."

It was weird, but the snow created a feeling of

safety, a sense of being in a cocoon. Beyond the car hood, streetlights were blurry and everything looked like an old photo. For a kid who'd lived most of his life in the Southwest, this was pretty cool. Graham couldn't believe he was actually excited about the weather. "We'll be okay."

The signal dropped and he lost contact.

Probably for the best, Graham thought, pocketing the cell. Because Alastair might try to play the grandfather card and tell him to come home.

He stopped at a red light.

No other cars on the street. There was no sign of life other than shop window lights and traffic signals that changed even when nobody was there.

Kristin pulled out her seat belt strap, locked it, and leaned back in the seat.

"What do you think?" Graham asked. "It's five miles to Old Tuonela. The snow isn't that deep. It can't get much worse before we get there."

"I'm from Minnesota, where this would be considered a dusting. I say go for it."

The light turned green and he hung a right, then accelerated and made a run for the hill. The car lost traction and slowed to a crawl as they crested the peak. It picked up speed again and they both exhaled in relief.

They left downtown and the river behind, heading north. Once they broke away from the protection of the buildings the wind increased. An occasional drift slowed their speed and tried to suck them off the road.

"Should I slow down?" Graham asked, both

hands on the wheel as he crouched forward. "I'm not used to driving in snow."

"You have to go fast or you'll get stuck. You have to have enough speed to plow through the drifts. But don't slam on the brakes. Don't even touch the brake pedal if you can help it."

The car felt boggy. It wouldn't go straight, and he had to keep turning the wheel to compensate. "Look." Back and forth with the wheel. "I'm like a little kid pretending to drive."

They both laughed.

Maybe too loud. Maybe with too much enthusiasm.

Graham was nervous. Because of the rescue their relationship had taken a step somewhere, but he wasn't sure where.

"If you hadn't found me, I'd still be out there." Kristin looked through the passenger window. "I'd be dead."

That's what he'd been thinking. "It was really my dad who found you."

"But he wouldn't have looked if you hadn't gone to him for help."

She was right.

He felt proud of Evan. Proud of them both. And he'd been there. He'd held her while his dad drove. He'd gotten her into the hospital.

"Look out!"

The car veered to the left; then the ass spun around, and the next thing he knew they were flying backward. Everything moved incredibly slowly and incredibly fast, as if he were computing it all with two completely different parts of his brain.

Would the car ever stop?

At the same time he appreciated the fluidity of the movement, the gliding, flying, smoothness of it contrasting with what he knew would finally come.

The impact.

With a lurch, the car stopped. He and Kristin slammed forward and were immediately jerked back by their seat belts.

He sat there a moment, heart racing.

The air bags hadn't gone off, so the impact couldn't have been that bad. "You okay?"

Kristin stared straight ahead, both hands on the dashboard. "Yeah, I think so."

They took a little more time to collect themselves.

"I'll bet we're stuck," she finally said.

Graham felt like such a dumb shit. "Maybe not." The road was right behind them. He put the car in reverse. Tires spun, but the car didn't budge.

"We're stuck." Not a shred of doubt in her voice.

"It was your idea to continue on," he griped.

"You should have mentioned that you didn't know how to drive in snow."

Graham opened the door, stepped out, and sank to his knees. He buttoned his coat and squinted his eyes against the falling snow. He jammed his hands in his pockets, wishing he'd brought a hat and gloves.

They were near the turnoff. He was pretty sure of it.

He got back in the car. "We're close. We should be able to walk there in a few minutes."

"Always stay with the car. That's the rule."

"Since when do you obey rules, Miss Shoplifter?"

"Since I about died out there, asshole."

"We haven't met a single car. They probably won't start plowing until the snow stops."

"How much gas do you have?" She leaned over to look. "Quarter of a tank."

"That won't last long. We could be here all night. I say we walk." He reached over, opened the glove box, and found a flashlight. Pushed the switch. It worked.

"I'm not leaving the car."

That was insane. "I'm not staying here. We're close to the house. We need to get out of here before the snow gets deeper. If we stay, we'll end up having to hike out when the car runs out of gas, the snow is deep, and we're cold."

She shook her head.

She's still weak, he realized. She shouldn't be trudging through deep snow—at least until he had his directions figured out. "I'll go. You stay here, and I'll come back for you if I find the house. If I don't find it, I'll come back. Either way."

He left her there.

The headlights cut into the storm. He followed the twin beams until they vanished.

Chapter Forty-eight

Richard Manchester wiped the blood from his chin with the back of his hand, stepped over the dead body, and headed up the stairs to the ground level of the museum.

A sound caused him to turn.

There was the museum worker, the one who cleaned, standing in the stairwell staring at him, eyes wide, mouth hanging open. Richard contemplated killing him, but what was the point? He'd have to cross the expanse of polished floor to do it.

He turned and walked out the front door, down the wide steps, and into the snow-filled darkness.

Sh, sh, sh.

They were everywhere. His followers and his enemies. The ones who'd eventually turned on him.

Let them talk. Let them complain. They'd been foolish when they were alive; they were even more foolish dead.

The wind was powerful. It whipped his hair and stung his cheeks. *Wonderful.*

He lifted his face to the sky, closed his eyes, and inhaled deeply.

He could smell the river. He could smell Old Tuonela. He could even smell the polish used to shine the banister of his home. And *her*. He could smell her. Along with his unborn baby.

He flipped up his collar and put his hands in his pockets. With each step he grew stronger and felt the cold less. Down a brick street, up a cobblestone alley. Past the morgue, and out beyond the border of the new town, where the hills grew tall and sharp and the roads turned back on themselves.

Alastair's phone rang.

"Another call from the museum," the dispatcher said.

"Let me guess. The Pale Immortal is roaming around again."

"You got it."

Alastair sighed. "Tell whoever's on patrol to check it out. No need to report to me. I'll follow up in the morning."

"Will do."

Alastair hung up.

Had Graham made it home?

He pushed the autodial for Evan's number.

No answer.

Lights came at him, slowed, and stopped. A window was rolled down and a man leaned out. "Need a ride?"

Manchester shook his head.

"Sure?" Now the man was looking at him with strange curiosity, trying to see in the dark.

"Go on about your business," Manchester told him, getting into his head. His voice was smooth and hypnotic. "Go home."

Dazed, the man nodded, rolled up the window, and drove away.

People obeyed him. People did what he said. *Most* people.

He walked, and even though the snow was deep it didn't matter. He enjoyed the sensation. And even though he could see only a few feet in front of him, he didn't care. He knew where he was going.

He was close when he spotted something in the distance.

A car.

Chapter Forty-nine

"I have to go," Evan said. "I have to get away from you." *Before I do something bad.*

Rachel grabbed his hand. "You can't leave me here alone." Her voice was odd, breathless. She glanced past his shoulder to what was behind him. Victoria. The mummy child. "I'm having a contraction."

His stomach plummeted while the hand holding his squeezed so hard he thought his knuckles would shatter. As soon as she relaxed, he urged her forward.

Monster. I'm a monster.

He ducked and helped her through the rip in the door. With one arm around her, he grabbed the lantern and led her back the way they'd come.

At times the path was narrow, and they had to separate in order to move single-file.

He'd almost killed her.

If not for the fact that she needed his help, he'd run from the house right now and keep running until the sun came up and he evaporated in the day-light.

His mind shifted.

Strange thoughts flitting in and out before he could fully catch and absorb them. Snapshot images of a life that wasn't his.

The scary part was that he sometimes *got it*. Even looking from the outside in, things would tilt and he would slide and suddenly he understood the why and the how.

He got Richard Manchester, even when he wasn't Manchester, even when he was still whatever was left of Evan Stroud. He understood the craving that drove the Pale Immortal. He understood the mad love he'd felt for Florence.

They reached the kitchen, and Rachel sank to the floor, her back to the wall, eyes closed, face ashen. Evan put a hand to her belly and felt a tightening.

Another contraction.

She looked up, fear in her eyes. "I have to get to Tuonela."

He glanced at the shattered phone, fresh shame and self-loathing washing through him. "I could walk to the main road and try to get a signal with my cell phone, but if I did connect, an ambulance prob-ably wouldn't be able to get here."

He could feel the possession. It moved back and forth like a gentle, swaying breeze, or perhaps a pulse.

So seductive.

Wind rattled glass. It picked up objects and hurled them against the house. Snow swirled in the broken window, the temperature in the kitchen close to freezing.

He opened the door; snow blasted him in the face.

A whiteout. Zero visibility. Even if he hadn't tossed the keys in the snow, they wouldn't be able to get to Tuonela. The only thing to do was to make her comfortable, hope the contractions stopped, and wait out the storm.

Rachel was truly alone with him.

A monster.

He slammed the door. Another gust of wind and the red ceiling light flickered.

He tried his cell phone, but it was more for Rachel's benefit. Occasionally he could get a weak signal from the house. Nothing now. "We have to get upstairs."

Two minutes later they were in the bedroom.

He eased her back on the bed, a pillow under her head.

He hoped he wouldn't be delivering a baby, but he prepared for a birth just in case.

"Remember in grade school? When you got beaten up on the way home from school?"

"Which time was that?" he asked dryly. There had been so many.

"When I came to your rescue."

It was obvious that she was trying to keep him grounded, keep his head in her world.

He unbuttoned her coat, slipped it from her shoulders, tossed it aside. She was wearing a man's oversize flannel shirt.

"When you jumped on that Olson kid's back and

got beaten up yourself? Yeah, I remember." It was before his disease had taken hold; before things had gotten dark and strange.

"Remember what you used to call me?"

"Yes."

"Call me that again."

He covered her with a quilt. *"Enfant terrible."*

"Did you know I liked you? Even back then?"

"That's why I teased you so much. To lighten things and keep you at a safe distance." She'd had a crush on him, and he'd been trying to protect her, keep her from getting hurt, because at that time he'd thought of her more as an annoying kid.

"There's no such thing as a safe distance."

He felt a pain down deep in his soul. For what was lost. For the life they would never have. His thoughts moved backward and forward. "We couldn't have stopped it."

She immediately understood. "I don't like to think that we have no control over our lives. I can't believe that."

"Do you think I would be this way if I could do anything about it?"

She didn't answer.

"You're wrong. I didn't choose this. I didn't want this."

"Subconsciously I think you did."

"To be a freak? To almost kill you? Jesus, Rachel."

"The mind is a strange place."

He grabbed her hand and pressed her knuckles to his mouth. "I won't think that. I can't think that. *You* can't think that."

Sweet, sweet baby. Sweet, sweet Florence.

"Tell me you don't believe that of me," he begged. Was he right? *Oh, God.* "I have to hear you say it."

"Evan." She touched his face, his hair. The sorrow in her voice and face told him everything. She thought he was insane.

Was he?

That was far worse than actually being some hybrid, a cross between a human and a nonhuman. To know that all of this was coming from him, from some strange dreamscape in his head.

"You read the journal," she said.

"You're saying I'm reliving the past?"

Her gaze clouded and her thoughts turned inward. "If anything happens to me, you have to take care of the baby. You have to get it to a hospital."

"Nothing is going to happen to you." He wouldn't allow himself to contemplate such a loss.

"Promise me. You have to protect the baby."

He couldn't fathom a world without her, even if they could never be together. "I promise."

The light flickered again. He was surprised the power hadn't gone out. "I have to leave for a minute."

"No!"

"We might lose power soon. I have to get the lantern."

"Don't leave." Her gaze shifted and dropped. "That's his scarf," she said with renewed fear. "You're wearing his scarf."

He reached up to pull it off, then stopped. He couldn't make himself do it.

She inhaled sharply. "It's snowing."

Her voice was distant now. She stared up at the ceiling, her pupils large with pain. Flakes of snow drifted from the darkness to land on her cheek. "Snowing in the house. I wonder what that means. . . ."

"The wind's driving the snow through the cracks in the walls."

"No, it's something else. This is where it happened, wasn't it?"

"Where what happened?"

"This is where she killed him. Where Florence killed Manchester. Probably in this very room."

"Don't think about that."

"And maybe where my great-grandmother was born."

He'd already considered that likely possibility, but had hoped the thought wouldn't occur to her.

Why in the hell had he given her the journal? Why hadn't he kept it to himself?

Selfish bastard. Not that anything he did lately had much logic to it, but he did have moments of clarity. He'd convinced himself he was telling her because she would want to know, when deep down he'd hoped it would restore the bond between them. Now she was more like him than they'd ever known. No wonder they both felt such a strong attraction to each other. It went beyond a simple crush or lust or love. They both had strange blood in their veins.

She tried to get up. He gently forced her back down. "The baby's coming."

"I can't have it here."

"It's too late." He reached under the quilt to ease the elastic waistband over her belly; then he tugged off her panties and jeans in one movement. "Where it happens won't change anything. Maybe this is where you were meant to give birth."

Why had he said that? It was a thought he didn't want to solidify with words.

"I tried to leave," she said. "I tried to return to California. But all roads lead back to Tuonela." Another contraction was building. "All roads lead back to you."

I'd been turning the car on and off every twenty minutes or so, trying to conserve gas.

Maybe I should have gone with Graham. Where was he? Why wasn't he back? Should I go after him?

No, that would be stupid. That was the worst thing I could possibly do. But maybe he was right. Maybe nobody would find us until tomorrow—or later.

The car was covered in snow—a dark cocoon. The wind was blowing hard enough to send an occasional shudder through the vehicle, rocking it.

I started the engine again, then flipped on the wipers to clear a small patch. Turned on the headlights.

And saw someone.

Thank God!

I leaned forward, watched, and waited.

Hey!

Where was he going?

He was moving away.

I honked the horn. When he didn't respond, I honked again. "Over here, dumb-ass!"

He paused, so I knew he heard me. He tilted his head in what seemed like contemplation. Then he turned and headed in my direction.

The wind had died down some, but it was snowing harder, and the visibility was worse. I craned my neck. Was it Graham? Who else would be out wandering around in a blizzard?

Snow accumulated on the windshield. I hit the wiper button again, clearing a spot.

First he was far away; then he was close, just a few yards from the car.

He was coated in a heavy layer of snow that fissured and cracked where his arms bent.

Not Graham.

I hit the wipers again—one swipe, then tapped the brights.

His eyes.

Two dark, empty pits looked in at me.

Christ.

I couldn't breathe.

He reached for the door.

Without taking my eyes from him, I fumbled for the lock button, found it, hit it. Both doors clicked.

Evan once knew a woman who'd given birth to her first baby thirty minutes after thinking she was just having a bout of flu, but he was still surprised when Rachel's labor went so quickly.

The child didn't look that small, and it made a few gusty cries that promised all was well. He wrapped the newborn in one of his black T-shirts, followed by a small quilt.

A wave of tenderness washed over him. "A boy." His voice snagged, and he hoped Rachel wouldn't notice. He placed the bundle in her arms.

She was different.

Her hair was wet and her eyes were dark with exhaustion, but that wasn't it. Motherhood had already changed her. He sensed a gentle strength that hadn't been there before.

He was trying to hold himself together, but a flood of emotions tightened his throat and made him feel close to tears. Rachel, the woman he loved, and their baby.

Here. With him. In his house.

For the first time in years he felt joy sneaking into his heart, and he found himself contemplating the possibility of a future. Maybe they would have that garden. Maybe she would bring sunshine into his life.

He studied the unfamiliar feelings moving through him, finally recognizing hope.

It frightened him.

"I'm going to take the cell phone and walk to the main road. I should be able to get a signal from there. Will you be okay? Alone here for half an hour?"

She nodded, not taking her eyes from the infant, bemused serenity on her face.

Downstairs, a door slammed.

Rachel glanced up, a question in her eyes.

Footsteps. Moving through the kitchen, down the hall, to reach the bottom of the stairs.

"Must be Graham. A snowplow must have come through." Rachel and the baby would be able to get to a hospital.

Footsteps on the stairs.

Words of love were close to the surface, and Evan struggled to keep them from slipping out. Not now. Now was not a good time. It would be unfair to reveal his feelings at such a vulnerable moment.

Hope. He would savor it.

The door creaked.

All color drained from Rachel's face. Evan swung around.

Standing in the opening was Richard Manchester, the Pale Immortal.

Chapter Fifty

Rachel stared in horror at the apparition in the doorway. Without taking her eyes off it, she whispered, "Do you see that?"

"Manchester."

The dead had appeared to her at various times in her life, but this one was different. This one had a presence the others hadn't possessed. This one could have been mistaken for human except for his eyes. Or lack of eyes.

He came for the baby. He wants the baby.

"Oh, God."

We told you to stay away. We told you not to come.

And then it spoke. Jesus, it spoke. Directly to her, with a smile on its lips.

"Florence."

With a voice that sounded hollow. A voice with no depth, being pushed from a shell.

She worked with the dead and knew this was impossible.

She glanced down at the baby in her arms, its

little forehead streaked with blood. She wanted to clean the poor thing, wash the poor thing.

But there was a vampire in the room.

Evan hadn't moved, and now she became aware of his stillness. Hardly breathing, arms at his sides, staring at the door. At the thing in the doorway.

Without looking, Evan put out his hand as if to stop her from getting up or moving. "He's real. You have to play this like you see it."

"It will go away," she said, even though she wasn't sure this time. "They always go away."

"He's not going anywhere, Rachel. He's where he wants to be. He's home."

Her fear evaporated and suddenly she was angry.

If she hadn't had a baby in her arms, if she hadn't just been through labor, she would have rushed him. She would have pushed the silly hollow man down the stairs and watched him crumble to dust.

The baby made a strange noise. A nasal inhalation. Then he began to cry, his toothless mouth open wide, face red. Rachel jiggled him and made distracted sounds of comfort.

Manchester had been focused before, but now every cell zeroed in on the child. From a position of wild-animal awareness, he launched himself across the room. Rachel let out a scream, and Evan jumped in front of Manchester, blocking him.

The men grappled, locked together in a struggle. At first neither seemed to have the advantage.

But then Manchester picked up Evan and threw

him. Evan slammed into the wall and crashed to the floor.

Rachel put the baby down on the bed and inched her way to the side of the mattress. She grabbed the nearest weapon—a lamp—and tugged the plug from the receptacle. Manchester reached for Evan.

She charged with the lamp.

Manchester swiveled. His hand shot up and he deflected the blow. He ripped the weapon from her and swung it—hitting her in the side of the head. She staggered and dropped to her knees, dazed.

"Go." Evan gasped. "Get out of here."

She pushed herself to her feet. Evan did the same so that now Manchester stood between them.

"He wants you," Evan said. "He wants the baby."

And still she hesitated.

"He has the strength of ten men," Evan said.

Manchester smiled, and the pit of his mouth was as dark and as black as his eyes. "You speak as if I'm not even here." In one swift movement, he grasped Rachel from behind, one of her arms twisted so high she feared it would break. He wrapped his other arm around her waist and pulled her close, whispering in her ear, "I want the infant."

His breath was as cold and damp as a bog. "I will take what matters most to you. That's what you did to me."

"What will you do with the baby?" Rachel asked.

He pressed his lips to her ear and whispered, "What do you think?"

She had the sensation of tumbling headlong into a pit of decay and depravity. Of evil unimaginable.

He broke his hold, grabbed her anew, and tossed her against the wall. Pain receptors fired red. She was aware of a struggle; then darkness came and she slid to the floor.

When she regained consciousness, she was lying on her back. Evan stood against the wall, holding one arm as if it were broken.

"I came for something else," Manchester said. "Not just the baby. Not just my house. Can you guess?"

"The heart," Evan said, panting. "It's gone. I don't have it."

"Part of it is in you. I can sense it. You are me."

"I'll never be you."

"All men are capable of darkness."

"But all men don't welcome it."

"You're wearing my scarf. That tells me so much."

"Maybe I'm cold."

Manchester laughed. "You mean to tell me you never wanted to kill somebody?" A shift. "The heart. Where is it? I know it's here. I know it's close."

"Evan, don't give it to him."

Evan ignored her, reached in the dresser drawer, and pulled out the tin.

Rachel closed her eyes and let the disbelief and pain roll over her. When she opened them again, Evan had removed the lid. He shook the tin, peering inside. "I always wondered how much of this I'd consumed. Half, I'd guess."

Manchester held out his hand. "Give it to me." His voice shook. The first emotion he'd shown.

Breathing shallowly, Rachel backed to the bed and picked up the infant. Then, half crawling, she began moving toward the door.

"Will it make you whole?" Evan asked. "Make you just like you used to be? Will it give you a pair of fucking eyes?"

"Give it to me."

"Will it make you stronger than you are now?" Evan taunted.

"The heart."

"I'm not sure I like the idea of a stronger you," Evan said.

Rachel reached the open door.

They weren't paying attention to her.

"If it will make you stronger, it only stands to reason that it would do the same for me."

Evan reached into the tin and pulled out something shriveled and brown that looked like a dried mushroom.

While Rachel looked on in horror, he stuffed it in his mouth, and Manchester let out a cry of alarm. He flew at Evan, tackled him, knocking him to the floor. Manchester grabbed him around the throat and began squeezing. "Give it to me!"

Two madmen.

She must have made a sound, a note of despair.

Manchester swiveled.

The distraction was enough for Evan to lock a

heel to the floor and shove himself backward, out of reach.

He swallowed and broke into a sweat.

As Rachel watched, he changed before her eyes. He took on the characteristics of Manchester. A strange sensuality, a boldness. Then his eyes rolled back in his head and he lost consciousness.

She scrambled to her feet and ran.

Chapter Fifty-one

Graham was frozen.

He couldn't feel his toes or fingers. His face was numb.

He'd gotten lost, but now he was on track, because he'd finally found the lane. Walking was easier within the protection of the trees, and the wind wasn't as bad, but the damage had already been done.

He wasn't dressed for cold weather, and he began to think that maybe Kristin had been right. He slowed, alternated between high steps to clear the depth of the snow, and dragging his feet to plow right through. Why not run? Not some flat-out gallop, but a jog to get the circulation going and get him there faster.

It worked.

He began to warm up. By the time he spotted the house, his fingers and toes were warm.

Something in the driveway. A vehicle. He swiped a hand down the side. CORONER.

He frowned. Rachel?

He circled around to the back.

Chapter Fifty-two

With the baby in the crook of her arm, one hand on the railing, Rachel ran down the steps.

Black radiated inward from the edges of her visual field.

Don't faint.

On the first floor she walked rapidly to the kitchen.

Have to hurry. Before they come downstairs.

Before she passed out.

Snow blew in the shattered window. She pulled the quilt over the baby's head and frantically searched drawers, looking for anything to use as a weapon.

She found a butcher knife.

The kitchen door banged open and a dark form appeared in the opening. She lifted the knife high.

"Rachel!"

She hesitated—an almost physical stammer. "Graham?"

"Holy shit!" Graham's eyes took in her bloody

clothes, her bare legs and feet, the knife. "What the hell?"

The baby let out a whimper, and Graham's eyes got bigger.

Rachel put down the knife and thrust the bundle into Graham's arms. "Go. You have to get out of here. Take the baby and go."

He didn't move, and she turned him and shoved. "Go! Now!"

Graham vanished into the night, and she slammed the door, leaning her forehead against it.

She'd just sent her premature infant into a raging blizzard. But freezing would be better than death at the hands of the Pale Immortal.

With numb feet, she shuffled back to the table and picked up the butcher knife.

Those men upstairs. She would kill them both.

She laughed a little at the ridiculousness of the thought. As if she could kill two men, one who was already dead and one who was halfway there.

She collapsed on the floor.

Graham cradled the infant in his arms, unsure what end was what, unsure whether the baby was even alive. He hunched his body and leaned into the driving wind, trying to protect the child as best he could.

Evan must have gone completely insane. Graham hated to leave Rachel, but the baby . . . Had to protect the baby . . .

The snow was a foot deep, deeper where it had drifted, and progress was slow, his steps long, high, and awkward. The snow itself created an uneven surface, and he repeatedly slipped, only to catch himself at the last moment.

It was easy to stay between the trees that lined the lane. He didn't even try to figure out what was going on or what had happened back there. He had one focus, and that was to get the baby to the car.

He finally spotted the misshapen outline of the snow-covered vehicle. The headlights were off; the engine wasn't running. He staggered toward it with an awkward, step-plunge gait.

Locked.

The door was locked.

He wedged the flashlight under his armpit and brushed snow from the driver's window. "Kristin!"

Nothing.

He pounded a fist on the hood. "Kristin!"

The locks clicked. He opened the door; the dome light illuminated the interior. Kristin was huddled in the corner of the passenger seat, knees to her chest. "Graham?"

"You expecting somebody else?"

"Yes." She dropped her knees. "What's that?"

He passed the bundle to her. "A baby."

Alastair's phone rang. An officer calling from the museum.

It was late, but Alastair was still up. He was too worried about Graham and the storm to go to bed.

"I think you'd better come down to the museum," the officer told him.

"I'll stop by in the morning, once the storm's over. This guy's cried wolf too many times."

"Is it crying wolf if we have a dead body and a missing mummy?"

Graham cranked up the engine and turned on the heat.

The bundle squirmed and began to cry. Kristin gingerly pulled the blanket aside enough to reveal the face. "It has dried blood on it. Oh, my God, Graham. It's just been born."

"I'm going to walk back to Tuonela and get help. Or at least get closer so my cell phone will work."

"No. It was bad enough to walk to your dad's, but Tuonela is five miles."

"I have to."

She let out a sob. "No."

"I'll be okay."

"Lock the door."

"There's no reason to do that. Not in this storm."

"Lock it."

He did.

The baby started crying. "You can't go. Somebody's out there."

"Kristin—"

"I saw somebody."

"People see things around here. Things that aren't really there."

"He was here." She jiggled the baby and made hushing sounds, but it kept crying. "The Pale Immortal was here."

He recalled the terror in Rachel's face. Was it true? Was the Pale Immortal loose?

"Lock this when I get out. And shut the engine off as soon as you're warm. No telling how long you might have to wait."

She put a hand on his arm, made a sound as if to argue, then stopped. "Be careful."

He knew she was thinking how hopeless her words were, but she had to offer them. Leaning across the seat, he found her face in the dark and turned it to him. He gave her an awkward, blind kiss, then left.

Chapter Fifty-three

Evan felt the darkness curl over him. It grabbed at his ankles and pulled him under. It seeped into his pores, and when he opened his mouth to breathe, he pulled the inky blackness deep into his lungs. His tongue was coated with a layer of evil.

It tasted good.

He felt an overwhelming loss of self—the loss of the man being pushed out and dominated by this presence. He hadn't expected it to be so powerful. He hadn't expected it to be so seductive. His hope had been to make himself strong enough to stand up to Manchester, to defeat him.

Instead he'd ingested a parasite.

Parasites were strong. They invaded the host, changed the thinking of the host. Mice attacked by cat parasites began acting more like cats than mice. So why had Evan expected this to be any different?

Manchester was watching him. Evan sensed a connection that hadn't been there before. He understood Manchester's hunger and his lust and his anger.

With no words, he felt his amusement at the turn of events.

Manchester spoke. Or was it thought?

"That would have been my second choice."

Downstairs a door slammed.

Manchester tipped his head toward the sound. Curious, but calm. This was his moment. He'd waited a hundred years and he planned to savor it.

Yes, their minds were communicating.

Manchester was more evolved, yet had been unable to make the leap.

A link had been missing.

The baby is the link. The baby is the secret.

A result of a union between a partial revenant and the great-great-granddaughter of a vampire. The lineage hadn't been strong enough, and the offspring had appeared fully human. Rachel was an unaffected carrier. But now, with revenant carriers on both sides . . . The infant would span two worlds, the living and the dead. A super being.

Had Evan really even loved Rachel? Or had this been some preordained journey he'd been on since birth?

"Yes," the man with no eyes said.

Evan refused to believe it. "I love her."

"An illusion."

But what wasn't an illusion of some form? Life filtered through personal pasts and perceptions. Did that make embracing it any less important? Did that give someone like Manchester the right to destroy and torture and murder?

They were talking to him. One collective mind.

He could see it all. It wasn't linear, but rather a lake of information, with no beginning and no end.

A form of evolutionary life, a creature who could live forever under the right circumstances, grazing and feasting on the living, especially children, with no purpose other than to satisfy his hunger. Humans were nothing more than livestock to Manchester.

Until Florence had come along. She'd sparked something in him, nurtured by her own trickery. Her own hatred and lust for revenge was stronger than her desire to live. She would do what she must in order to achieve her goal: his death. She would sleep with him. She would have his child.

She'd meant to kill the infant once it was born. Drown it in a bucket of water like some stray cat. But when she'd looked into her baby's eyes, a mother's love had surfaced and she was unable to carry out her plan.

And now another infant had been born. Downstairs, just below them . . .

But Manchester hadn't figured on Evan's humanity. It hadn't even been a part of the equation, because someone devoid of humanity wouldn't consider it.

Would it be enough?

Manchester heard his thoughts; he smiled a black smile and exhaled on a laugh. "You can't fight it."

"I don't want to."

A gust of evil floated across the room and touched

Evan's shoulder. It took him by the arm and pulled him toward the door, toward Rachel and the infant.

Come. Together we will conquer.

Evan felt stronger than he'd felt in his life. Physically he'd changed. His back was straight. His chest, though still pale and scarred, was broader. The broken arm was no longer broken.

He motioned toward the door with a regal sweep of his hand. "Let's finish this."

Chapter Fifty-four

Alastair called someone from the highway department to pick him up and take him downtown. It was either that or walk.

"Victim is Gabriella Nelson," the officer on the scene told him when he arrived at the museum. "Throat was sliced."

Bloody footprints led up the stairs to ground level. Alastair crouched to examine one of the more defined prints. Narrow, with an unevenness that indicated a worn leather sole. He spotted a brand—or rather a stamp. From a shoemaker that hadn't existed in the area for a hundred years.

His cell phone rang. He straightened and answered.

Graham.

He had to strain to hear. "Repeat that." He must have heard wrong.

Same thing. "I'm on my way." He folded and pocketed the phone.

• • •

Graham waded down the middle of the highway. Or what he figured was the middle of the highway, judging by the occasional signpost. Should he try to make it back to the car? Or should he keep going toward what he thought was Tuonela?

Too hard to figure out. Too hard to think.

So he just stopped.

He stood there a while. Head back, he shone his flashlight up at the sky, watching the flakes come down. *Pretty cool.*

The light went out.

He shook the plastic flashlight. Nothing happened.

He'd lost track of where he'd come from. Maybe this way. No. This way? Maybe. Maybe not.

He dropped to his knees.

So tired.

And the snow was soft. Like a bed . . .

He fell asleep. For a second. Or maybe for an hour.

A rumble.

Followed by faint lights that grew steadily brighter.

A vehicle. Heading his direction.

What d'ya know?

He staggered to his feet and stood there, legs braced apart. When the truck got closer, he waved his arms. But he didn't jump. He was too tired to jump.

Behind the truck was another vehicle.

Graham's brain was muddled, and it took him a

moment to figure out that the snowplow was cutting a path for an ambulance.

Cool.

The plow stopped. Alastair jumped out, ran to him, and hugged him tightly. They got in the cab of the truck and headed toward Old Tuonela, Kristin, and the baby.

Right where he'd left them.

They got them out of the car and packed them into the ambulance. Two EMTs bent over the baby while Kristin sat in the corner and watched, hugging herself, shaking with cold. Alastair put a hand on Graham's shoulder and gave him a shove. "Get in."

Graham turned around to argue, and collapsed.

He seemed to be doing a lot of that lately.

With Alastair's help, he got to his feet and crawled into the back of the ambulance. The doors slammed behind him.

Chapter Fifty-five

Evan and Manchester found Rachel sitting on the kitchen floor. Evan took in the scene before him with strange detachment.

Rachel's lips were blue, her skin transparent. Limp tendrils of dark hair framed her face. Her legs formed a vee, the bloody flannel shirt falling between her thighs. One hand on her lap, one behind her. She had dark circles under her eyes, and she trembled violently.

Manchester made a visual sweep of the room. "Where's the baby?"

She looked up at him with defiance. "I threw it out with the dishwater."

Evan laughed. How fitting. They were all insane. All three of them.

With one swift motion, Manchester had Rachel by the throat. He lifted her into the air. "Where's the baby?"

A knife appeared in her hand. She raised it and plunged, her movements blind and desperate.

"You can't kill me," Manchester said.

Rachel.

Evan watched her struggle. The power of his feelings for her encompassed the past and the future; it spanned generations and reached beyond his own questionable existence.

He dove, breaking Manchester's hold. Rachel crashed to the floor, dropping the knife with a clatter.

Manchester whirled, grabbed the knife, and stabbed Evan in the arm. He pulled out the blade and drove it down again.

Evan slammed Manchester's wrist against the wall.

You have to cut off his head.

Manchester heard the voice too.

Evan released him and sidestepped. Without taking his eyes off Manchester, he backed away, moving toward a dark corner of the kitchen.

Evan's fingers wrapped around the handle of the sword. He let out a roar and charged, the heavy blade held high. He swung.

One long, clean stroke.

Alastair saw a faint light deep inside the house. He jumped from the snowplow and ran to the front door. Locked.

A woman screamed.

With his handgun, he fired at the lock, then kicked the door open.

Something rolled across the floor and hit his foot.

It took him a moment to realize it was a severed head.

He looked up to see his son standing in the kitchen, the hilt of a bloody sword held in both hands.

Chapter Fifty-six

Air brakes hissed as the bus bound for Minneapolis pulled to a stop in the terminal. I picked up my bags, got to my feet, and waited for the arrivals to disembark. Third person out was a girl about eighteen. Cute. Short blond hair with yellow barrettes and a fuzzy knee-length coat. She had a cell phone to her ear.

"I just got into Tuonela. I'll call you later." The girl disconnected and tucked the phone into her pocket.

Then she was gone.

I boarded and grabbed a seat near the back, but not too close to the bathroom. The bus filled up, and a twenty-something guy sat beside me. He was fidgety and nervous.

"I've never been out of Tuonela," he confessed. "I'm going to Minneapolis to check out the U of M. How 'bout you? Have you ever left?"

"I was just visiting. I'm going home."

That seemed to scare him. Stranger danger.

Would I ever come back to Tuonela? I didn't

know. At this point I was just glad to get the hell out of there.

The driver closed the door and put the bus in gear. With a lumbering roll, the vehicle moved out of the terminal.

Minneapolis, here I come.

I unzipped my backpack to make sure the video-tape was still there. I'd found it in the glove box of Graham's car. It contained footage of the death pit, along with two interviews: the one with Graham at Peaches, and the one with the old guy outside Betty's Breakfast. Even with the videotape nobody would believe me.

But I would make my little movie.

Would it unfuck my life? I smiled at the guy next to me and offered him a piece of gum.

Probably not.

Evan sat at the kitchen table as Dr. Henderson opened the black leather bag he'd had ever since Evan could remember. Years ago, when Evan returned home after extensive medical tests, Dr. Henderson had used the protocol outlined by the specialists for treating a patient with an allergy to sunlight. They had a long history.

Now Evan removed his shirt and the doctor leaned over and examined the knife wounds. "That's amazing," he said. "They've almost healed. But I can't help but notice you seem nervous."

Evan stopped jiggling his knee. "I've had some strange thoughts lately." Dr. Henderson was trust-worthy, but there was only so much Evan was willing to share. That he was afraid he might be well on his way to becoming a one-hundred-percent non-human was not one of them.

"That's understandable in your position. You feel trapped, claustrophobic. I'm surprised you haven't mentioned the symptoms before this."

"Can you give me something for it?"

"A couple of things. One medication you can take once a day. It will suppress those common desires and frustrations. I call them good-behavior pills. Another medication—a strong sedative—for occasional emergency use. One tablet will make you sleepy as hell. Two will knock out an elephant, so be careful."

Evan nodded. "That's what I need."

He planned to keep on with the excavation. The Tuonela Historical Society was going to help. The bodies would be given a proper burial in the Old Tuonela graveyard. Victoria and her daughter would be buried next to each other. Maybe that would stop their restlessness, if the end of the Pale Immortal hadn't.

Dr. Henderson was old-school. He poured some pills into a brown medicine bottle and wrote out the instructions.

Evan picked up the bottle. "Lithium? Isn't that for schizophrenics?"

Dr. Henderson tucked the pen in his pocket. "Works extremely well for them in some cases, but we also use it for various personality disorders. I know that's not what you have, but it can suppress certain unwanted tendencies, thoughts, and urges. I think you'll find it useful."

Evan wanted a normal life. He wanted to be there for the people he loved.

He would take the pills. He would suppress whatever was inside him.

Alastair turned on the basement light and headed down the steps. *All's well that ends well.* That's what he always said.

He felt pretty sick about suspecting Evan of the murders, but what a relief that it was over and everything was back to normal. They'd burned Manchester's body and head, making two different fires. Once that unpleasant business was done, they'd put the remaining ashes and bones in containers. One of those containers was at Evan's house; the other was here, upstairs in a safe. No telling what might happen if the contents met. Probably nothing, but you couldn't be too careful.

In the basement, Alastair opened the freezer. He shoved the packages of meat around, looking for the skin. He was going to burn it too. Be done with it once and for all. A fresh start.

No skin.

He went through the packages once more.

The skin was gone.

Graham shut the cash register and bent down to arrange the food in the case. He had a new job working at Peaches. It was temporary, because he'd be leaving for college in the fall. Peaches was one of his favorite places to hang out, so it was cool.

"I'd like a large café mocha with almond syrup and whipped cream."

He shot straight up to stare at the girl on the other side of the counter.

"You quit returning my text messages," Isobel said. "Why?"

Looking at her hurt. Everywhere. His heart, his hands, his eyeballs. "I got kind of busy."

She shook her head. She didn't believe him, but she played along. "With school?"

"Other stuff."

"What kind of stuff?"

He picked up a white flour-sack towel and made a big deal out of wiping his hands. "Nothing very exciting." He wouldn't brag about the lives he'd saved, or how he would come running if anybody tried to mess with his baby brother.

"What time do you get off?"

He shrugged. "Now, if I want."

She smiled. "Like to share a mocha?"

He made the drink. She tried to pay.

"It's on me." He carried it to a dark corner table away from the few people who still littered the café. He sat down. "What are you doing here, Isobel?"

She took a seat across from him. "What do you think?"

"I thought I wouldn't see you again," Graham said. "That's why I quit replying to your messages. You were having so much fun. You were in France and Italy. Prague. Abbey Road. You saw Abbey Road. You were meeting so many cool people. I mean, you met the damn queen." Using two fingers, he pushed the cup across the table at her.

"The queen." She made a dismissive gesture with one hand. "Pfft."

Unable to make eye contact, he repeated, "I thought you weren't coming back."

"Doesn't everybody return to Tuonela? That's what I've been told. Once it's in your blood, you can't shake it."

"Tuonela? That's why you're here?"

"Silly boy. I came back for you."

He smiled, and the tenseness drained from his body. Isobel had always been too damn confident. He liked that in a woman.

Rachel sat in the hospital bed cradling the sleeping infant. She couldn't quit looking at him, marveling at him. Tiny hands. Tiny fingernails. Tiny perfection.

She heard a movement and looked up to see Evan standing in the doorway. The room was dark, but faint light from the street lamp below cut through the window blinds, falling in a broken pattern on the wall behind him.

She'd wondered if he'd stop by to see her. With Evan it was hard to say.

He came in and tossed his wool coat on a chair. "How are you? How's the little guy?"

"They say they've never seen such a healthy premature baby."

Evan's relief was obvious. Then he surprised her by sitting down on the bed, his back to the headboard, one arm braced behind her. She could feel his calm. Feel his normalcy.

He'd eaten the Pale Immortal's heart, but Evan wasn't a monster. Yes, some hard-to-believe things had occurred. Richard Manchester had walked and talked and almost killed them. She didn't know how, but it had happened, and she would never again live in denial. But Evan was okay. Their baby was okay, and the truth of his ancestry was locked away in a safe in the morgue.

Evan leaned close and pressed his lips to the top of her head. "A name?"

"Not yet. All along I thought I'd name him after Dad, but he needs his own name. He needs a name that isn't clinging to the past."

"Who are the daisies from?"

"Graham and Kristin. They stopped by earlier today. Sweet of them, wasn't it?"

"And the roses?"

"David Spence."

"From school?"

"Yeah."

"I thought he was married."

"Not anymore."

"He's a little white-bread, wouldn't you say?"

"Don't be mean."

"How's that mean? I never said he wasn't a nice guy. Just boring and predictable, that's all."

She looked up. In the dim light she caught a glimpse of dark lashes and a pale jaw. "Not everybody can be a vampire."

He laughed. "Very funny."

Let him think she was kidding, but she'd seen him take on the traits and features of the Pale Immortal.

He reached for the baby, cautiously touching a small, perfect fist. Smitten. "I've been thinking about our garden," he said softly.

Could it work? "So have I."

"What flowers should we plant? Other than night-blooming jasmine?"

"Daylilies." In brilliant shades of orange and red.

"How about lavender?"

"I think that's considered a plant, not a flower."

"I like the way lavender smells." He paused. "I love the way it smells."

The baby whimpered. Unfocused eyes opened and little arms moved frantically.

"Poor sweetie. Do you need to be changed?" Rachel pressed a button on the bed's control device, and muted blue light fell across the sheets.

Father and son simultaneously flinched and turned their faces away.

ONYX

ANNE FRASIER

PALE IMMORTAL

The sleepy town of Tuonela, Wisconsin, is known for one thing: the killer who stalked its streets one hundred years ago, drinking the blood of his victims. And when the drained corpse of a young girl is found, the citizens fear their past has risen from the grave—and point their fingers at one man....

Evan Stroud can never see the light of day. The prisoner of a strange and terrible disease, he lives in tragic solitude, taunted for being a "vampire"—until the son he never knew he had shows up in Tuonela, and is drawn into its depraved, vampire-obsessed underworld. Then Evan must rely on coroner Rachel Burton, his childhood friend, for help. But the evil that they face is powerful and elusive—and about to take them to the very brink of madness.